The Captain's Boy

SAM STEVENS

PROWLER BOOKS

THE CAPTAIN'S BOY

First printing December 1999. Printed in Finland by Werner Soderstrom Oy.

web-site: prowler.co.uk
• ISBN 1-902644-23-9

British Library Cataloguing in Publication Data.
A catalogue record for this book is available from the British Library.

ONE

Robert Henry Marchant fastened the last strap on his long, leather riding boot and stood, admiring his reflection in the full-length gilded dressing mirror. A slight adjustment to his cravat should do it, he smiled to himself. Perfect. He knew that he had never looked more handsome. His bright blue eyes sparkled, his firm mouth betrayed a love of the good life. He was dressed in style, overflowing with elegant confidence, his beige long-skirted coat and satin riding breeches were considered the very height of fashion in this year 1798. A soft, grey three-cornered hat topped his chestnut hair, pulled back and tied with a scarlet ribbon. Robert looked upon the practise of powdering the hair as not quite "the done thing" for a young gentleman of refinement. Why over-paint perfection? He was constantly aware that he was one of the finest young gallants in the county of Hampshire. He also knew that, as such, the world lay before him. His future was certainly secure. As one of England's most eligible batchelors, he would no doubt end up marrying a pretty young thing with a slender figure, who would bear him any number of healthy, strapping sons to carry on the Marchant dynasty. But not if he could help it.

'Have you been introduced to Abigail Hartford yet?' Lady Mary Waterstone's insistent voice had carried piercingly across the dining table the previous evening. Her gaze was equally compelling. 'I think she would make the perfect wife for you, dearest Robert. She is not only attractive and well-educated in all the feminine arts, but plays the harpsichord divinely, rides horses with skill, and furthermore she is Viscount Hartford's eldest daughter. A better wife than dear Abigail would be exceedingly hard to find.' Lifting a large spoonful of sugared strawberries, and shovelling them into her rose-painted mouth, she continued without pause, spattering small globules of the masticated fruit over the starched tablecloth. 'Well? I do think you should consider her. Now that you have reached your twenty-first year, it is time you settled down. I am sure your dear father would be delighted if you were to present him with a grandson soon, wouldn't you, Cedric?'

Shifting her considerable bulk around in the groaning chair, she turned to Robert's father, Lord Cedric Marchant. He was deep in conversation with the wife of the County Sheriff, and had managed to blot out the shattering tones of Lady Waterstone, a practice that he'd made into something of an artform.

Robert spoke quickly and determinedly, before Lord Marchant could reply. 'My father will have his grandson in due course, Lady Mary. I see no reason to rush into marriage simply to please other people. I will marry when I feel the time is right for me, and not before. More strawberries?' He gestured to the family butler, a soldierly figure called Presland, who appeared silently at Lady Mary's elbow with a silver dish loaded with the delicious berries.

Like his father's adroit ability to become deaf when required, Robert was adept at changing the subject. He had spent years talking animatedly about the weather, the state of the harvest, or the lastest gossip about the wavering health of the King. The current topic of conversation around the country's dinner tables was the threat of war with France, an increasingly violent nation, which had just come through the throes of a bloody revolution, brutally executing their King and Queen. Although of great general interest to Robert, it had no actual bearing on his life. France was such a long way away.

The more pressing matter for Robert, at present, was how to tell his father that he had no intention of providing him with an heir. He had known for many years that the company of men was preferable to the company of women. He also knew that the joys of being sexually involved with a man far outweighed any sensation one might have with any waspish female. No woman could hold you in a strong embrace, could match your manly strength or know how certain intimate actions felt, and, from this innate knowledge, reciprocate fully in the wondrous sex act. Robert had only really started seriously "going" with other men in the last few months. Of course there had been the obligatory adolescent games at his boarding school. He would often smile at his happy memories of playing the "Circle Game": as many boys as wanted to participate stood naked and erect in a circle and each would then pull off the boy on his right hand side, as quickly as possible. The last boy to come would have to do the dormitory chores for a whole week. Robert had never been last.

Until recently, he'd been rather afraid of doing anything more intimate. Afraid that if he did, a thunderbolt from above would sizzle down and smite him. Afraid that someone would find out about his secret desires for men. All he had really done so far was look at, admire, and have the occasional fondle with any willing partner. There had been one rather unpleasant experience a couple of years before, with an older man in London, but he'd since put that unwholesome escapade from his mind.

At any time, he could recall vividly that recent first full sexual experience, as it was etched on his heart, the thought of it still making his pulse quicken. The act itself was over in a few short moments, but was incredibly important to him. He had made the acquaintance of a travelling apothecary in the local village, who had led him to a deserted barn on the outskirts, knelt before him and taken his cock in his mouth. It had only lasted but a handful of minutes, the astounding sensation sending Robert into paroxysms of delight. He had come quickly, his whole body shaken. The nameless pedlar then picked up his cases and vanished, leaving Robert sitting on a bale of straw, unable to speak or move for the next half-hour. Whenever he desired, he could bring that afternoon back perfectly to his mind, the exact feel of the cool breeze on his cheek, the rough texture of the pedlar's coat sleeves, the exotic smell of the hair tonic that this stranger was wearing. But, try as he might, he could not recall the man's face or name. Perhaps the act of sexual congress had been more important to him than the person performing it? Since then he had sought out other willing men, young studs from around the county, rich or poor, it mattered not, to satiate his lust for men. Not always succesfully, though. On one occasion he had mistaken the signals he had been given by a farmhand. What Robert had interpreted as sexual interest had, in fact, been just friendliness. The worker seemed none the wiser, though, and Robert vowed to be a lot more careful in future.

All of this was still secret though, and would remain so. Lord Marchant must never know the sordid details, but soon he must be told the truth about his son's proclivities, that a marriage between Robert and some winsome young woman would never happen. But what was the point in rushing to make his father unhappy? The truth could wait.

With a final glance in the mirror, Robert ambled to the dressing table, picked up the fierce riding crop lying there, and thwacked it against the side of his boot, the satisfying sound echoing around his plush bedroom. With a deep, satisfied breath, Robert strode from the room. Today would be a good day. He loved his early morning rides, thundering around the estate on Prince, his new thoroughbred Arabian stallion, a gift from his father on the event of Robert's twenty-first birthday, five days earlier.

That day also held happy memories for Robert. He had been woken from a rather pleasant dream by the sound of pebbles being thrown at his window. Hastily pulling a dressing gown over his naked form, he pushed the window open and looked down into the smiling eyes of his father, holding the reins of the most beautiful horse he had ever seen. Throwing some clothes on, he dashed downstairs and immediately took the horse out for a canter before breakfast.

Robert chuckled at this more recent memory as he dug his heels in and spurred Prince on into a gallop. It was a lovely autumn morning. The leaves on the trees still had their colour, and the sprinkling of dew on the grass made everything smell like new. The balmy blue sky had a dusting of feathery, white clouds. The feel of the black beast between his legs was somehow strangely erotic. The rising and falling of its haunches against Robert's groin sent ripples of pleasure through his entire being. As he reached the brow of the hill at the edge of the estate, he pulled Prince up sharply and looked down at the glorious sight that lay before him: the verdant, undulating lawn that led down to the lake, and beyond it the gleaming white portico of the family home, Marchant Hall. He never grew tired of this view, the house that he loved, that he had grown up in, that would one day be his.

'C'mon Prince,' he yelled excitedly as he cracked the riding crop and forced the horse into a trot, getting faster and faster as they careered down the hill towards the lake.

Suddenly a shot rang out. Prince, galloping along the edge of the lake, started and reared up with a neigh of fright. Trying to hold on, Robert pulled at the reins, but they slipped from his grasp. Badly frightened, the horse galloped off toward the house. With a cry, Robert felt himself falling sidelong into the brackish water.

'Master Robert!'

Benham, the gamekeeper's assistant, came running around the side of the house, a rifle hanging from his shoulder. 'Are you hurt, Sir?' He threw the rifle to the ground and reached out a strong, bronzed arm. Robert sat up, slightly dazed, and, realising he was sitting in only a few inches of water, began to laugh. He took Benham's arm and squelched to his feet.

'Thank you, but I seem to be alright now.'

'What happened, Sir?'

'Oh, my horse bolted. There was a shot, and he just panicked. No harm has been done.'

Benham looked shamefacedly down at the ground and began to nervously scuff the dust with the toe of his boot. 'I'm so sorry, Sir. That was me. I was cleaning Mr Willoughby's rifle when I dropped it and it went off. Nearly blew my head off. Please forgive me. I don't know what to say.' The young man stared up at him, his full, brown eyes giving the sensation of boring right through Robert. It was a rather unnerving feeling. Robert shook his head and smoothed his hair back, disquieted by the attention.

Wringing the water from his coat tails, Robert took a slow look at this young man. He had never taken much notice of him before. Hadn't he only recently joined the estate staff? He rcalled that Willoughby the Gamekeeper had spoken highly of him. He was conscious of an uneasy feeling in his stomach as he looked up and down this rather attractive young buck.

'Do not worry, no bones have been broken. I'm only a little wet.' He paused. 'William, isn't it?'

'Yes, Sir.' Benham kept his eyes downcast, looking no higher than Robert's waist. 'I could go and look for the horse for you, Sir.'

'She'll come back in her own time.' Robert was conscious of the fact that his soaked riding breeches were clinging tightly to his well-muscled legs. Benham seemed aware of this too, as his eyes seemed to linger around Robert's private area. Something stirred and Robert knew that the outline of his aroused manhood was now quite obvious. Was this young man interested in him? Robert was a little unsure, but quite curious to know for certain. He pulled at the waistband of his breeches, hauling them up, emphasising the bulge at his groin. Benham's eyes were glued to that slowly growing mound. That settled it.

Although Robert had been born into a privileged class of society, and lived in a world that had both an elite and a working class, he knew that all men were equal in the eyes of God, and where a person came from should have no bearing on how you treated him. William Benham was employed as a servant, but he was also a man, and an attractive one at that, thought

Robert. Small of stature but perfectly formed, his body seemed extremely fit. Those piercing eyes, that firm, round face surrounded by a mop of ruffled brown hair, held a promise of something deeper. His shirt was open to the waist, revealing a few wisps of auburn chest hair, and his smooth, unblemished skin had a sun-browned hue, as many who worked on the land had. He might only have aspired to be a Gamekeeper's assistant, but he obviously had hidden depths.

The logical thing to do now would be to go back to the house and dry himself off, then change clothes. But who said one should be logical? Robert chuckled silently.

'I should really get out of these wet things, young man. Don't you think?'

William Benham hesitated for only a second before rubbing his chin in mock perplexity. 'Hmmm. I think so too, Sir. The Gamekeeper's cottage is just across the way. I have some towels in my room, if that would be of use to you, Sir?'

Without waiting for an answer, William strode off around the house, the knowledge that Master Robert was following, absolutely certain. He wasn't wrong. With a jaunty step, and whistling a jolly tune, Robert stepped out after him.

As he reached the small, ivy covered cottage on the outskirts of the woods, Robert saw the front door had been left ajar. He pushed it fully open and poked his head inside. 'Ho, there! Is anybody home?'

'Up here, Sir.' William's voice came from an upstairs room. Robert headed for the narrow wooden staircase and stealthily made his way up. He crept along the darkened landing until he came to the last room. Pushing the oaken door open with a creak, he beheld William, stripped to the waist, laying out two large dry towels on the bed. 'I think you should get out of those wet clothes, Sir. You don't want to catch a chill.' Robert moved toward the bed, slowly untying his cravat and throwing it across the back of a chair. William reached forward and helped Robert slip out of his sodden coat, which fell to the floor with a watery flop. Robert took the opportunity to look over this friendly young man. He obviously worked hard, his chest was well defined and there were the beginnings of muscular ripples on his stomach. A very fine specimen of manhood indeed. Running his hands through his mop of brown hair, William stood waiting. A distant clock ticked laboriously. The air of the room was slightly musty. Seeing a chair in the corner of the room, Robert lowered himself into it, his breeches squelching as he sat. Although he felt exceedingly uncomfortable, he didn't want to appear too eager... as eager as William seemed to be. The boy's eyes never left Robert's. They had a charming twinkle about them, a determination that showed William wasn't just an unthinking servant. He had character and self-worth. He might be an interesting person to get to know.

'So how long have you been working here, William?' Robert's voice trembled a little, and so he gave a cough to try and cover his slight nervousness.

'Six months, Sir.' William held Robert's gaze, his eyes large and inviting.

'Good. And how old are you?'

'Nineteen, Sir, and five months.'

'Very good. And are you happy here?' Robert hated small talk, but he was unsure as how else to proceed at present. Remembering his previous unfortunate misunderstanding with that farmhand, he wanted to be completely sure that William was offering himself for sex, and not just being overly helpful.

'Very happy, Sir. In fact, this is the most pleasant position I have ever had. I once... ' He trailed off, the red glow of embarassment spreading over his face, his eyes looking down at the floor. He realised he was going to start sharing a private memory, and it wasn't the done thing to be intimate with your betters. Unless asked of course, and Robert had been singularly unforthcoming.

There was something very appealing about this boyish naivety, and Robert was beginning to become aroused again. He opened his legs wide and let his hand rest lightly on his groin, the tips of his fingers gingerly brushing the tip of his enclosed cock. This was the invitation William had been waiting for.

Cautiously taking a step forward, William gave a hint of a smile, a tiny suggestion of impropriety in his manner. 'I should take off those wet things now, Sir. The sooner you do, the sooner they'll be dry. Let me give you a hand.' Standing now at Robert's side, he was irresistible. Levering himself up, Robert let the boy untie the bows on his shirt front, easing the garment off, sliding the sleeves from his arms. Robert lifted his arms and ran his fingers across his head, smoothing his hair and giving William the added sight of his flexing muscular biceps. He wasn't sure if he noticed a slight grin of appreciation, or not, from the Gamekeeper's lad.

A thought crossed Robert's mind and he pulled back sharply. 'What about Willoughby? Where is he?'

'Don't worry, Sir. He's out catching rabbits, he'll be gone all morning, most like.' That was all the encouragement Robert needed. He let his fingers stroke William's face, a few dark bristles poking through the soft skin. Their lips gently met. William opened his mouth and his tongue tentatively darted out. They began to kiss passionately, grasping each other's bodies tightly, gasping for breath and feeling the warmth of another willing man, holding each other tight for what seemed an eternity.

Robert ran his hands up William's leg and felt, firm, muscular thighs. His fingers stopped at the large mound, which gave away the size of the cock. It strained for release from the confining material of his trousers. Kneeling, Robert began to gently work his way down the buttons, until the trousers fell to the ground around William's ankles. He stared with delight at the engorged penis which stood there. He was pleasantly surprised by its size, about seven inches long and quite thick. There was a large tuft of soft hair at the base which grew upwards before trailing off to a few strands just below the navel. Underneath, resting between his thighs, were the balls, not too large but beautifully shaped. Above them, the cock was hard and waiting, and curved upwards, the foreskin just pulling back slightly, showing the slit at the end of the bulbous head, a drop of liquid oozing out from it.

Robert stared at this treasure, almost too afraid to put it into his mouth. The head suddenly jerked. He looked up at William and their eyes met.

'Please take me in your mouth, Sir.' William seemed to be almost pleading.

Leaning forward on his haunches, Robert took a deep breath and inhaled that heady smell of musk and sweat... the smell of a man. Their eyes never left each other's as he let his tongue flick across the tip of the enraged cock. Grasping the shaft, Robert slid the foreskin back to reveal the purple head beneath. Licking it again, he let his tongue snake along the underside, leaving a trail of glistening saliva. Realising that it was now or never, Robert slid the monster prick into his mouth until it filled his throat, the tuft of pubic hair tickling his nose. Slowly pulling back he let his wet mouth plunge down the length again and again. He determined that this young man would have an experience to remember, and he was now starting to really enjoy this.

Swallowing hard, he took the weapon down again until it touched the back of his throat. William began to moan. Gripping the back of Robert's head, he pumped his cock in that wonderful warm wetness, fucking the mouth with long, even strokes, pulling right back before plunging in deeply once more. Robert sucked for all he was worth, his tongue rolling around the column, drawing the length of William's manhood down, past the tonsils without even gagging. It was as if he wanted to draw the very life out if it. The pressure of the sucking was so intense and so glorious that William could have stayed like that forever. The young nobleman worked his lips all along the solid shaft, grasping the sides of William's waist, grinding his face against the soft, curled hair of his groin. The Gamekeeper's lad stiffened and Robert instinctively knew that an explosion was imminent. Sitting back, he stopped this oral assault and smiled up at his young friend.

'Not yet, you beauty. We have so much more to do before you come to the end!' Robert stood up and swiftly undressed, his cock responding to the feeling of freedom by growing bigger before William's appreciative eyes. The young man reached a hand forward and stroked it. The skin was silky smooth, a few veins stood out along the length and he saw that it was circumcised. He gripped it tightly and started to pump his fist up and down the huge tool.

Robert smiled at William's obvious enjoyment. His cock was larger than William's but it stood up at less of an acute angle. He knew what he had to do next. He put a finger in William's mouth and the young man hungrily sucked on it, making it very wet. Robert then took the lead. He held William by the shoulders for a moment then spun him around and pushed him over onto the bed. Spreading his buttocks apart, Robert slipped his hand between them, feeling for the arsehole. He gently probed the opening. William gave sharp intake of breath andRobert felt the whole of his muscular young body tremble. His finger dabbed gently at the puckered muscle-ring, letting the tip push past the pulsing sphincter. With his other hand, he swiftly kneaded and stroked the flesh around his arse cheeks. After some considerable time spent probing and tenderising the inviting pink ring, Robert knew that this young man was ready. William's breath came in short, sharp bursts. This was it.

Spitting a large gob of saliva onto the hole, Robert centred his hardened cock against the hole and pushed, impaling William on the first two hardened inches. William cried out with shock and pain, but was stopped by a hand placed over his mouth. He could feel the solid dick pushing up inside him, inch by inch, convinced that he would be ripped apart. He had never known such a sensation. Another man had entered him, and he loved it! He began to relax and tried to accommodate the rigid mass.

Robert pulled back before thrusting forward again, his balls touching against the downy skin of William's arse cheeks. He ran his fingers down so that he could feel his cock stuffed inside that throbbing hole. Once more he pulled out slowly, and felt the pressure ease around the thick shaft, then forced it back up, sensing the walls of the young man's arse stretching, becoming used to such an invasion. Gradually he increased the tempo as he started to push harder and with more speed. William bit into the flesh of the hand covering his mouth. He was in a haze of ecstasy, he had never known anything like this before. The pain of the first thrust had felt like a bolt of lightning surging through his entire being, as didthe knowledge that he was filled with an incredible sensation... another man's cock deep inside him. Through his deep breaths, Robert whispered in William's ear, 'Let us finish together!'

His fucking got faster, fand he felt the tightening of his own balls, which meant an eruption was not far away. William reached down and grabbed his own hard cock and began to stroke it furiously, the dual sensation now finally bringing him to a shuddering climax. 'Ohhh! I cannot hold it any longer!' He came in great heaving bolts as Robert pulled out and shot across his sweat-covered back. Hot spurts of white fluid erupted from them both. As their rasping breaths gradually slowed and their bodies stopped shaking with the intensity of their orgasms, Robert fell onto the bed and started to tenderly kiss the back of William's neck, whispering to him. 'Hell's teeth! That was wonderful, William. I hadn't expected it to be so good. This cannot have been your first time?'

'No, I have had sex with a lad from the village a few months back, but we only sucked each other. I have been fucked before, but this will be my second time only.' He eased himself round so that they lay face to face, their cocks touching and stiffening once more.

'Did you enjoy it?' Robert asked, in a hushed voice.

'More than I can say, Sir.' As he started to speak, an outpouring of emotion came tumbling from his lips, as if a dam had burst. 'You don't know how long I've been wanting to be with another man in this way. I am so glad that it was you who took me. I've been aware of you since I came to work here. You've made me feel special — that I'm not just a nobody that no-one cares about.'

The depth of feeling in William's speech touched Robert intensely. Here was a young man who had obviously kept his passion at arm's length for ages, never daring to do anything about his natural needs. Here was a young man to be treasured. 'Are you honestly telling me that this was only your second time being fucked?'

William was about to reply when the door was thrown open.

Willoughby, the Gamekeeper, stood framed in the doorway, speechless, his mouth agape at the sight of his apprentice and his master's son, naked and erect in each other's arms.

TWO

'You will explain yourself, Sir!' Lord Marchant glared furiously at his son, who stood before him, hands clasped behind his back. Robert stared back at his father, trying to find the words to describe how he felt. 'Father, I have something to tell you, that you will not want to hear.' He moved away from the fireplace and strode toward the imposing french windows across the room. The heat in the library was becoming unbearable. Rivulets of sweat coursed down Robert's face. This was the hardest thing he'd ever had to do. His future lay in the balance. Everything that he held dear could be snatched from his grasp in a second. Something deep within his psyche told him not to tell his father the truth, that this was not the right time.

All of Hampshire knew that Lord Marchant was fiercely proud of his son. What father wouldn't be? He was handsome, well educated, intelligent, an excellent swordsman and good with horses, quite a catch indeed. Even though he idly spent his days at leisure, frequently indulging in hunting, shooting and fishing, and seemed to have no solid plans for a future career, he was Lord Marchant's only hope. As an only child, Robert was expected to continue the family line — but four hundred years of the Marchants would probably end with him. This situation required the utmost tact and delicacy.

With a cough to clear his throat, Robert faced his father. 'I... I... Please understand me, father, this will never happen again. It was an aberration.'

'Of course it was an aberration. You were found in bed with another man, God knows what you were doing. There is no reason on this Earth for two men to be lying together, unclothed. Apart from devilish feelings of evil, wanton lust. No son of mine is going to be one of those degenerate effeminate types.' Lord Marchant's face was like a block of stone. No emotion showed on it as he spoke slowly and precisely. ' I will not allow it. This is a proud and well-respected family. People look up to us. I will not let you bring shame upon us. As my only child, you are my sole heir and you are the only one who can further the family line.'

Lord Marchant paused as if weighing up what he was going to say next. 'As my only child, you will be bound to inherit this house, and the fortune that goes with it. But that will be on two conditions only.'

He paused and took a sip of water. Robert watched the small vein on his father's forehead twitch, as it often did when he was angry. 'I want to make a proper man of you. You must prove to me that this was an error of judgement on your part, that will never be repeated.' He gripped his lapels and stared forcefully at his son. 'Tomorrow, I am riding to London to seek an audience with His Majesty the King. He knows me well, and looks fondly upon the Marchant family. I shall ask him for a commission for you in the Royal Navy. You shall go to sea as a midshipman and learn the ways of the sea, and the ways of being a man. Then, in three years' time, you shall return and marry the bride I shall have selected for you.'

Robert's mind was in a turmoil. The happenings of the morning, plus the effect of several glasses of madeira wine, had a giddying effect on him and he slumped into an armchair. Most of the time his father was a good-natured man, always seeing the best in people, never having an unpleasant word for anyone. He had never seen Lord Marchant like this before. He didn't know how to deal with him.

Should he agree to the plan and hope that in the morning Lord Marchant would have calmed down enough to have his mind changed? If he remained obdurate, then Robert saw himself being shipped off, like the victims of the notorious 'press gangs', to a life of slavery on the high seas. Midshipmen were treated little better than the ordinary Jack-Tars, and worked to the limit of their endurance, scrubbing decks, polishing brass, unfurling sails and hauling tar-covered ropes. They had no off-duty time, as they would be expected to learn such things as navigation, trigonometry and handling weapons. Ship's food was a disgrace, salted pork and hard biscuits, their quarters a shared cabin, with no privacy, and they were invariably bullied mercilessly by the rest of the crew. "Mids" were kept on the run from morn to night, and half that night was spent frozen to death, perched precariously in the crow's nest high above the ship.

These thoughts plunged Robert into a pit of despair. He had to say something. 'Father. I cannot agree with this. A life at sea would be a living hell. You cannot surely wish that upon me for this one mistake.'

Lord Marchant turned away and gazed up at the portrait of his late wife, Robert's mother, Lady Eliza Marchant, and his voice dropped. 'Robert, I confess I am shocked and puzzled by your behaviour today. You are my only son, and I love you dearly, but this dilettante life you have so far led has to stop. You are twenty-one and need a firm direction in your life to follow. This is the only way I can think of to make you face up to the harsh realities of the world. You cannot go through your life just wandering aimlessly. I have made my mind up. You will do as I say.'

'And if I refuse, Sir?'

'You will not refuse. I will this very evening be adding a codecil to my will, disinheriting you forthwith if you do not act as I have ordered. I shall take it with me to London tomorrow, and lodge it with our solicitors. My word is final.'

Looking away from his father, Robert cleared his throat. 'And what of William, I mean Benham, the Gamekeeper's lad? What will happen to him?'

'He has been sent packing. It is quite clear that he led you to partake in this indecency. I can no longer countenance his working here. Do not try to see him. If I learn that you have, you'll regret your actions dearly.'

With a last look at his son, contempt vying with pity, Lord Marchant turned away and slammed the door behind him.

Robert sat on, thinking madly. There was no way he would submit to this gross indignity. He had to change his father's mind, or else his life would be purgatory. He felt terribly alone. If only his mother were here. She would have been able to soothe his father's wrath. But gone were the days when he could run to her arms and feel safe against the world.

Perhaps he should run away? If he departed that night, leaving a long letter of regret and apology to his father, perhaps he might be forgiven. All his father needed was time. Yes, that was it. He would pack a few things into his saddle-bag and ride for the coast. The bustling sea-port of Portsmouth would be a fine place to spend some time, and in a week or so he would return and beg an audience with his father. Surely by then he would have relented, and his anger would have subsided.

He sprang up from his armchair and slipped upstairs to his rooms. From around his neck he pulled a key tied to a red ribbon, the key to the large wooden chest in the corner of the bedroom. The key turned easily in the lock.

Lifting the lid, he knelt beside it. Pushing aside packs of letters and various battered wooden toys, he felt around for a small velvet box. Inside this box lay many gold sovereigns. Robert counted out twenty and dropped them into a leather drawstring purse. That should be more than enough to pay for a week's stay in Portsmouth. Fixing the bag to his belt, he then re-locked the chest and sat down at his writing desk to compose a letter to his father. Dipping the quill into the ink, he wrote:

My Dearest Father,

Please do not think too ill of me, but I cannot abide by your wish that I go to sea. It would be unutterable hell and would, I fear, change me too much for the bad. I beg you to reconsider your actions and delay speaking to the King. I am going away for a short while to afford both of us the time to ponder our futures... I have some little money and will be fine. Please do not try to find me, I hope that when I return I will have the honour of attaining your love and trust once more.

Your loving and wayward son,
Robert.

He sprinkled this letter with sand, sealed it with a blob of sealing wax, and sat back to wait for night to fall.

As the grandfather clock in the dining room struck midnight, Robert crept stealthily down the great staircase, carefully avoiding the creaking floorboards in the hall, and slipped out of the kitchen door. The sound of his tread upon the gravel path seemed as though it would wake the whole house. Biting his lip, he made his way to the stables and saddled up Prince, who had come ambling home during the afternoon. The great black horse sensed his master's touch and whinnied appreciatively.

'Quiet, you stupid beast, or I'll sell you to the butcher!'

A rustling noise came from the straw in the hayloft above his head. Looking up, Robert could make out a crouching, darkened figure. 'Who is there? Come down here at once.'

It took only a moment to realise that it was William, clambering down the ladder. The young man rushed to Robert's side and flung his arms around him.

'Alright, William, it's alright. What happened to you?

William looked up with tears in his eyes, bits of straw poking out of his tousled hair. 'Well, after Mr Willoughby found us, I put on my clothes and followed him to the house, where he told his Lordship what had happened. Lord Marchant just sat there dumbstruck and told me to go, without wages, or a reference, or nothing. I don't know what to do. I've got nowhere to go, not with my parents being dead. I've just been sitting up here waiting for you. I knew you'd come and find me. We could go away together, eh? Somewhere remote, and quiet, and be together always. Please say yes.' Silent tears coursed down his face, and his body trembled with cold and fear. Robert felt a stab of remorse and enfolded William in his arms. He had never had to look after anyone else before. Could he do it? William was steadfastly relying on Robert to see him through his immediate problems. He would just have to try.

Robert kissed the top of William's head and whispered, 'Don't worry, I'll sort everything out. I'll look after you. You can come with me to Portsmouth and we'll have a lovely week there together, and we'll try and find you a wonderful new job.'

Their eyes met and they gazed at each other for what seemed like hours. Robert could feel his companion's body becoming aroused, and so was his own. He bent forward and kissed William on the forehead, before placing both hands on his shoulders and roughly pushing him down to his knees. William went willingly, and then hurriedly began to unfasten the waist-buttons on Robert's trousers. He reached in a hand and released the straining cock. Without a moment's hesitation he quickly plunged his mouth down over it. He must have done this before! William sucked hard, drawing back and then sliding down the whole length of the shaft, tightly holding it with his mouth and tongue. He ran his lips up and down the firm pole, exploring every inch, licking around the swollen head. This incredible attention caused such a spasm of delight to thrill through Robert that he arched backward, pushing his groin further forward. He wanted to shriek with joy at the intensity. Even William was squirming with delight at the thought of the wonderful experience he was providing for his new friend and mentor. Robert tried, but could hold back no longer, and he gave a cry of wonder and shot his pent-up fluid all over William's tear-streaked face. Unable to believe how much there was of this milky juice, Robert's body convulsed with the intense pleasure of orgasm.

After a few minutes, William used the sleeve of his shirt to wipe up, and then Robert took him by the arm and helped him to his feet.

'It's time to go.' He finished saddling Prince and then swung himself onto the horse's broad back, letting out a hand to William, who climbed up behind him.

The ride to Portsmouth took many hours. Prince trotted along the darkened country lanes, happily bearing the two young men towards the coast. Bats shrieked overhead, and owls hooted suspiciously as they passed by. They broke the journey at what Robert guessed was the half-way point. Sitting together under a broad plane tree, William resting his head on Robert's chest, their fingers entwined, they talked. Telling each other their family stories, their dreams, hopes and fears. On hearing that William had had an awful childhood, Robert immediately grew even more protective of him, and hugged him tightly.

'It seems like a terrible story, Robert, but I have known others who have fared worse than me.' William slid down, rested his head on Robert's lap and continued. 'I was an only child. My mother didn't seem able to have any more babies after I was born. Nobody knew why. I think my father blamed me for that, for causing some upset to her system. He desperately wanted more sons to carry on with his business. He was a wheelwright in Paddington, and he had inherited the business from his father.'

An owl hooted somewhere above them. William paused and listened intently to it, as if deciphering some secret message. When all had gone quiet, he carried on speaking. 'As I grew up he always seemed to resent me, never having a kind word for me. I was given menial tasks to do, and if I slipped up in any way, I would be beaten. Some nights, when I'm in bed, I can still see him coming at me with his big, studded belt in his hand and a look of pure hatred on his face. Sometimes I couldn't sit down for weeks. Many was the time my mother would soothe my wounds and then rock me to sleep, singing a lullaby, her body heaving with sobs for her poor baby. I loved her so and still miss her every day.'

Robert saw that tears were falling from William's eyes and landing silently on his jacket, a damp patch spreading slowly on the suede. 'But everytime I think of her, I think of my father and I hate him all over again. He made her life a misery, and she deserved so much better than him. Somehow I managed to grow up a fairly normal, well-adjusted boy. I was a bit of a loner, though, and had few friends. I would enjoy getting away from Paddington and catching a ride to Battersea Village to see the great lavender fields. The air would have a blue haze and the whole place would be heavy with their wonderful smell. I would always bring my mother a posy of lavender back, and she'd wear it on her breast. Then some days I would go down to Blackheath and watch the richer children flying their kites. Did you know that Blackheath was where they buried lots of the plague victims? It's true. In fact, the lullaby my mother would sing me to sleep with was the one about the plague... how did it go...?'

William scratched his nose and sang quietly to himself.

'Ring a ring of roses
A pocket full of posies
A-tishoo, a-tishoo
We all fall down.'

He closed his eyes for a moment before continuing. 'I would also love walking up to Hampstead and strolling about the heath, listening to the birds and looking for nests with eggs in them, or rabbit warrens. I remember I found an injured rabbit once, it can only have been a baby, and I wrapped it in my coat and carried it home. My mother helped to tend its broken leg and I kept it in a cage in my attic room. I loved that animal, and called him Alexander. He would look up at me and wrinkle his nose, and know that I was caring for him. One afternoon, I came home from a walk at Hampstead and found his cage empty. I ran downstairs, crying for him, yelling his name. My mother was standing in the kitchen, a sad look on her face, and my father was sitting at the table, with Alexander's crumpled body in front of him. I'll never forget his words. "You worthless little bastard. I didn't say you could keep vermin in my house. I've wrung his scrawny neck, and we shall have a rabbit pie for supper, right Mum?" All I could do was sit at the table and watch as my poor mother skinned and gutted the creature. At supper, under my father's watchful eye, I took a mouthful of that horrid pie, and had to run outside to be sick.' He stopped for a moment to wipe his eyes with the back of his sleeve. Robert gently stroked his hair, wondering if he had ever spoken about this before to anyone. He felt honoured that William had trusted him enough to want to open his heart like this. 'Go on, finish your story.' Robert's voice was soothing.

'I was about fourteen when I came home one day to a dreadful scene. There had been a fire at a laundry down the street from our house, and the whole street had burned down. My mother had been trapped upstairs in the bedroom. One of our neighbours told me that he'd seen my father lolling drunkenly in the street, waving a bottle of ale at her and saying good riddance. His words were "I hope you burn, you miserable witch." She died in that fire. I couldn't bear to live with him after that and so ran away.

'I eked out a living for the next three years, travelling about, doing odd jobs, sleeping rough most nights, and when I was seventeen, I found myself among a group of boys in Brighton, who moved about the country, from town to town, offering their bodies for money. Somehow I knew this was wrong, but I tagged along, because for the first time in my life I was treated as an equal, as a human being in my own right. I couldn't bring myself to do what they were doing, but the whole thing fascinated me. I had never really been interested in girls, I found that I got more excited being near a man, someone strong and masculine. I never did anything about it because I was too scared.

One of the boys, their leader, a big eighteen-year-old called Colin, tried to get me to do some business with a butcher that he knew in Hove, but I just couldn't. Colin took me to a shabby room in an old house where I was introduced to the man. He was very nice, but when he tried to touch me I froze, broke down in tears and ran from the room. After that, Colin didn't try to set me up with anyone again and he let me be their watchman, keeping an eye out for them when they were doing the business in any public place. The number of times I was chased by the local beadle and his men is countless. Luckily, I was small and fast on my feet.

In time, it became the most natural thing in the world for one man to be with another, and I finally did have sex last summer, with a French-Canadian sailor, when the boys and me were in Southsea. He was on shore leave, and saw me in a local inn notorious for its street boys. I had heard that the innkeeper also kept a male brothel in another part of town. I was sitting in a corner with a glass of rum, and Franck, that was his name, came over and started talking to me. I had no intention of going with him, but his voice was so beautiful, and he was so handsome and charming that I fell for him there and then. We went up to one of the empty rooms upstairs. The inn-keeper, who fancied me I think, let me have it for half the going rate, and we had sex. It was wonderful. He was a marvellous lover, tender and giving, but also forceful when he needed to be. That first time I sucked a cock was a glorious life-changing experience. I cannot describe the joy of that moment, and when he did the same for me, I thought I would die of ecstasy. He fucked me that night, and although the pain was excruciating, I loved every moment of it. The feeling of another man inside me, and he wasn't small by any means, was indescribable.

'We stayed together all night, and when the time came for him to go back to his ship, I just hugged him and didn't want him to go. But he had to. He left a five pound note on the pillow and left without a look back at me. I will always be grateful to him for that first time, and often wonder where in the world he is.

'I decided to move on after that, and worked my way across country, learning the ways of the land from farmers and poachers. I had never lost my love of the countryside, and animals.Then I met Mr Willoughby, who seemed to like me, and took me on as his assistant at Marchant Hall. The rest you know.'

Robert did know. William had apparently met Jacob Willoughby, Lord Marchant's Gamekeeper, at the village market six months previously, and had greatly impressed him with his knowledge of animal trapping. Willoughby had taken him on, and he was thrilled to be working at the house of a famous Lord of the realm. He had watched as Willoughby trapped animals without hurting them, which was a great advantage to the animal-loving William. He turned away when they had to be killed, but took great care in helping breed new colonies of rabbits and game birds. He had seen Robert around the estate on numerous occasions, but hadn't had the courage to speak to him. Now that he had, and they had suddenly become intimate, William wasn't going to let him go. He hadn't known such a special and caring man before, whose sexual prowess outshone even Franck's.

William wasn't stupid, for he knew that such a relationship as theirs would not be easy. It would be frowned upon by society, for many reasons, not least of which, the fact that they were two men, as well as being from different social classes. It would be difficult, but with strength they could win through against those closed-minded bigots. Couldn't they? Snuggling into Robert's lap he felt safe, perhaps here was the man to finally look after him for the rest of his life. Wiping his nose, and giving Robert a gentle kiss on the cheek, William helped him to his feet, and clambered up onto Prince's strong back for the rest of the journey.

It was around 9 o'clock in the morning when they found themselves riding along the port's main street, clopping their way past the bustle of the day. Grand carriages, attended by postillions and footmen in gaudy liveries, clattered along the dirt road, counterpointing the somber brown and black worn by the local countryfolk. Most people were heading for market, baskets carried on their arms or atop their heads. A rich variety of goods graced the many shop windows, tempting passers-by to stop and look. The street was so crowded that Robert had to steer Prince with extreme care. Every now and then delicious smells would waft toward them, fresh baked bread, malty ale or some other spicy scent. It occurred to them that they were hungry and that buying some breakfast might be a wise idea.

Heading toward the quay, they found a half-timbered inn named The Olde Oake, which looked inviting. Having tied Prince up to the rail and let him take his fill from the water trough, Robert led the way inside. A roaring fire was crackling in the grate and the walls were hung with brasses and ancient portraits of different ships, all engaged in multifarious nameless sea battles. The inn-keeper, a thin, wiry man with a shock of grey hair, nodded as they entered. He was listlessly wiping the bar but, sensing money in his guests, he sprang forward. A one-bedded room would be three shillings a day, if shared. He looked slightly disdainfully at William, shuffling behind Robert's coat-tails.

Robert drew himself up and stared imperiously at the inn-keeper. 'That will be sufficient. Now we would like to purchase some breakfast. What can you give us?'

The inn-keeper, who said his name was Walter, showed them to a table by the fireplace and proceeded to serve a rather palatable meal of fresh bread, cheese and cured ham, washed down with a jug of surprisingly good Bordeaux wine. Having sated their hunger, both men felt their exhaustion rolling over them, and so decided on retiring to their room to take a nap before exploring the town.

The room was small but clean. As expected, there was only one bed, but that mattered nothing to either of them. After pulling back the counterpane and sliding between the crisp, white sheets, William gave Robert a tight hug and quietly said 'Thank you.' He closed his eyes and in a moment was fast asleep, curled up in a tight, foetal ball. Robert lay on his back, his arm nestled against the back of his young friend, and considered. This wasn't an unpleasant place by any means. They could stay here for a week, explore the town and its environs, go riding in the forest — perhaps even a little fishing in the Channel might be amusing. Things weren't so bad after all, he thought, as he also drifted off into a deep, dreamless slumber.

Robert awoke with a start, at a loud crash and furious shouting from outside in the street. He looked at William who was still out to the world. Softly easing himself out of bed, he crossed to the dresser and picked up his fob watch. Four in the afternoon. He hadn't expected to sleep so long. Quietly dressing and slipping out of the room, he made his way down to the saloon of the inn.

A fit-looking young potman, with almost jet black hair, in a leather apron, was washing tankards in a large china bowl and whistling to himself. 'Afternoon, Sir. Enjoy your nap?'

Robert ambled over, adjusting his collar and straightening his tie. 'I certainly did, young fellow-me-lad! I have been riding all night, and I must have been more tired than I thought.' The potman grinned cheekily. 'Well as long as you're wide awake now, Sir. Besides, if you feel the urge to fall asleep again, just come and see me... I'll keep you up, Sir!' He winked broadly and carried his bowl through a door behind the bar.

Hesitating only slightly, Robert followed and putting his head round the door asked, 'Is Mr... er...Walter here, boy? I'd like to talk to him about... er... the room rates.'

'No he isn't, and my name's Jack, not boy,' the potman chuckled, his back to Robert now, his hands seemingly engaged in something in front of him.

Robert licked his dry lips. 'So there is no-one else around at the moment, then?'

'No there isn't. Perhaps you should come over here, Sir, and pull the door shut behind you.'

With a last look around the saloon, Robert pulled the door until the latch clicked solidly. He moved cautiously toward Jack, who spun round and lifted his leather apron. His breeches were already unfastened and his cock was standing proud and free, of average length, but exceedingly broad and thick.

Robert gazed appreciatively over the thick-set man standing before him. Almost as tall as Robert, with a short trimmed head of very black hair and a square-cut jaw, Robert imagined him as a prize fighter rather than a glorified washer-up. He watched as Jack lifted the apron and threw it dismissively to the ground. He lifted first one leg and then another as he unlaced his boots, and kicked them aside. Slowly and teasingly he lifted the grubby white shirt that stretched taughtly across his stomach, pulled it over his head and let it dangle from his hand, then let it fall.

Standing there naked, except for a spotted handkerchief tied loosely round his neck, Jack was like an ancient Roman statue, muscular and perfect, atop a marble pedestal, an example of man's beauty, except his cock was much bigger and harder than the Romans ever dared to portray. Did he know how breathtaking he was? Robert wondered if this was Jack's first time, but then swiftly pushed that idea from his mind. Of course it wasn't. He had the confident air of an expert.

As his tongue flicked lightly across his lips, Jack let one hand wander up to his chest. His manual work at the inn, carrying wooden barrels and casks of ale, had certainly given him some incredible muscles. Robert stared entranced as Jack's hands wandered across the well-defined torso, the fingers lingering around the nipples, tweaking and pinching. Unable to move, Robert stood rooted to the spot. Somehow Jack radiated an aura of control and power, and Robert didn't know how to react to this. Sensing Robert's uneasiness, Jack gestured with his head and gave a crooked smile. Stepping forward, Robert bent his head and sucked on those large, pink nipples, licking and gnawing until the tips were sore, and they stood firm and defiant. He caressed the neck and shoulders, first with his hands, then with his lips, all the while feeling the constant twitching of the cock, just out of sight. Several times Robert reached down and squeezed this firm pole, and fondled it between his sweaty palms.

Jack let his hand wander downwards over the taut belly toward the V-shaped muscle at the base of his stomach, leading to a whispy tuft of dark hair. This framed and seemed to emphasize the extraordinary dimensions of his erection, and knowing that Robert was now staring at it, Jack began to fondle it himself. Long, sensuous strokes, up and down the rigid cock, closing his eyes, letting the feeling take over his whole body.

Robert decided he had waited long enough. He reached out an arm and pulled Jack roughly to him. With still-closed eyes, Jack assented, not letting go of his dick, and without missing a stroke.

With a sigh of pleasure, Robert went at Jack's chest, again licking around the nipples, first one, then the other, teasing and gently nipping with his teeth. The soft moans of pain and pleasure flowing from Jack's mouth, made Robert shiver. He let his mouth move down the stomach, tongue lingering over the muscled ridges, before kneeling and heading for the crotch. His cock jerked in anticipation, then Jack muttered with a cracked voice, 'Go on then!' Inhaling deeply, Robert opened his mouth wide and with some difficulty enveloped the rigid prick in one swift movement. Jack gasped at the sensation, his cock buried tightly in this stranger's throat, right down to the heavy balls, which slapped against the chin. Robert slid back and let his tongue flick across the tip, around the head, and in and out of the slit, which was now oozing semen. He savoured the drop of fluid, knowing it was a foretaste of what was to come.

Without a warning, Robert began to suck again, his mouth rocked back and forth along Jack's cock, held in place by Jack's hands, entwined in his hair. The wideness of the shaft stretched Robert's mouth wide, and he felt the beginnings of an ache in his jaw. The potman was enraptured, watching the action with a grin on his cheery face. Robert stopped suddenly and let his mouth drop down to the balls. Taking one, then the other into his wet mouth, he sucked with a fervour he'd never experienced before. At a stretch he could take both the saliva-covered orbs into his mouth. Jack's body shook and he tried to pull away, but Robert's hold on his bollocks was so tight he couldn't move. Shuddering as they popped out of his mouth, Robert immediately dived back onto the cock, sucking again, with a violent suction, plunging from base to tip. It wouldn't be long now.

Jack started to shake, his breath became heavier and he twisted his fingers tightly in Robert's hair. Ignoring the pain of this, Robert quickened his pace, until Jack pulled out and shot his hot stream of white milk across Robert's face, pouring out bolt after bolt, it ran down Robert's cheeks and chin, dripping down onto his coat.

Robert staggered to his feet and leant back upon a beer barrel. 'That was fun. And very unexpected! Do you do this kind of thing often?'

With a laugh, Jack began to wipe and rearrange himself. 'It depends on who comes into the bar, and if I like the look of them!'

'You must have liked the look of me?'

'Oh, yes. As soon as I first saw you I knew I wanted to have you back here. And If you'll stop and have a drink with me, then I'd like to do to you, what you've just done to me.' He grinned again, a cheeky, infectious grin. Robert felt for his watch and noted the time. 'Normally I would have been delighted, Jack, but time is pressing. I should wake my companion. We need to purchase some new clothes and other toiletry items.'

Jack sniffed. 'I saw him with you earlier. Is he your lover boy?'

'Well, in a way, yes.'

'Have you run away, then?' said Jack.

'Not as such. We are both... having a short holiday break. Taking some time away from home. I am looking after him, as he has no family.'

'Sounds very cosy. Perhaps I could visit the both of you in your room, this evening? You will be around here this evening, won't you?' All of a sudden, he appeared slightly nervous.

'Perhaps.' Robert didn't dismiss the idea of a three-person sex session, as it had certain exciting dimensions to it, but this odd change of character puzzled him. 'We may see you later. Will we find you down here?'

'You can rely on it. In fact, I shall be totally free after 'time' is called. Come and find me back here.' Robert finished wiping his face with his handkerchief. 'I may well do that.'

The afternoon was warm and bright. Having bought some new shirts and underclothes, Robert and William headed toward the quay. Sitting on a wooden bench, with a bag of flavoured sugar crystals, William linked his arm in Robert's and sighed. 'This is so nice, here, with you. I don't ever want to leave.'

Robert pulled back slightly and pushed the arm away. 'You must be careful, when we are out among people, Will,' he said sternly, realising they had gotten a glare of distrust from a white haired, grizzled fisherman, seated a few yards away, surrounded by a mass of fishing net.

Knowing the truth in what Robert said, William sat back chastened, and looked out over the busy quayside.

'If we are to stay here for a while, we must be careful not to draw attention to ourselves.' Robert said, still watching the bobbing fishing boats.

'People don't understand our kind of feelings for each other, so try and be circumspect when we are in public.' William nodded.

'It's just that I've never met anyone like you before in my whole life, Robert. You are kind, and handsome, and you treat me like an equal, not just a work-slave. I so want to be with you always, I know you'll always be good to me.'

This blind faith was a little shocking to Robert. In his life so far, he had known many friends and occasional lovers, but never anyone who totally relied on him for all his needs. He wasn't sure if he was up to the task. Perhaps this is what marriage would be like? Having somebody else constantly with you, always reliant on you to take care of them, and provide for them, as well as never sleeping with anyone else ever again. But could he abandon this helpless young man now? Especially after he had found a period of stability in his so-far troubled life, and also as it was mostly his fault William had been fired. He couldn't bear the thought of the distress he'd cause if he dumped the boy. This needed some thought.

The rays of the setting sun cast long red streaks across the herring-bone clouds. A gentle breeze blew across the quay-side, making Robert shiver. 'Look, it's almost supper-time. Let us go back to the inn, freshen up and have some food. I am feeling quite hungry now. How about you?' William nodded and, standing up, led the way back to The Olde Oake, avoiding Robert's eyes, hands thrust deep into his pockets.

The bar was fairly busy. Sailors and villagers sprawled at tables and benches, supping ale, and a happy buzz of conversation and laughter hung in the air. Seated in their usual place by the log fire, the two lovers heartily consumed a filling meal of pork pie and baked apples. The Hock wine, imported from Germany, quickly went to William's head, and he began to relax considerably. As Robert was about to order a third flaggon, he felt a light touch on his shoulder.

'Hello there!' It was Jack, freshly scrubbed, and carrying a jug of beer. 'I was hoping I'd see you two.'

William looked puzzled at the way this stranger seemed to know Robert. 'Aren't you going to introduce me then?' Jack slumped down beside William and put out a hand. Sensing William's uneasiness, Robert leapt in, 'This is my friend William Benham. William, meet Jack.' He turned to the potman. 'I don't think you told me your surname?'

Jack fingered the towel hanging from his belt. 'I didn't. Jack is all you need to know.'

'Well, Jack works here at the inn. We met earlier this afternoon and... er... chatted for a while. He was keen to meet you. We all seem to have much in common.'

With a slight slurring of words, as the alcohol took further hold, William shook hands firmly. 'Very pleasant to meet you.'

'Pleased to make your acquaintance too, I'm sure,' Jack said in an exaggerated manner. The cheeky grin he gave melted any reservations William may have had, and he smiled back. Robert sat back and folded his arms happily. 'I think William has had a little more of your excellent wine than he should have!'

'That's alright. He needn't be sober for what I've got planned.'

'And what might that be?'

A momentary look of anxiety flitted across Jack's face. 'Oh...er... you'll find out.' He stood up and took the beer jug back to the bar, passing a dark-bearded man, who nodded at him. The man reached into his pocket and pulled out a small money purse which he deftly slid across the bar to Jack. Grabbing it, Jack gestured toward the two friends by the fire and quickly dashed out of the inn.

The heat in the saloon and the smoke were having a strange effect on William. His head slumped forward onto the table. 'Will, please, get up.' Panic gripped Robert. He was supposed to be looking after this young man, and here he was on the verge of unconciousness. 'Come on, you need some air.' With a grunt, he slipped his arm around William and helped him to his feet. Pushing aside benches, he guided his nearly comatose companion to the door. Lifting the latch, he pulled it open and stepped out. Before he had a chance to even inhale a breath of cool evening air, he was aware of someone shifting nervously near the door. With a swift movement, something hard and sharp came crashing down on the back of Robert's head. William's inert body fell to the ground as Robert saw stars, a violent shower of twinkling lights, then utter blackness.

THREE

It was the rasping cry of a distant seagull that eventually penetrated Robert's brain. The constant shrieking ripped through him. In his dream-like state, he was sure it was the neighing of a giant black horse, chasing him through the woods at Marchant Hall, his father astride the great beast, waving a whip and shouting wildly at his son.

With a wince of pain, he sat up and felt the large, egg-like lump on the back of his head. His eyes began to focus, and he looked around him in dismay. He was in a small, darkened, wood-beamed room. He tried to stand up but the floor lurched beneath him, and he pitched forward onto his knees. A bolt of fearful realisation jagged through his entire being. He was on a ship. All he remembered before blacking out was helping William from the saloon of The Olde Oake, and being hit on the head. With a sigh of despair Robert immediately knew what had happened. He had become another victim of the notorious 'Press Gang'. Groups of unscrupulous ruffians, kidnapping unsuspecting men for a couple of shillings, and bringing their inert bodies to whichever ship's Captain needed extra hands.

Shuffling on his knees to the door, bumping into the slumbering bodies of several others, he turned the handle, but it resisted. It was obviously locked from the other side. For the moment there was nothing he could do. Stiffly, he lay back on the hard floor and tried to visualise his situation. If he was out at sea, then there seemed no immediate hope of rescue. He would have to wait until they docked somewhere before trying to make a run for it. His name would carry no weight either. No-one cared who the extra, unwilling sailors were. The fact that he was heir to Lord Marchant would be as nothing. It might even mean he'd be treated worse than the others. If his fellow tars knew he came from a privileged background they would treat him abominably because if it. Until he had a firmer grasp of where he was, he would keep quiet. He felt for the money purse on his belt. Of course it had gone.

But what of William. Where was he? Had he also been captured? If he had, then it might make this hellish place slightly easier to bear. Thoughts of Jack filled his busy mind. His strange behaviour the previous evening suddenly made sense. Jack must have been a lookout for the Press Gang, searching out any strangers who came to the inn. Anyone running away from home or seeming to be hiding somethingwould be a prime target for the kidnappers. And the odd-looking man at the bar must have been the one who knocked him out. How could Jack have been so deceitful? Scheming bastard.

Robert had thought he was a nice chap. He had certainly seemed so when he was sucking his cock. Next time I'll be more cautious, he thought. Perhaps growing up in the lap of luxury, cossetted from the horrors of the real world, was not the best way to be raised? If he had only experienced more of life, and realised that people were not as nice as they pretended to be, then he wouldn't be lying here, a prisoner, with no possible means of escape. He closed his eyes and drifted off to sleep, the creaking of the ship's boards strangely soporific.

The shock of a bowl of freezing cold water being thrown over hi, woke Robert with a violent start. He gasped for breath, and tried to stand up. A strong pair of arms lifted him to his feet and dragged him from the room. Vaguely aware of a blur of faces, Robert was unceremoniously bundled out of a hatch and kicked onto the ship's deck. A loud cheer went up from the assembled crowd. Focusing his eyes on his surroundings, he saw he was only one of about a dozen men cowering on the deck while all about them the crew jeered and snarled abuse. The others were a motley bunch, from differing backgrounds, of course, in a variety of clothes. It seemed to Robert that he was probably the highest-born among them. A hush settled on the crew and all eyes turned upward to the bridge. Robert scrambled painfully to his knees and looked up into the glare of the man who'd just taken his position above them all. Tall, stocky, grey-haired, and with steely black eyes, the Captain waited until he had everyone's attention.

With a piercing gaze, he scanned the entire crew, before drawing himself to his full height and addressing them, his voice booming out authoritatively.

'I am Captain Greer. You are all upon His Majesty's warship, *The Valiant*. Some of you are here willingly, some of you... well let me just say that some of you needed a little "pressing". This is one of the proudest warships in the fleet, and it will continue to be so, be we just patrolling our coastline or engaged in bloody warfare. I am sure that some of you will be unaware that this country is now at war with France. It is a situation that has been brewing for many years. Finally Prime Minister Pitt has declared war on that despot, Napoleon Bonaparte.' A murmur of unease rumbled through the crew. 'I will do my utmost to ensure that the French will gain no hold on the Channel. Henceforth, I will be your mother and father. I am also your teacher and your God. You are now my loyal crew and will do what I say, when I say it. Your lives are no longer your own. Every task you perform, every thought you think will be at my command. I run this ship tightly, with Officers that I can trust to act as I deem fit. Any insubordination will be punished. Anyone who tries to defy me, or any of my Officers, will wish they had never been born.' Slipping his hat under his arm, he turned to his First Officer, a dark-haired, thin, but well-muscled individual. 'Mister Crook, get this rabble into shape. I want a first-class fighting force ready for action in one week from today. If you fail me, Mister, then you'll feel the bite of the 'Cat o'Nine Tails' yourself.'

Crook gulped and saluted. No-one ever argued with Captain Greer, one of the Navy's most feared sailors. He had risen through the ranks with a grim determination to reach the top, and he finally had. Being granted the command of *The Valiant* was a supreme honour, and Greer wasn't going to let his King down.

Spinning on his heels, Crook made his way down to the main deck. 'Now, you worthless bastards… the Captain wants us ready for action in one week, and by God I shall make sure you are. You there, Stubbs, take these new ones down below. At twelve of the clock I want the crew on deck and ready for drill.' A weather-beaten, surly-looking sailor gestured to the twelve men and led the way down to the lower hold, to where they would all sleep, cramped together with one blanket apiece. 'Here's your home for the forseeable future. Make yourselves comfortable!' Stubbs laughed, a wheezy, phlegm-rattling chuckle. You have one hour, then be up on deck. Anyone who's late will wish they weren't.' With a hacking cough, he spat out a blackened lump of chewing tobacco, which landed at Robert's feet.

Robert stood in the middle of this terrible place and pulled his coat about him tightly. This couldn't be happening to him. This was a bad dream. What kind of vengeful God would have put him in this appalling place. Was it a punishment for his desires and lusts? Surely not. He had to find a way out. Even if it meant swimming for it. If England was now at war with France, then it was likely that the ship was in the English Channel. With luck they might not be too far from the coast. He was fit and young, he could swim any great distance, couldn't he?

Another kipnap victim crawled from a corner and slumped down beside Robert. A hand poked out from the rough blanket covering his head. It grasped the leg of Robert's trousers, and as the blanket slid back, Robert suddenly found himself gazing down into the frightened eyes of William Benham.

FOUR

None of the experiences of Robert's fairly uneventful twenty-one years could have prepared him for the extreme horror of life on board a warship. He had imagined that things would be tough, but the severity of his new existence stunned even him.

That first afternoon had been a nightmare. In years to come he would look back on that day and shudder at the despair that had permeated his entire being.

Apart from the shivering shadows cast by the candle's flame, the hold had no light or heat. It smelt dank and foul. Stubbs's laughter echoed down the corridor after he had left them to settle themselves in, pointing at a pile of rough woollen blankets in a darkened corner, and telling them to get ready for their first taste of a naval drill. As the sound of his laughter and footsteps died away, Robert sank down to his knees. The floor didn't feel as hard as he had expected, so he judged that it was covered with straw matting. After a few moments, a faint scuffling sound from the far corner of the hold caught his attention. Robert jumped to his feet and flattened himself against the wall. He couldn't see them but he knew that there were rats there. Robert was no coward, he knew that he was a fine swordsman and could hold himself tall against any opponent, but the thought of hundreds of tiny, razor-sharp teeth nibbling at his flesh sent a spasm of terror down his spine.

'Robert. Please, Robert...' William's pleading voice shot through Robert's consciousness, a violent stab of remorse bringing him back to reality. He had to pull himself together and help William now. It was his fault they were in this terrible situation. 'Come here, William. Sit by me. It will be alright. It has to be. We will find a way out of this awful place, but it might take some time. We have to be strong, and try and cope with whatever happens here.' He lowered his voice and spoke gently into William's ear. 'We must also try and be extra careful because... I mean we musn't show any affection if... We cannot be open at all about our relationship. People here won't understand. In fact, we could even be put to death if we are caught doing anything. Is that clear?'

With a nod of his head, and a sob of despair, William assented and, grabbing a blanket, curled up into a tight ball, rocking back and forth. Something about the helplessness of this young man touched Robert's heart. He was in this terrible place because of Robert's desire for him. If he had only curbed his wanton urges and not had sex with him, then none of this would have happened. He watched the poor boy rocking himself, utterly dejected, and realised that he did have strong feelings for him. His openness and honesty stirred deeper emotions in Robert. Whatever happened, he had to get them both out of this awful situation.

Steeling himself for the worst, Robert staggered to his feet and shuffled forward a few paces in the darkened hold. His hands met the wooden wall, which felt moist. He followed the wall around until his fingers found the edge of the door, he gripped the handle and turned it. The door opened with a creak. The corridor outside was deserted. 'Good', thought Robert. 'That means that we aren't guarded. Either we aren't important enough, or they assume there is no way of escape, so why bother to keep an eye on us'. Pulling the door closed behind him, he crept along the corridor, listening carefully for any sounds. At the end of the passage he came upon a steep stairway, leading sharply up to a door. Tentatively, Robert began to climb, pulling himself up with a length of knotted rope that hung down the stairwell. The ship was rolling quite vigorously now and it was not easy getting to the top, but with some effort Robert stood before the door and pushed it slowly open.

He found another empty corridor, with cabins on each side of the passage, leading ahead to another stairway. A sound from a door just by him made Robert start. He stood, petrified, against the wall and waited. The door was pushed open and Robert found himself face to face with Crook, the First Officer.

'What in God's name...?' Crook seemed shocked. 'What are you doing here, may I ask?'

Unsure as how to react to his superior, Robert stuttered and looked sheepish. 'Er, I was just... um... having a look about the ship'

'You will call me Sir!' Crook looked down his aquiline nose as if he was a bird of prey, sizing up his next meal. 'What is your name, boy?'

'Robert, Sir. Robert Marchant.'

Crook looked puzzled at this. 'Marchant, eh? I believe I know you. You are Cedric Marchant's son.'

'Yes, I am. But...how did you know?' Robert was astounded. To think that anyone would have recognised him in this frightful situation was incredible.

Crook smiled, knowing that he had this young man at a disadvantage. 'You may remember a costume ball, some two summers ago, held at Marchant Hall. I was a guest, along with half of Whitehall. I believe your father was trying to ingratiate himself with several high ranking members of the Admiralty, and so therefore many of us, all subordinate officers I should say, were invited to attend and swell the numbers. You may not have noticed me, but I certainly noticed you. As I recall, you were dressed as the god Pan, with cloven hoof, padded haunches and little else.'

Blushing slightly at the memory of one of his more excessive japes, Robert gave a grin and pushed his hair back out of his eyes. 'That's right, and it was jolly uncomfortable to wear. What did you have on?'

'Oh, I came as a Roman Soldier. And I seem to remember that you only had eyes for a pretty little thing in a milkmaid's costume. What was her name?'

'Rose. I think she was the daughter of some Duchess or other. Rather a bore, actually.'

Crook looked Robert over with an appreciative glance. 'So did you ever marry?' He folded his arms and waited.

'No. I haven't met the right girl.'

'I am sure you haven't. But how do you come to be here? I didn't have you down for a sailor.'

With a sigh, Robert explained about the Olde Oake Inn and the Press Gang, leaving out the more personal details of why he and William were there. Throughout, Crook smiled knowingly. 'Oh, yes. I know the Olde Oake. Captain Greer usually gets a good breed of pressed hands from there. Did you meet up with the potman, Jack?'

'I certainly did. It was that bastard who is responsible for us being here.'

'But I expect he made you feel welcome before, though?

'I don't know what you mean.'

Scratching the side of his nose with a long finger, Crook stared firmly at Robert. 'Of course you do. A handsome, virile young buck like you would have been irresistible to Jack. He has an eye for the more delicious things in life. You would have been just his cup of tea.' Crook spun on his heels and pushed open the door behind him. It swung open, revealing a desk covered with books and charts, and against the far wall, a narrow bed. 'This is my cabin, Robert. Do come in for a moment.' He held the door open and watched as Robert squeezed past him.

Closing the door and clicking home the lock, Crook took a step toward Robert, who was sitting back against the desk. Crook knew that this beautiful young man was far from home, in an unplanned-for situation, and would probably do anything to make his life on board ship easier. He cleared his throat and began to speak softly. 'I hope that you realise that there is no way out from your current predicament. Anyone who is caught trying to escape is hung from the yard-arm. Punishments on board ship are swift and terrible. But you can make life easier for yourself, and I think you know how.' Crook's hand moved down toward his crotch and he began to slowly squeeze himself.

Robert's mouth was dry. This was an unexpected turn of events. What should he do? Crook was his superior officer. To deny him would be to land himself in deep trouble. But on the other hand, if he pleasured Crook, then life might get easier for him, and by association, for William. He took this chance to really study the man opposite. Although he was at least twice his age, he still seemed very fit. His dark hair framed his spare face, his angular features very well defined. Not what one would call handsome, but not ugly either. Robert had experienced sex with worse-looking men before now. He realised that he had to do it. But should he make the first move? Crook seemed to be waiting.

Moving away from the desk, Robert stretched out his hand and touched Crook's thigh. The First Officer gave a sharp intake of breath, as he knew that he had succeeded in persuading Robert of his desire, and that this young man would do anything he wanted. Grasping Robert's wrist tightly, he pushed his hand toward the rapidly swelling cock. It was of a monstrous size already. 'Very good, Robert.' Crook's voice had a hard edge to it. He was in control and that is how he was going to stay. With swift, sharp movement he pulled his trousers down, letting his organ spring free. Even though Robert wasn't really in the right frame of mind for this, he reluctantly had to admit that it was a very fine example of manhood, long and thick around the middle before curving up to a large pinkish head that held a gleaming droplet at its slit. 'I think you know what to do, Robert, don't you?'

With one hand holding on to the rim of the desk for support, Robert crouched down and grasped the shaft of Crook's penis. He looked at it for a moment. It was one of the biggest he had ever encountered, and its size was a little frightening. He wondered whether he would be able to get it all into his mouth. He had to try. He had to put all his natural reticence aside and make the most of this strange situation. After all, one wasn't presented with such a magnificent specimen as Crook had jutting from his groin every day. Putting out his tongue, he licked the pearly drop from the tip and savoured the taste. It was salty and very strong. Leaning forward a little, still gripping it tightly, he let his tongue lick around the quivering head. At the merest touch, Crook shuddered. Perhaps he was so sensitive that it might be all over very soon, Robert conjectured. Licking his lips and filling his mouth with saliva, Robert let the head into his mouth. Breathing through his nose, he slid the rigid shaft down his throat. The width of it stretched his mouth wide, uncomfortably so. He was only halfway down, when he realised that his mouth was full and he could take no more. Crook had other ideas.

Grabbing the back of Robert's head and twisting his fingers in his hair, Crook gave one mighty thrust and pushed the whole length of his massive cock down the young man's throat. Robert was unable to cry out. He felt the solid mass push down past his tonsils, filling his throat completely. It went so far down, and filled his mouth so fully, that the need to gag was dissipated. Robert was surprised at himself. He had sucked cock before, but never got one so far down inside. This was a rather pleasant experience. Deciding to really enjoy himself, Robert sank to his knees, wincing as Crook's fingers held tight in his hair. He pulled himself back and let most of the moistened shaft slip from his mouth, but still keeping his lips around the head. He felt with his free hand for the bollocks, swinging heavy in their sac below, and he pulled them down sharply in a vice-like grip, making the cock even harder, if that was possible. Crook exclaimed with a cry of deepest pleasure.

Having sucked down the whole member, Robert confidently knew he could do it again. He let it pass the lips and slid his wet mouth down to the very base, letting it fill his very being. This was an experience he wouldn't forget in a hurry. Crook thought he was in control, but Robert knew that at this moment he was the master of the situation. He began to suck, deeper and stronger, the onslaught getting faster and faster, as he held Crook in his mouth, his hand now squeezing and massaging the egg-sized balls. Robert's throat seemed somehow to expand to take the whole of the engorged cock, his lips and tongue worked with ferocious speed, as he looked up into the eyes of Crook.

The First Officer stared down in wonderment at the pleasure that Robert was giving. He had had men sucking on his admittedly large cock before, but no-one had given such sensations as this. He sometimes thought it was a curse to have been born with such a gargantuan weapon, most people couldn't cope with it in any of their bodily holes. He would have to see if Robert could take it up the arse. That would be exciting. Somehow, deep inside, he hoped that he could.

The sliding wetness of Robert's mouth and throat were astonishing. Knowing that he would soon be at a climax, Crook pulled back and started to fuck that gaping, moist hole. The strokes got longer and harder. He knew he was about to explode. Robert had also sensed this. He gripped the balls tighter and pulled them, feeling them tighten in his grasp. Abruptly, Crook withdrew, and with a yell of exquisite pleasure, he pumped handfuls of creamy semen across Robert's upturned face.

As his breathing grew more regular, Crook pulled a handkerchief from his pocket and wiped the sticky mess from Robert's face and neck. 'That was exceedingly well done, Robert! I think that we shall get on very well with each other on this voyage. Don't you think so?'

Sitting back on his heels, taking the kerchief and finishing off the mopping-up, Robert smiled. 'I can be very good to you, Sir, if you'll be good for me. There are many things that I can do for you, and do *to* you... I am no innocent and I think you know that. But I cannot live in squalor. Down below is a completely terrible place, and no-one should have to exist in those conditions, certainly not one of good breeding like myself. Please do what you can to help me... and my friend William Benham, who is still down there.'

'Would he be your lover, then?' Crook sneered lasciviously. 'This young thing I must see.'

Robert looked down at the floor. 'Well, yes, I suppose he is. But I am willing to do anything to make our lives easier. And I do mean *anything*.'

Crook laughed, an unnerving, sinister chuckle. 'You have nothing to worry about on the matter of your accomodation. New recruits are always put down below for their first few days, to see the hardship of a life at sea. After two or three days, they are given a better place to sleep, and the gratitude they show is immense. They will then do anything they are ordered to do, and they realise that their Captain is a man who can take with one hand but give graciously with the other. That way you engender complete devotion in a sailor. Quite simple, really.' He chuckled again. 'You just tell your young friend to hang on for a couple of days and everything will improve, I promise you.'

Robert had no reason to doubt what he was being told, so he knelt forward and pulled up the trousers that had gathered around Crook's ankles and hoisted them gently up. 'I did enjoy that... Sir. I must admit to never having seen such a big cock as yours before. I think that I shall have fun getting to know it.'

A knock on the cabin door stopped Crook from replying immediately. 'What is it?'

'Captain wants all the new men on deck, Mister Crook, Sir. He wants you there too, Sir.' A nervous voice came through the wooden door.

'Very well. I shall be there forthwith. Now away with you.' He turned back to Robert who had finished re-fastening Crook's trousers and putting away the now-soft giant. 'We shall certainly have fun, I believe. But not a word to anyone. If you let anybody know what we do, then I shall have you flogged to within an inch of your life... and that young friend of yours, too. I hope I make myself clear?'

Without waiting for an answer, he unfastened the door and strode out, head held high. Robert sat back and stuffed the come-soaked kerchief in his pocket. From outside the door came the sounds of people being herded along. He stepped outside and joined the queue of the new recruits, heading up on deck for their first taste of a life in the Navy.

The rest of that day was long and exhausting. After many hours of climbing about the ship's rigging and jumping to attention down on the deck whenever the Captain showed himself, an interminable amount of time was spent winding ropes, and scrubbing the wooden planks of the deck itself. Knowing that the best thing to do was to try and meld with the crowd and not draw too much attention to themselves, Robert and William just did whatever they were ordered to. The unpleasant and gnarled seaman Stubbs was the one in charge of the day's activities. He seemed to want to make everything as discomforting for these new recruits as possible. He took a great deal of pleasure in strolling about with a small braided whip, giving short, sharp strokes to anyone who apeared to be lagging. He also seemed to sense that Robert and William had some sort of close bond, and so split them up at the earliest opportunity. All they could do was steal the occasional glance at each other from opposite sides of the ship.

The regular crew lazed about on the upper decks, revelling in these new tars' misery. The old hands had chosen this life and were well-prepared for all it threw at them, and so watching the miserable attempts of these new boys was enormously entertaining.

A sudden buzz of stifled comments flew around the upper decks as Stubbs called for silence and the attention of the new crew members. The old boys knew what was now coming. This was going to be good.

'Now, we can't very well fight those damned Frenchies if we cannot see where they are bloody well hiding themselves, can we, my beauties?' Stubbs puffed out his chest and surveyed the exhausted men, scattered in various positions before him. 'It's now time for one of you *charming* young gentlemen to learn all about the crow's nest. What do you say, lads?' He looked up to the older crew and winked. This was the part he always looked forward to. Sending some young inexperienced whippersnapper up aloft, watching their terror as they try to cling to the rigging, whilst inching higher and higher, afraid that one swell of the rolling tide would send them plummetting deck-wards.

It was the custom to send the smallest sailor up to the precariously perched crow's nest, and so Stubbs cast his eye over the assembled men. His gaze lit upon William, who was crouching by the side of the ship, half obscured by a large coil of rope. 'You, come here.' Stubbs pointed a knobbled finger at William and beckoned slowly. 'Look up there. Do you see that basket, up at the top of the mast?' William nodded dumbly. 'That'll be the crow's nest. Someone'll have to climb up and keep a lookout for French ships. Someone agile, and with a head for heights. Someone with a big voice, who can shout at the top of his lungs if he sees so much as a French flag. I think that you'll be just right for this job, my young friend.' He stood with his arms crossed and waited. 'Well? Get climbing, or you'll feel the bite of my whip.'

Robert watched uneasily as William hauled himself to his feet. He had watched him scrubbing the deck for hours that afternoon, and his hands looked raw and blistered. The tortuous climb to the top of the mast would be almost impossible. He wanted to say something but knew that if he did they would both be in deep trouble. It was agony seeing William attempting to lift himself up, hand over hand, trying to get his balance before hoisting himself upwards on the rungs of rope rigging, spasms of pain crossing his tear-streaked face. The boy's bravery and courage was obvious to Robert.

As William reached the first horizontal crossbeam of the mast, he faltered and flung his arms around the mast, holding on as though his life depended on it. He looked down at Robert, fear in his eyes, unable to go any higher.

Stubbs laughed, a toothless, unpleasant grin contorting his features. 'Get on up there, boy, or you'll regret it.' William had frozen, and his eyes were now tightly shut. It was apparent that he wasn't moving any further. Stubbs could see that he would have to send someone up to prise him lose. He shouted up with a cracked note of triumph in his voice. 'If I have to get you down boy, you'll wish you were somewhere else. My little whip has a nasty sting, and your back will feel its teeth, by God it will!' He gestured to one of the men slumped by his feet. 'Climb up there and get that scared little fucker down. Extra grog rations if you do!'

The thought of an extra cup of watery rum had its desired effect and the sailor pulled himself up and started to climb. It didn't take him long to reach the first level, where William still stood petrified. Holding firmly to the guide rope, the sailor managed to prise William's fingers free and, as he did, Robert saw him talking animatedly to the scared young man. William appeared to be listening and after a few seconds began to descend, carefully and tentatively. As he reached the lowest rung, he jumped down to the deck, where Stubbs pulled him by the arm, and with a voice like thunder began to shout wildly at him. 'You useless little worm. Can't climb a rope? You aren't even worth a dollop of my shit. Captain Greer needs real men on this ship, not scared cissies, if we are to beat those French bastards. You need to learn what it takes to be one of His Majesty's sailors. Stretch him out.'

The last command was aimed at two of the lazing seamen on the upper deck, who leapt from their viewing positions, clambered quickly down the stairs, and grabbed William by both arms. Spinning him round, they ripped the shirt from his back and spreadeagled him against the foot of the mast. Each sailor held an arm tight, and William found himself unable to move. Stubbs looked up at another of the regulars. 'Fetch the Cat,' he sneered. The seaman opened a rough wooden chest and lifted out a fearsome looking whip, made of long strips of blackened leather, periodically knotted along each length. 'This is the 'Cat o' Nine Tails', my lad. This won't be the last time you'll be meeting, I'm sure. It loves to get acquainted with smooth, lily-white skin such as yours.' He gave it one lash against the side of the ship, and the crack it made sent a shiver through Robert. This was a nightmare. He had to do something. He couldn't let William take this brutal punishment. Some men never recovered from the severity of the flogging, their minds broken and jarred. It could even kill him.

Stubbs licked his cracked, sun-burned lips and raised the whip.

'NO!' Robert threw himself at Stubbs, who was caught off-guard. He stumbled back and hit his shoulder against one of the huge iron cannons that lined the deck, the whip thrown from his hand. For a moment he didn't know what had happened. Shaking his head he stared vehemently at Robert, sizing him up. With a yell he rushed forward, knocking Robert off his feet. He reached down and gripped Robert around the throat, the fingers tightened, wanting to squeeze every drop of life from this insolent cur. Robert choked, finding it hard to breathe. He wasn't going to let this foul-smelling bully get the better of him, but the sailor's grip was firm. Robert began to feel a sharp pain in his lungs from the lack of air. If he didn't break this man's hold on his windpipe, he would be done for. With a grunt he pulled his legs up in front of him and pushed back with a mighty kick, sending Stubbs sprawling on the deck. A hearty cheer erupted from the crowd of onlookers. Some of them had waited years to see Stubbs get a good beating. Today might be the day it happened.

With a cry of anger, Stubbs rushed at Robert, his hands again going for the throat, but quickly Robert struck up with his right fist, catching Stubbs in the eye. He recovered momentarily and came staggering back towards Robert, throwing a punch at his stomach, winding him and doubling him over in pain. Pulling a sword from his belt, Stubbs brought the hilt down upon the back of Robert's head. He fell forward, hitting his nose on the deck, a gush of warm blood spewing forth over Stubbs boot. Through clenched teeth, and gulps of wheezing breath, Stubbs addressed the crowd. 'This dog has gone too far. I shall flog him until every gasp of air is forced from his rebellious body. Stretch him out.'

Through a haze of blood and pain, Robert felt himself being manhandled to his feet, much as William had been, and was stretched out against the mast. Rough hands ripped at his clothes, pulling apart his shirt and breeches until he stood naked, held firm in the grasp of two determined sailors.

Without warning, the first stroke came. The whip cracked through the air, the leather thongs biting into his back. Robert cried out but found a hand placed over his mouth. The pain was indescribable. The searing, stinging lash left violent crimson streaks across the flesh on his back. Suddenly the whip cracked again. This time it bit lower down, striking across his buttocks, feeling like a thousand hot knives, cutting apart his skin. He knew that he couldn't take any more. He looked out and his gaze met William, who stood unable to move, silent tears of anguish streaming from his horror-filled eyes, hugging himself tightly.

Steeling himself for another blow, Robert tensed. But it didn't come.

'STOP!' A voice from above penetrated Robert's mind. A voice he thought he recognised. Looking up through poorly focusing eyes, he saw Crook standing on the upper deck, hands placed firmly behind his back, watching the scene. 'That is enough Mister Stubbs. I think he has learnt his lesson.'

'But Sir, he attacked me… I want my revenge.'

'Revenge is for savages, Mister Stubbs. We are British and proud of it. I believe that this man has suffered enough for what he did… coming to the aid of a fellow sailor is not a crime, and that is what he did. Take him down to my cabin immediately.' Crook spun on his heels, leaving a stunned Stubbs to obey his order.

Robert felt the iron grip on his arms relax and he fell to the deck. The last thing he saw before passing out was William's concerned face.

FIVE

'There, there. This salve should help those wounds of yours.' Crook's soothing voice penetrated Robert's consciousness, as he slowly came to, lying face down, naked, save for his boots, on Crook's bed. 'What happened?' Robert asked in a shaken, trembling voice. He tried to sit up but the stinging pain from his lascerated back made him fall back and cry out with a yelp of anguish. 'You must just lie here and let me help you, Robert.' Crook sounded almost concerned. Perhaps he was, thought Robert to himself. Turning his head slightly, he could see that Crook was holding a large glass jar, filled with some sort of pale ointment. 'Now this might sting a little, but bear up, it is for your own good. We don't want any lasting damage on that beautiful skin of yours, do we?'

Crook took a small amount of the salve and started to smear it into the vivid red wheals. It felt like someone was stroking a hot poker across his back. The temptation to cry out was incredible, but Robert just bit back the scream and pushed his head into the pillow.

Amazingly, after a few moments, the balm seemed to take effect and the pain started to ease. Crook continued to rub in the potion, lingering over the contours of his muscled back, letting his hands gently massage further and further down towards the firm buttocks. Sensing that Crook had another agenda, rather than his patient's well-being, Robert pushed his arse up a little, squirming around so that the cheeks parted, affording a clear view of the puckered arsehole. Robert could feel Crook's body stiffen. He moaned quietly as the First Officer's finger, lubricated with ointment, began to probe his pink hole. Tenderly, he pushed one finger deep inside, feeling the muscles clamp tightly about it, before pulling it free and inserting two together. Crook looked down at the graceful curve of Robert's spine, the delicately soft skin, now sadly defiled by the efforts of the deranged Stubbs. He saw the strong shoulders tapering down to a slim waist, the sinews of the back leading down to the extraordinarily beautiful bottom.

Robert could hear the rustling as Crook quickly shed his clothes. Through the corner of his vision, he could see Crook standing beside the bunk, naked, his hardened prick standing firm and ready. He watched as Crook took another handful of the cream and slathered it on himself, before kneeling up on the bunk, nestling between Robert's thighs, pulling them apart, revealing the almost hairless bollocks pressed down against his own quickly stiffening member. Crook could restrain himself no longer. Using his moistened fingers, he positioned the head of his solid shaft against the trembling opening. He eased forwards and felt the hole part slightly. With just enough pressure to imbed the tip inside, he pushed. Robert groaned as the iron-hard weapon began to slide in. Crook balanced himself, trying carefully not to push the whole length inside yet, just managing to keep the tip in place, held tight by the pleading grip of Robert's anus.

Robert raised his arse higher, wanting that final full thrust to come soon, to be completely impaled upon that monster, and whimpered, 'Please, do it... do it now!

The excitement mounting within Crook finally reached boiling point and he swiftly gave one heaving thrust. Before Robert knew what was happening, the entire rigid pole had slid inside. He gasped in shock and delight as his muscles clamped tight around it and held it firm for a moment, before relaxing his grip and allowing Crook to pull it right back, again leaving just the head inside. With another swift stroke he plunged forth, his bollocks smacking against the underside of Robert's groin.

Unable to contain his desire any longer, Crook started to fuck Robert, with serious strokes, getting faster with each one. He slid his arms beneath Robert and held him about the chest. Each time he pushed forward he could feel Robert's body respond, pushing back and enveloping his shaft, becoming as one with it. Their passion grew higher as they began to buck more ferociously together, Crook driving with an ever-increasing force into Robert's willing hole. Robert was unaware of any other sensation but the pounding domination of this huge cock, he even had to remind himself to breathe, gulping in large lungfuls of air in between each staggering assault.

It was obvious to both men that this astonishing onslaught couldn't last forever, as Crook's own breathing became heavier and more laboured. Robert knew that the moment of fulfillment was almost imminent. He tried to hold the cock tighter within him, waiting for that instant of eruption. With a cry of ecstasy, Crook thrust deep and delivered his full load, a steaming flood of come poured into the warm blackness. Robert cried too, grasping his own hard cock and pumping himself to climax, never letting the still throbbing cock free from the confines of his arse. His fist banged swiftly, encouraging the streaks of sticky fluid to bolt out onto the blanket.

Both men lay still, breathing hard, still joined for a few minutes. When the blood had eased its thumping in their heads, Crook slowly pulled himself out, the little sighs of satisfaction Robert gave as it slid free keeping him hard. Reaching for the towel at the end of the bunk, Crook started to wipe clean the evidence of their carnal act. 'I am amazed at you, Robert.'

'Why so?'

'Because in the many experiences I have had with other willing men, I have never met anybody who could take the entirety of myself within them. Most had to give up after a few inches. I know it is large, but there had to be someone who could accommodate its dimensions.'

'You surprise me! It was a wonderful experience. You knew how to handle yourself, and how to make it good for me, too.'

'I think this could be a very happy spell of duty for me, Robert. If you will be around for me to call upon and are willing. I wouldn't want to force myself upon you. I am not the unpleasant man that people think I am. I cultivate an air of superiority and disdain because my position demands it.'

Robert shifted himself, and sat up on the crumpled blankets, moving slightly so as to avoid sitting in the pool of his own jism. He moved quite easily, the pain on his back now just a mere ache. 'I can see that you aren't a bad man. Anyone would have to be tough and uncaring to survive in this terrible environment.'

'That's right. A ship such as this cannot exist without authority and discipline.'

'Why did you join up though? Did circumstances conspire against you?'

Crook sat back and stared at Robert, his cock slowly softening. 'They certainly did. I was born an only child to parents who despised each other. My father was an Admiral and so it was assumed that I would follow in his footsteps. I had no choice but to do so. My mother was only interested in her many suitors, and my father was blind to the scandal. I joined the navy as soon as I could, working my way up through the ranks. If all goes well on this particular tour of duty, and we mete out some well-deserved puishment to those damned French, then I can seriously hope to be made Captain and given my own vessel to command.'

Talk of parents made Robert sadden a little. He wondered what his own father was doing now. Would he still be angry at him? Would he have forgiven him for his indiscretion and welcome him home with open arms? Whatever the outcome, he had to find out. There had to be a way off off this ship. Perhaps Crook could help him. Was now the time to take the risk and ask him?

'I am sure we can make the best of it… but must I call you Sir? Especially when we are alone?' Robert looked up through the strand of hair that flopped across his eyes, and gave his most winning smile.

'Whenever we are alone together you can call me Joseph.' Crook ran his fingers through the strand of hair, brushing it clear from Robert's face. 'But anywhere else, you must act as if we are strangers, even enemies. As I have told you before, no-one must know of what we do.'

Robert leant forward and took Crook's hand in his. From somewhere on an upper deck, a bell rang sharply, twice. Crook started and leapt to his feet. 'Two bells… five o'clock… that's time for food. There are some spare items of clothing in that chest. Get dressed as quickly as you can. Anyone who is late goes without food and drink. I shall hope to see you later.'

The meagre rations given to the men — salted pork, hard biscuits and watery lemon juice — hardly provided a filling meal. The only provision of any interest was the grog, a thin mixture of rum and water. At least it helps ease the aches of the day, Robert mused to himself, hunched over his tin cup of that insipid brew. The evening was drawing in slowly, and was bringing with it a cooling breeze. The day's work over, the men were free to do as they wished. Some talented soul was playing an accordion at the far end of the deck for some of the more energetic seamen to dance jigs to. Such forced jollity appalled Robert, but then he supposed you took your pleasure and relief where you could on this God-forsaken vessel. His mind drifted back to the afternoon's happenings. His back still ached, but was nowhere as bad as it could have been, thanks to Crook's medical ministrations. Thoughts of Joseph Crook flooded his mind. What an odd man he was. In public, a seemingly miserable, heartless officer, but in private, a tender loving man, with depth and a great deal of heart. He would have to keep their liasons secret, especially from William. His young friend had suffered much and was relying on Robert's strength to keep them both alive and well. He couldn't let him find out that he'd been dallying with another man. William assumed that Robert only had eyes for him. That lie must be kept up. Crook had the opportunity to be their way out from this dreadful place. If played in the right way, he could help them escape. How this was to be accomplished, Robert didn't know at present, but he was certain something would happen soon, something would present itself, and he would be ready.

Sitting astride a bollard, Robert downed the last drop of grog and surveyed the scene before him. An endless stretch of rolling sea, in the far distance the twinkling lights of the French coast. Robert guessed it to be somewhere around Cherbourg. He looked at the lights and thought of the ordinary people sitting in their homes, eating, drinking, sewing, singing, unaware that, out here in the English Channel, men such as him were waiting to engage in warfare with their sons, their brothers and fathers. Life was sometimes very strange indeed. Why did country fight country? England and France were but a small number of miles apart, but over hundreds of years there had scarcely been a period of peace between them. Again these two great nations were about to fight to the death. This time at the behest of Napoleon Buonaparte, an inconsequential young Italian soldier, who had risen through the ranks to exalted heights. His military strategy had been superlative and for his successes he had been created a General. Subsequently, in his late twenties, he had become the ruler of France and changed his name to the more Gallic-sounding Bonaparte.

Robert had often wondered what this strange little man was really like. He had heard tell many stories from the London gossips about Bonaparte's courtly habits. He expected to be treated as royalty, honouring close family and friends with titles and Governorships. He had developed a court around him that fawned on his every whim and tried to stay in favour with him. He had taken to wife a dark haired, well-rounded woman, Josephine de Beauharnais, a society beauty with charm and elegance but, unfortunately, rotten teeth. The couple doted upon each other and their abiding love was the talk of Paris. Through all this, Bonaparte had sadly believed himself to be the saviour of

France. He had created himself Emperor of Austria and his plans for total control of the rest of Europe were underway. His only stumbling block was that damned country sitting smuggly across the Channel. He had drawn up an invasion plan for England and was soon to start carrying it out. Many of his ferocious warships patrolled this small stretch of water, but the skirmishes between French and English ships had been few and far between up until recently. It seemed likely that bloody battle must soon be on the cards.

Some men had delusions of grandeur, insane notions of domination, and they had to be stopped, Robert thought to himself, there had to be freedom among any nation's people. Hadn't the French just fought a blood-soaked revolution to be free? Still, Bonaparte must have some kind of charisma to get to where he was now. Perhaps he had exerted some mesmeric influence over the citizens of France, and so they could only see his good side, and were unaware of his faults.

As Robert sat, watching the water lap around the ship's hull, some black shape caught his eye away in the distance. It seemed to be large and irregular and was growing slowly bigger. It had to be a French ship. Throwing his tin cup down, he jumped up and hoisted himself aloft to the bridge, where the bo'sun was standing at the wheel, listening with half an ear to the music of the accordion. Grabbing the sailor by the shoulder he pointed out the black mass. 'Look, there! Is that a ship? We must get away from here now. We aren't ready to fight!'

The bo'sun pulled out a telescope and fixed it on the dark shape. Identification wasn't easy, owing to the failing light. 'It's the Frenchies alright. It's a thirty-six gun frigate, if I ain't much mistaken, and they're coming our way. Looks like we don't have any choice in the matter… they've seen us and they're coming to get us.' He grabbed the bell rope and started wildly ringing it. The men at the aft end of the ship broke off their dancing and came running up in consternation. Almost immediately Captain Greer appeared, pulling his uniform jacket on hurriedly. 'What's all this commotion?' he snarled at the bo'sun.

'The French, Sir. A frigate is off the starboard bow, heading toward us, south by south-west. By my reckoning they'll be upon us in half an hour.'

Greer stroked his chin. 'Which means firing range within twenty minutes. Mister Crook!' His yell brought Crook running from below deck. 'Are the new men ready for battle?'

'No Sir, they've had no battle drill yet.'

'Well then, they'll be learning by experience. Get the crew up here. Get the cannons stoked and issue every man with a musket. Show the new ones how to load their firearms. If it means a fight, we won't go down like cowards. Get to it!' He turned to the man at the wheel. 'Steer us up the Channel toward Dover. We may be lucky and meet up with a ship from the Dover Squadron, which may scare the French off.'

It took but ten minutes for every sail on the ship to be hoist. The wind caught the billowing sheets and sent the ship scudding away from their pursuers. Nervously, the crew stood at their positions along the side of the deck, everyone holding tight to their loaded muskets. Experienced war veterans crouched by the canons, explosive and shot at the ready.

The shadows had deepened now and Robert stood alert, hoping wildly that night would fall and they would be able to outrun their pursuers. A moment later, he heard a sharp retort, and saw a plume of white smoke billow up from the French ship. He guessed that the enemy had fired a warning shot to try and bring them about. Surrender, though, would be worse than dying in battle. All they could look forward to as a prisoner of the French would be an agonising, long drawn-out death, rotting away in rusty shackles, chained to the oar of a French warship. The gun boomed again, and Robert watched the shot bounce across the waves, some ten feet away from the ship's hull. They were getting closer. He looked about him and couldn't see William anywhere. Up above, on the bridge, Captain Greer was deep in hurried conversation with Crook, both of them looking a little worried. Greer's hands were clasped tightly behind his back, and with a bravura tone he called out to the crew, 'Do not fire until they are within range. That is when we will inflict the most damage. Hold steady now...'

A third shot sent a canon ball clanging loudly against a iron lantern swinging wildly at the ship's stern. Another explosion came and with a whistle and a terrifying crash, a canon ball smashed through one of the masts, bringing it tumbling to the deck, swathed in tattered rigging and sails. 'FIRE!' Greer shouted at the top of his voice.

Robert found himself deafened by the terrific cacophany of sound. Firing guns, exploding canons, men screaming, splintering wood. All around sailors were being mown down by grapeshot. As he looked about him he saw an explosion on the bridge, throwing Greer up in the air, the force of the impact kicking him over the side of the bridge to land with an almighty splash in the freezing water of the Channel. Without warning, a canon ball caught Crook squarely in the back, cutting him in half and spraying his blood all over the bo'sun at the wheel. Tears sprang to Robert's eyes as he realised there was nothing he could do for Joseph now. The battle seemed lost. He had to find William. With a deep breath he started to make his way down the side of the decimated ship. 'William, William. Where are you? It's Robert. Can you hear me?' Robert yelled as loudly as he could but the noise of the battle swamped his words. Another ball smashed into the deck a few yards in front of him. He realised he was in danger of losing his head.

As to what exactly happened next, Robert wasn't entirely sure. He heard a cry from somewhere ahead, 'Robert… it's me… I'm over here!', then there came a dreadful splintering of wood, and something hit him on the back of his head, knocking him off his feet, and throwing him forward. The next thing he knew was that he was in the water, his mouth full of blood and salt, his heavy boots dragging him down to a watery grave.

SIX

Robert prided himself on being an expert swimmer. Ever since he had been able to walk he had delighted in showing off his skills in the local river, demonstrating different strokes in front of his proud father. But at this moment, plunged into the icy waters of the English Channel, he had great difficulty in recalling any of them. His clothes were an encumbrance, their sodden mass pulling him down. Salty water filled his nose and mouth. If he didn't act now, he would drown. With a surge of energy, he kicked his feet and forced himself upwards. As he broke the surface, he took several huge gulps of sweet evening air and tried to stay afloat by treading water. Wisely, he decided against shucking off his coat and shoes, for if he reached shore he would need them.

After a while, he looked around and tried to take in the situation. Bodies floated about him, some still oozing blood, some missing limbs, their faces frozen in attitudes of terror and pain. The general detritus of the destroyed ship bumped into the bodies, trunks, sections of the hull, masts, rigging. He listened hard and, above the sloshing of the waves, could hear the triumphant cries of the French. He couldn't call for help, as he would be taken prisoner by them, and so realised he had better stay silent and try and find something substantial to cling onto. He watched, dismayed, as the French frigate began to tow the battered hulk of *The Valiant* in her wake, wondering if they had taken anyone captive, and if William was one of them. But for now there was nothing he could do.

His prospects looked grim. The water of the English Channel was bitingly cold, and he knew that if he just remained floating there, things would soon look very dark indeed. Aware that he needed to stay alive for some considerable time, before there was any chance of rescue, Robert decided to try and find something sturdy to cling onto. After what he judged to be half an hour, when the French had sailed some distance away, he swam to a length of rope which was tied to a section of mast. He managed to gather three more shattered sections, and with the rope he lashed them together, creating a makeshift raft. Hauling himself up, he smiled grimly at his efforts. It may be makeshift, but it would bear his weight and keep him afloat for a while. His one hope was that at last he had some chance of staying alive until morning, when he may be able to paddle himself towards England, or even be picked up by a passing fishing vessel.

For what seemed an eternity, Robert lay back on his temporary craft and looked up at the stars. They twinkled away brightly, reassuring him. His mind whirred madly, thought after thought wildly jostling for attention. He thought of home, of happy childish summers at Marchant Hall, of a loving father, always ready with a smile and open arms. He thought of Joseph and those astonishing few hours they had spent together on board *The Valiant*, and Joseph's delight at finding such an accommodating young man. With a pang of regret, Robert realised he would miss Joseph. His death had been unnecessary, and he hoped that he had gone to a better place. And of course he thought of William. That beautiful young man who had given his heart and soul to Robert, and who was now either a prisoner of the accursed French or lying at the bottom of the Channel, his silken skin being eaten away by fish. Shaking his head to clear away that frightful image, Robert saw a few strands of light beginning to weave their way across the horizon. It would soon be morning.

He had been lying on the raft, soaked, for most of the night. With a grunt, he began to jerk his arms about to try and restore some of the circulation in them. A desire for sleep was creeping over him, but knew that he had to stay awake. If he dozed he might fall from the raft, and that could prove fatal. With an effort of will, he began to recite to himself the rulers of England, the plays of Shakespeare, anything that would keep his mind alert. As long, whispy clouds floated across the sky and the sun slowly rose behind them, Robert thought he heard something. He turned his head and saw a small sail-boat being rowed towards him. He scrambled to his knees and balanced precariously on the mast raft. Within minutes, he was being hauled aboard.

'Are you alright?' Robert silently thanked God for their English accents.

'Yes, thank you.'

A blonde young man, handsomely uniformed, put a blanket about Robert's shoulders, and ordered the two others in the boat to row them back.

'Back to where?' Robert queried.

'Why, our ship, of course. Look there, *The Merry Megan*.' Robert stared ahead with relief at the ship lying at anchor ahead of them. The young man stood as they reached the side of the ship and helped Robert to climb the rope ladder to the deck, where willing hands pulled him on board. He was shown to a cabin where a hot bath had been filled and dry clothes laid out on the bunk. 'The Captain says you are to make use of the facilities and when you are ready he will be pleased if you will join him in the galley. Breakfast will be served at eight o'clock.'

Robert stuttered a few words of thanks to the blonde chap in the uniform who had helped him to the cabin. 'I don't know what to say. Thank you... Mister...?'

'Good. Daniel Good. First Officer aboard the merchant ship *The Merry Megan*.'

'So this is a trading ship?'

'That is correct. Out of Portsmouth and heading for the West Indies.'

Robert was hit like a bolt. 'The West Indies!' he exclaimed with astonishment. 'I have to get back to England. I cannot go to the Indies.'

Daniel Good scratched the tip of his nose. 'I am very much afraid that you have no choice. The Captain is determined that we shall make good time in our journey to the island of Dominique, and there is to be no turning back.'

Robert sat on the bunk, his shoulders slumped in utter dejection. 'But I must get home. Can you not let me take the small rowing boat and let me chance my own way?'

'That would be very unwise, especially with the number of French warships out there. Look, Sir, why not have a warming bath, put on some dry clothes and join us for breakfast. That will give you time to adjust to your change of plans.' Saluting smartly, Good turned and pulled the door shut.

Robert sat for a moment, his mind a kaleidoscope of jumbled images. Having survived the bombardment of the French attack and escaped the horror of life on board *The Valiant*, he found himself on a merchant naval vessel bound for the other side of the world. He had to try and get off this ship. Nobody was actually holding him here, the crew seemed kindly and obliging. They should surely agree to his request. William was out there somewhere and he had to find him. He had to know if he was still alive. If his friend was suffering in the hands of the enemy, he would rescue him, come what may. If he was dead, then appalling as that news would be, he had to know for sure. Spending days idling aboard *The Merry Megan* would be of scant use to him in that search for information. A sudden pang gripped his heart and a strange twisting feeling filled the pit of his stomach. Was it hunger, or was it love? If he never saw William again he would be utterly desolate. He would desperately miss the look of total trust in his large, brown eyes, miss the delightful way his nose wrinkled when he laughed, and miss the thrill of his firm young body, ready and quite willing to please in any way. Whatever happened, Robert had to find him again. He knew that his life wouldn't be complete without him.

Steam was rising from the bath, and Robert's muscles were beginning to cramp. Unable to resist its pull any longer, he threw his damp clothes in a heap on the floor and slipped smoothly into the tub. A cake of soap was hanging from a string at its side and so he generously began to lather his chest and neck. He had almost forgotten the luxury of a hot bath, and this was one of the best. Sliding forward until his head was submerged, he let the water's warmth permeate his skin. As he emerged and shook his head, a cascade of water droplets fanned out across the floor. 'Excuse me.' A voice came from the doorway.

Wiping the soapy water from his eyes, Robert looked up at Good, who was standing there with a smile of amusement creasing his boyish features. 'I forgot to leave a towel. I did knock, but you obviously didn't hear me.' He stepped into the cabin and laid the towel across the foot of the bunk. 'If there is anything else you need, just ask for me. I'll be glad to provide anything I can.' He grinned, a full smile pulling apart his mouth, showing perfect white teeth, his eyes large and blue, an exquisite compliment to his white-blonde hair. Moving to the door, he reached for the handle and began to step out.

'You could help rinse my back.' Robert found himself saying automatically. Should he be getting involved with another man, when his poor William was still out there, who knows where, perhaps in deadly danger? But was Good offering what he thought he was? Did that twinkle in the eye mean that special interest? Even if it didn't, the thought of this young officer completely naked, made the blood rush to Robert's crotch and his cock began to swell rapidly. Unable to control his highly sexual nature, Robert kept his hand under the soapy water, wrapping his fist around his hardening tool, and slowly started to stroke it. Daniel Good quietly clicked the door shut, and moved into the room. He stooped and picked up a large pewter jug, filled with cold water. With one swift movement, he began to pour the water over Robert's head and back. The crystal clear stream clinging to the contours of his smooth skin. Gasping, Robert ran his fingers through his hair, and blew a few drops of water from his face. 'This is the most enjoyable bath I have had for many weeks. Thank you.'

'I am here to please. All our passengers need looking after. Some more than others. Can I help you with your towel?'

Robert placed his hands on the side of the tub and slowly inched himself up, his back toward the young officer. As he rose, Daniel watched appreciatively, his gaze never leaving the wet form of Robert's masculine young body. Finally standing at full height, Robert stepped from the tub and turned to face Daniel. With a murmur of delight, Daniel stared down at Robert's hard cock, standing proud, dripping with soap suds. Without saying a word, Daniel leaned forward and grabbed the towel, moving to a few inches from Robert. He raised the cloth and began to dry his back, firmly mopping up the wetness and massaging the muscles of his back and neck simultaneously. Moving slowly down he let the towel pat around his torso, lingering for a moment around the buttocks and then to the muscled and hairy legs. Dropping to his knees in front of Robert, and with a grin of satisfaction, Daniel moved his towel-clad hands to the jutting cock. The twisting veins had etched themselves along the surface of the penis, the head swollen and firm. 'Now that is a very wondrous sight,' Daniel said softly, before he let his mouth envelope it with its warmth and wetness. He slid the cock right down, where it struck the back of his throat. Robert was caught off guard and cried out in wonderment. Daniel seemed to be taunting and playing with it, pulling back and just letting a string of saliva stretch from mouth to prick, then licking its quivering head. Robert's eyes watched absorbed as he saw Daniel take down just the head and suck on it as if it were some hard candy lollipop, then he would suddenly stop and let his tongue trace the length of the shaft to the base, touching his lips against the hanging scrotum, and with an inbreath swallow whole the balls in his mouth. His lips closed about them and he ran his tongue around their firmness.

Falling backwards, Robert sat upon the edge of the wooden bath tub and lifted both his legs. He placed them around Daniel's shoulders, imprisoning him between his thighs. The message was clear. Don't stop.

Daniel's lips released the straining bollocks and let his mouth return to the cock-head. His hand reached up and his fingers traced a pattern on Robert's chest. They lit upon the nipples, and each hand began to play with a nipple apiece. In turn, teasing, tweaking, rubbing and pinching swiftly, every sensation drawing sighs of pleasure from Robert's lips. Feeling his cock slide again down the throat made Robert's brain swim. A frantic euphoria crossed his mind, a rushing, pounding pulse linked directly from groin to brain. If this exquisite torture didn't stop soon he would erupt. With the knowledge that he was on the verge of an astounding climax, Robert pulled himself to his feet, and let the cock slide from Daniels's mouth.

'What have I done?' Concern streaked across the officer's face.

'Nothing. It is incredible. Take off your clothes. I must have a taste of you.' Robert feverishly started to unbutton the uniform jacket, while Daniel pulled off his boots, and shucked his trousers in an instant. He stood facing Robert, saliva around his mouth, his white-blonde hair tousled. Robert stared at this stunning example of manhood. His chest was hairless, and so seemed to emphasize the contours of the torso. The chest had strong ridges of muscle leading down to the cock, swinging free, swelling rapidly, lifting itself into a full blown erection. The pent-up masculine energy that seemed to emanate from this young man overwhelmed Robert. Whisps of blonde hair curled around the hardened column, the balls hung heavy beneath. It stuck straight out in front, a fairly narrow shaft, but with an enormous head, waiting to be engulfed by a willing mouth.

Robert took hold of the gorgeous prick and held it tight, sliding back the foreskin to reveal the end beneath. The head was smooth and crimson, the slit quivered with a drop of its juice. Unable to wait any longer, Robert pushed Daniel back onto the bunk. Then shifting himself around, he lay on top, head to toe, squirming down so that their mouths could reach each other's cocks. They reacted as one, both opening wide and swallowing each other deeply. Robert had done many things with many men, but never had he experienced this. To be sucking a man, while having your own cock buried in another mouth was mind-blowing. The smell of Daniel's musky maleness was incredibly sensual. Robert knew that it was one of the most evocative scents in the world.

Daniel's hips bucked and thrust, his own shaft penetrating Robert's throat to its full length, while his own tongue worked and slurped with circular motions against the top-side of Robert's weapon. The rhythm they fell into, with a regular rocking stride, meant that each was giving the maximum pleasure to the other. Daniel seemed to want to give the very best he could, and Robert tried hard to match it. Moans of satisfaction and joy flew from them. Daniel reached out for Robert's bollocks, holding them back, preventing their slapping against his brow and eyelids. Robert stiffened in his mouth further, and his cock twitched with pleasure. Using his entire fist, Daniel encircled the balls and pulled them up, massaging and rolling them around. He let them fall, and with a huge breath sucked them into his mouth. Shocked, Robert pulled away from his actions for a second. 'Oh, that feels marvellous!' he said, his voice cracking. With a grin, he renewed his efforts on Daniel, sensing that his balls were beginning to tighten. If Daniel was on the brink of shooting then he would aim to come at the same time.

Pushing his cock deeper into Daniel's face, Robert started pumping, while letting the suction of his own mouth increase. He could feel the fluid begin to surge, rising steadily upwards. With a gargantuan effort he tried to hold back, but the shock of Daniel's cock spurting out, and hitting the back of his throat, caused him to erupt also. Gushes of creamy semen filled Robert's mouth and throat. He drank it down, feeling Daniel doing the same as his own spunk poured out. As the last drops were forced from the depths, both men shuddered, letting the faintly softening penises slip from their exhausted mouths.

Moving around, Robert slid up the bunk toward Daniel and curled his arms around him. Daniel responded and so the two men lay, their eyes holding each other's intense gaze, while their arms held tightly the other's sweaty body. Daniel's lips quivered slightly and he let his tongue moisten them, tasting the saltiness of the sperm he had just swallowed. Robert leant his head forward and planted a tender kiss on those lips. 'Thank you.'

'What for?' Daniel's brow creased, his eyes still twinkled.

'For a marvellous welcome to this ship. But I find myself in two minds now.'

'Why is that?' Daniel smiled and touched a tiny kiss on the end of

Robert's nose. 'I cannot imagine such a forceful man as yourself being perplexed about anything.'

'Oh, but I am. You see I have a friend. Someone who was on board that other ship with me. When the French attacked we were seperated. I cannot stop wondering if he is alright. He... he relied on me and I have to know what has happened. If I go with this ship to the Indies then I could be away for months, perhaps a year at least. If William is alive then he'll think I've abandoned him, and that is the last thing I would do.'

'I am certain that if your friend is alive, he will be well. I wish I could help you. But here is nothing you can do. We are heading for the Indies and that is that. I suggest you accept the situation with as much good grace as possible and try and enjoy the journey. After all, there will be lots to see and do!' He wriggled around in Robert's tight grasp, their legs inter-twining. 'You are the most exciting man I have ever met, and the most beautiful. The moment I saw you, clinging to that raft, I knew that, one way or another, I would have to possess you.'

It seemed there was little else he could do but accept his present circumstances. It would appear that he was heading for Dominique. Robert gave Daniel another tight squeeze. 'As wonderful as this is, I am rather hungry. Did you say something about breakfast before?'

'You are invited to join the Captain in the galley at eight o'clock. If you look in that trunk you will find some dry clothes. In fact, time is moving along, we should get ready.' Pulling himself free from Robert's clutches, Daniel began to dress, then after smoothing his fingers through his hair he slipped a fob watch from his inner pocket. 'As I thought, we haven't long. I should hurry. Clothe yourself and I'll take you to the galley. We don't want to keep the Captain waiting.'

Even though England was at war with France, many of the trading companies refused to be cowed by this fact. Thousands of vessels still sailed around the world, importing and exporting goods to faraway places. Its seamen were efficient and the rewards for one such journey could be enormous. They had nothing to do with the activities of the press gangs, and so every sailor on board was there of his own volition. The Captains of such ships were invariably educated and experienced men, who would often let passengers hire cabins for the journey to whichever exotic shore was their destination.

Many rich personages took this opportunity to visit their plantations in the New World, or to try and purchase vast areas of land in such undeveloped places as the West Indies, Burma or Ceylon. It was at breakfast that morning that Robert made the aquaintance of such a group of people.

With a salute, and a well-concealed wink, Daniel had shown him into a largish room at the poop deck of the ship, where a motley collection of passengers sat around a sizeable wooden table. A bluff, hearty-looking man at the far end stood and put out a hand. 'I am Captain Samuel Cartwright. Welcome aboard *The Merry Megan*.'

Taking the offered hand and shaking it warmly, Robert smiled around the table. 'Robert Marchant. Thank you for your hospitality, Captain Cartwright. Though you do find me in somewhat reduced cirumstances.' Sitting in the vacant chair beside Daniel, and opposite Cartwright, Robert told his tale. The assembled company hung upon his every word, scarcely believing the bad luck that had befallen him so far. 'And so I lay upon the raft and hoped that someone friendly would come by and find me.'

'Incredible!' The Captain exclaimed. But what of *The Valiant*? Did they sink her?'

'No, Sir. She was towed back to France. I daresay to be plundered and cut to pieces.' A murmur of unease rumbled around the table. Sensing this, the Captain gazed about him and with a look of grim determination addressed the diners. 'I assure you all, as I have done since before we set sail, that there is nothing to fear from the French. By now we will have moved on out into the Atlantic, where those damned villains do not dare to cross swords with us. Your only worry will be how to fill your time over the next two months.'

One of the company, a smallish, red-faced man in an ill-fitting frock coat, raised a hand and coughed politely. 'Captain Cartwright, will the journey be any shorter? I am sure His Majesty would want me to take up my duties as soon as possible.'

Cartwright chortled and downed the rest of his glass of wine. 'Even His Majesty has no control over the elements, Governor Trench. With a favourable wind we should hit the Indies in around eight weeks' time. I can do no more, and I would think that the King would expect no more from you, Sir.'

Throughout the sumptuous breakfast of cold meats, bread, fruit and wine, Robert learned more about his new travelling companions. Uppermost among them was Fergus Trench, the recently appointed Governor to the island of Dominique, which had been claimed by the English forces for His Majesty the King, some months before. His entourage included his wife, Amy (an inconsequential little mouse of a woman), his Private Secretary, a dour Scotsman named Hamish Dee, and a plethora of servants and skivvies. They occupied the best cabins amidships, while the rest of the rooms were taken by a variety of merchants and their wives, out to see what money could be made with land ripped from those uneducated souls 'out west'. Everyone openly tried to welcome Robert, most showing great sympathy for his plight. He engaged in easy conversation with a number of them, sometimes with great difficulty in concentration, as Daniel's leg brushed against his occasionally. Whenever Daniel's hands were beneath the table, he let his fingers stroke the inside of Robert's thigh, sending a tingle of erotic delight through him.

Breakfast proved to be a relaxed and charming meal, the company generally educated and chatty people. Throughout the meal, Robert tried to learn and memorise the names of his fellow passengers, and generally succeeded. There were a number of merchants from around the British Isles, mostly amiable men with their wives; Mr and Mrs Barnes, the Tuptons, the Taskers and the Russells, as well as a couple of unmarried men, both who seemed intimate, in constant quiet conference with each other. They nodded at Robert with a conspiratorial air and introduced themselves as David Martenson and Richard Fitch, cousins from London, travelling to the Indies to see if they could make their fortune.

The only fly in the ointment so far was Trench, who spoke to Robert with perfect politeness that nevertheless seemed to hide an apparent disdain for him. His wife had nothing to say for herself, either before, during or after the filling repast, and so Robert dismissed her completely. Dee, on the other hand, watched the others with suspicious eyes, joining in the light conversation with only a grunt, or a grudging one-syllable answer. Robert noticed that whenever he had cause to look Trench's way, the Governor was staring at him intently, this unblinking scrutiny causing a light unease somewhere deep in Robert. This was a dangerous man, and someone to watch carefully. He would be a terrifying enemy and Robert decided to keep out of his way for as much of the journey as he could.

Captain Cartwright appeared unaware of any tension amongst his passengers, and kept up a stream of light and engaging chatter. He was happy to explain the details of their intended passage, heading south to Spain, taking on supplies at Lisbon, and then relying on the North-East Trade Winds to carry them unhindered across the Atlantic. They were apparently on schedule and all that was left for the assembled paying passengers to do was to enjoy the journey. At the end of the meal, as everyone stood, and made their way out on deck, the Captain took Robert by the arm and pulled him to one side. Lowering his voice he said, 'You must realise by now that these other people have paid quite a considerable sum to undertake this journey on my ship. It happens that someone pulled out at the last moment, and so a cabin is free. I accept that you have had a dreadful time recently, and have no money with which to pay your way. But I do know who you are, and who your father is, and I assume that on our return to England you will do the gentlemanly thing and pay me what I am owed for this hospitality.'

'Of course, Captain. I wouldn't dream of leaving you "out of pocket", as they say. You have my word upon the matter.' Robert put out a hand and they shook, no more needing to be said.

After a short spell on deck, taking in deep gulps of fresh sea air, and amusedly watching one of the merchant's wives, Clarissa Tupton, a fat, jolly woman, trying unsuccessfully to gather enough people together for a game of quoits, Robert retired to his cabin for a snooze, as he had gotten very little sleep the previous night and the heaviness of his breakfast now lay dully on his stomach. He pulled the curtains across the small cabin porthole and, throwing off his clothes, fell into a deep, dreamless slumber the moment his head touched the pillow.

Vaguely aware of a persistent knocking at his door, Robert sat up in bed, and pulled back the darkened curtain. A stream of daylight flooded in. 'Who is it?'

'It's me, Daniel. I came to see if you were alright. You haven't been seen on deck all day.'

'What time is it?'

'Almost five. Will you be wanting any tea? It is being served shortly.'

'No thank you, Daniel. But I will get up. Just a moment.' Staggering to his feet, rubbing the sleep crusts from his eyes, Robert lifted the latch on the door and let it swing open. Daniel stepped through and took Robert in his arms. With his uniform on he appeared to be much taller and broader than he had seemed earlier. Perhaps it gave him an air of authority. Whatever it was, he wore it well, Robert mused. Without a word of invitation, Daniel pulled Robert's face towards him and kissed him fully on the lips, his tongue forcing its way down the throat, meeting Robert's tongue, which reciprocated. They stood in that position for many minutes, mouth to mouth, tongues moving and sliding against one another. Daniel finally pulled back. 'My word! You are extraordinary. I cannot say how much I am going to enjoy this journey. It was just going to be another routine sailing to the Indies, but then you came aboard, and everything changed. I haven't been able to stop thinking about you. I even called the Captain "Robert" by mistake. I managed to cover up my slip, but he has looked at me strangely ever since.'

Twining his fingers among Daniel's, Robert pulled him closer and spoke softly. 'This life is a very peculiar one indeed, Daniel. Nothing ever works out the way you expect. Just look at me. A few weeks ago I was heir to a family fortune, but fell victim to a ruthless group of men, survived a battle at sea, and now am standing here in your arms. We must take what we can, whenever we can, because tomorrow we may die. I have often said to myself that I do not want to leave this world with the words "I wish I had…" on my lips. Let us enjoy each other's company and this journey will just fly by. But we musn't expect that all will be plain sailing. Come on. Let us have some of that tea you spoke of.'

Opening the door and stepping through, Robert thought he heard a scuffling noise from the end of the corridor, and looking up, caught a glimpse of coat-tail vanishing around the corner. Had someone been listening at the door? He wasn't sure, but from now on he would have to be extra vigilant. He didn't care what people thought of him, but he wasn't going to get Daniel in trouble. That was the last thing he wanted to do. If somebody on board was interested in Robert he would have to make sure that this somebody discovered nothing that could possibly make Daniel's life uncomfortable. Robert followed Daniel along the corridor, hands in pockets, brow creased, hoping desperately that he wasn't heading into a dangerous situation.

SEVEN

In the galley, tea was being served in a charming Sevres porcelain service. Robert marvelled at its fine delicacy, and wondered what would happen in a storm at sea. 'Ah, you've noticed the porcelain, Mr Marchant. We may be out on the ocean waves, but I still insist on the finer things in life.' Captain Cartwright chuckled heartily and handed Robert a cup.

'Thank you. I completely agree with you, Sir. Why must we behave like savages? If we can eat and drink off of Sevres, then why not?!' Robert swiftly downed his tea and took a plate from the table. He helped himself to some almond shaped biscuits, but as he reached for another cup of tea someone jostled his elbow. Startled, he looked down into the ferret-like gaze of Governor Trench, who stood at his side, cup and saucer in hand. 'Are you feeling any better after your terrible ordeal, Mister Marchant?' he enquired in a nasal whine. His skin was reacting badly to the sun, and red blotches had already begun to develop on his face and hands. 'It must have been quite dreadful, under fire, someone of your obvious well-breeding, with no-one to turn to for support and succour?'

Robert paled slightly. 'And what, may I ask, do you mean by that?'

Shifting his posture from one foot to the other, Trench stared boldly up at Robert and lead him to a quiet corner of the galley, 'All I meant was that one must take comfort where one can, in times of hardship and privation.'

'I still do not understand what you are trying to say. If you insist on making such snide insinuations about my character, then I shall make an official complaint, to the Captain, even if you are a "Governor".'

'You may make all the complaints you like, my young friend. Captain Cartwright has been given a sizeable amount of money to take me to my destination, he won't hear a word said against me.' He paused, mopping his brow with a grubby lace kerchief. 'You may think your secret is safe, but I assure you it is not. I should be very careful, young man.'

An expression of puzzlement stole across Robert's face. 'Secret? What secret?' Deep inside, a feeling of unease stirred. A distant memory started to coalesce and form, a memory that Robert had pushed to the back of his mind. Was Trench in any way familiar? A twinge of recognition sparked, and Robert's thoughts crashed back to a day, several years ago, when Lord Marchant had taken his son on a trip to London. He had been visiting some naval big-wig in his office at the Admiralty, and Robert had been left seated in an airless corridor outside. Some concerned clerk had brought Robert some orange water, and made a pass at him. He had taken Robert to a small ante-room, and kissed him, his hands fondling Robert's private parts lasciviously. Robert had only gone with him because of a sense of intrigue, and because he wanted as much contact with other men as possible. Here was his chance to experience it, with a man at least fifteen years older, not too unattractive, who seemed to desire him. Why not see what happened? He had examined this clerk's cock and balls carefully, eager to see what other men were like. He was extremely surprised at their smallness. The clerk was delighted to be able to hold and caress this youngster, this beautiful young man with an outstanding prick. Nothing much had happened after the initial undressing, a few nervous fumblings, but then the clerk appeared suddenly jumpy, and stuffed his shrivelled genitalia back inside his breeches before quickly ushering Robert back to his seat.

Stunned, Robert tried to visualise Trench fifteen years ago. 'The Admiralty. That clerk. Was that you?'

'Oh, yes, it was, my friend. You may have forgotten me but I have never once let your face be from my mind. You were a tantalising little trollop, who gave me signals, who teased me and led me astray.'

'As I remember it, you were the one who was interested in me.'

'Not so. You wanted to have me and so I took you to an ante-room. As I recall we were disturbed. Since that day I developed urges and desires for other men, for which I would go to any lengths. I hung around commons and the privvies of inns, looking for the slightest sign of interest. I realised that my degenerate behaviour would have to cease when I was promoted to head of the department, and it was only a short amount of time before I rose to prominence and the King noticed my capabilities. I had to give up that life of perversion and debauchery, and marry.'

Scarcely unable to comprehend what he was being told, Robert glanced at Trench's wife, standing across the room, mutely listening to the loud guffaws emanating from Mrs Tupton. 'That poor woman. How could you decieve her like that?'

'She was grateful. I plucked her from a dull country parsonage, and gave her respectability. She is now the wife of the Governor of Dominique. She knows her place.'

The full picture of what Trench was saying had permeated Robert's mind. 'So you believe that I am responsible for your "desires"? You think that I made you like that?'

'Of course. And I shall have my own back. You shall regret the day you ever tried to trifle with my affections. The time will come very shortly when I will denounce you in front of the entire ship, the entire country if need be. Just know for now that I know all about you, and all about that pretty little officer you have been so intimate with.'

Fuming, Robert clenched his fists and pulled himself to his full height, in an effort to tower over Trench. 'If you say one word to anyone about him, you shall regret it.' He lowered his voice as he saw Daniel enter the room. 'I warn you. Keep away from me, and keep your mouth shut.' He spun around and strode toward the table. Gripping the table rim for support, he took a few deep breaths.

'Whatever is wrong? You don't seem well.' Daniel looked concerned as he approached. Noticing Robert's knuckles had turned white, holding tight to the table rim, and that he was silently shaking, he put his hands around his shoulders and helped him from the room. 'Sea-sick!' Daniel. told the room as he stepped outside onto the deck, ignoring the odd looks they were getting.

Leaning on the side of the ship, Robert looked down at the foaming waters beneath. His head was in a whirl. He had known that being the son of a famous nobleman had many advantages, but constantly being recognised by all and sundry was very wearing. It was unfortunate that Trench knew him... and even more unfortunate that they had met before. It seemed obvious to Robert that Trench's desires had lain dormant for many years, that he'd never had the courage to do anything about them. Robert had been the catalyst for those feelings, and Trench had used Robert as a scape-goat, someone to blame for his own failings. Why blame yourself when you can lay the fault on another? It makes one's guilt easier to bear. Trench was a man who held a grudge, and Robert knew that the rest of the journey would be exceedingly difficult. He would have to try and stay clear of Trench and his entourage, give him no cause for anger. Having no fear of others' condemnation, Robert knew that Daniel must be protected. He was a kind, loving man, who had fallen into a state of passion for Robert, which was nothing to be punished for. People should be free to love whomsoever they desired, and Robert would be damned if he was going to let Trench ruin this young officer's life.

'Are you alright?' Daniel squeezed Robert's shoulder, concern on his face.

'I am fine, just help me to my cabin, and hold me. I need some affection. I feel out of sorts.' Putting an arm around his shoulders, Daniel lead the way down, kicking open the cabin door with his foot, and helping Robert to the bed. 'Now that we are alone, and out of earshot, tell me what is wrong. I know that Governor Trench said something to upset you. Tell me.' Daniel's voice had a pleading note to it. He took Robert's hands and stared at him. Realising that he needed allies, Robert told the tale of what happened those few years past, and what Trench had insinuated to him. When he had finished, Robert sat back and smiled. 'So there you have it. I have a dark past. I shall quite understand if you want nothing more to do with me.'

A throaty chuckle was Daniel's answer. 'If anything, I respect you even more. It is quite clear that Trench led you on, and is blaming you for his own guilty feelings. I shall tell him what I think of him when I see that odious little man next.'

'No, you must not do that.' Insistent, Robert took Daniel by the shoulders and his voice lowered. 'Please, say nothing. Promise me. It will only lead to trouble for you. I can handle anything that is thrown at me, but I do not want you to lose your position over a problem of mine.'

After a moment's pause, Daniel nodded. 'As you wish. But I shall find it very hard to be civil to that man.'

'You must try.' Robert noticed a small tear drop from the corner of Daniel's eye. Lifting a finger, he wiped it away. 'What's this all about, silly?'

'I hate the thought of someone like Trench getting the better of you. I can see that you are a good person. I think I love you.'

No words came from Robert's mouth. He had never met anyone like

Daniel. Someone who had given his heart after so few hours. William had confessed his passion for Robert, but wasn't that all it was? Passion? Did William love him? And, more to the point, did he really love William? Robert was unsure. All he could see at the present was a handsome young officer, perfect in every way, offering himself unashamedly. He knew that he would be a fool not to take this opportunity with both hands. 'Come here.' Robert pulled Daniel to him and kissed him, tongues darting ferociously in their mouths. It took but an instant for both men to become aroused. Standing, and heaving Daniel to his feet also, Robert hurriedly ripped off the officer's jacket and shirt. Then with one practised motion, he pulled down the trousers, so that Daniel stood there with his cock free and his trousers bunched around his ankles.

Unable to wait any longer, Robert pushed the young man back on the bed and lifted his legs high. The sight of the puckered pink hole, trembling, pulsing, made Robert draw a deep breath of lust. Kneeling, he buried his face hard within the crack of Daniel's arse. The smell was intense — maleness and soap — and it turned him on and meant that he had to have this man now. He put out his tongue and let it lightly pass across the wrinkled skin, watching it twitch with excitement. The hole spasmed suddenly, squeezing tight, then relaxing as if encouraging further action. Robert's tongue got to work. He licked around the tight knot of muscles, inching closer and closer to the hole itself before plunging his tongue deep inside. The muscles relaxed sufficiently for most of his tongue to slide in. Keeping up the motion of pushing in and sliding back, Robert doused the arsehole in saliva, making it wet for his next attack. All the while Daniel kept up a steady and pleading moan, his hands holding his legs high and apart.

A sudden flash of inspiration crackled through Robert. Standing, he grabbed Daniel's legs, still with the trousers gathered about them, and lifted them higher, over his head, toward the wall behind the bunk. It took only a moment to fasten the belt around the curtain pole above the small porthole window, leaving Daniel unable to move, his muscular legs held firm in a fixed position, the arse exposed and free for Robert's attentions. Hurriedly falling back to his knees, he started to lick more frenetically, Daniel's cries of delight filling the cabin.

Stopping what he was doing, Robert adopted a stern tone. 'Be quiet. Try not to give the game away. We must be quiet!' Resuming, he looked appraisingly at the wettened rosebud, and flexed his index finger. Gently, but with assurance, he probed the hole with the finger, letting it just enter, feeling the ring clamp about it. As it relaxed a touch, he pushed further in, until it was embedded in the dark warmth, up to the knuckle. He drew back and began to fuck the hole with his finger, slowly and rhythmically, praying that Daniel could continue to keep his moaning to a minimum. His other hand reached up and grabbed the free-standing cock, sliding his fist along the hardened shaft. The double attention that Daniel was getting only served to make him moan more. 'Ssssh. You must stay quiet.' Robert knew how difficult it was to be silent in a moment of passion, but it had to be so.

It took but a second for Robert to heave himself to his feet. Standing squarely and firmly, he spat a large gob of saliva down onto his own inflamed member, rubbing the wetness over the head, before leaning forward on the bed and positioning it against the moistened opening. Daniel drew in his breath as he realised what was coming. The pressure of the cock against his hole was increasing. Sooner or later it would push itself forth and slide in. The officer tried to relax his sphincter muscles to allow this to happen. Without a warning, the hardened bulk was pushed inside. The relaxed muscles clung tightly to the rod within them, clamping about the rigid pole, never wanting it to withdraw. But it did. Robert sensed that Daniel had gotten over the initial shock and began to pull back slowly, tenderly easing the shaft out of the hole, which gently shrunk back to its closed state. Unable to hold back any more, he forced the cock into the arse, seemingly feeling every muscle contort and expand to accommodate its size. Daniel, realising the need for circumspection, gritted his teeth and held back his cries of pain and delight.

A wave of lust poured over Robert and he began to pound away, sliding his cock back and forth, fucking Daniel's arse with practised strokes, grinding away with relentless strides, filling Daniel's very being with his manhood. His legs pinioned above him, Daniel felt as if a fire was blazing within him. The warmth and searing fullness was overwhelming, there was no other sensation in the world, only this astonishing pummelling from Robert's huge cock. His own penis had grown steadily from the actions of Robert's hand, and it thrust up from between his sweat-covered thighs. With a little effort, he slipped a hand down and grabbed at his organ, and lifted his arse even higher, encouraging a deeper thrust from Robert's weapon. The motion of the fucking intensified, making Robert's breath come harder and faster, and causing Daniel to grip his own cock tighter and start a pounding with his fist. This couldn't go on much longer, the exquisite torture of the embedded tool was producing a cascade of ecstasy in Daniel, and he knew that a climax was imminent. As if aware that his victim was about to explode, Robert fucked with an increase of speed and, if possible, depth, the strokes getting longer each time. His head was spinning as he heard a cry escape from Daniel's lips, and he could hold back no longer. Looking down, he saw spurts of thick, milky juice pouring from the boy's cock, shooting across his chest, leaving a trail of ecstatic evidence. He watched his own solidity fuck the hole, and felt that intense wave of climax build, before he pulled out and let his come pump out over Daniel's chest and stomach.

Daniel lay, breathing heavily, his exposed arsehole still looking enticing, as his legs were held aloft. His chest was covered in bolts of semen. Some had even reached his face, a trail of cream over his clean-shaven chin. Robert had never seen such an erotic sight. With one hand he unfastened the belt buckle and let Daniel's legs fall back to the bed, then reaching for a towel, began to wipe him clean.

'You are incredible,' Daniel panted, watching the mopping-up intently. 'Where did you gain such experience?'

'Oh, here and there. You were amazing yourself, though. Have you done this before?'

'A couple of times. Once in Portsmouth with a boy of the street, and once on my last tour of duty to the Indies. It was with a black manservant, who was prodigiously endowed. I didn't think I'd be able to take all of his length,' he paused for effect. 'But I did!' Robert smiled and buttoned his trousers, then helped Daniel to his feet. 'I must admit that this unexpected journey is getting better and better,' Robert said. 'With each other for company, we will be at the Indies in no time!'

EIGHT

The voyage of *The Merry Megan* passed quite amicably. The first stage of the journey, down to Spain, proved uneventful, with favourable winds aiding the sailing The days aboard were long, but the passengers seemed to find enough things to do to pass the time. Mrs Tupton was a pillar of strength, organising deck games, ornithology lessons and Bridge tournaments.

Robert and Daniel managed to see quite a lot of each other, occasionally finding opportunities to be alone, sneaking away to each other's cabins to enjoy their bodies.

It was on their eighth day out of Lisbon, where fresh supplies had been taken on, that a series of storms raged about the ship. During the afternoon, the weather got worse, and visibility decayed. The ocean's swell increased and many of the passengers had to retire to their cabins with bouts of sickness. The crew seemed unaffected, as was Robert, but they were in the minority. Throughout the night, the pitching and tossing of the ship caused much lost sleep, and the Captain found a very depleted company at breakfast the next morning.

On the second day of storms, needful of some fresh air, Robert managed to scramble up to the deck, where he tied himself to a mast for security. The ship pitched from side to side, and waves came crashing over the deck, but Robert stood firm. Drenched to the skin, he declared it an exilarating experience. The storm raged for a further four days, during which little headway was made. Captain Cartwright seemed unworried by this, and tried to reassure anyone who asked that the ship could withstand any amount of buffeting. There were times, though, that Robert thought their end was in sight. Gales of wind shrieked through the rigging, and the wooden timbers groaned and creaked, as if she was about to fall apart. The passengers were in a state of terror, expectant that each crashing wave would finish them off, sending them to their graves in the ocean's depths.

On the fifth stormy afternoon, the weather eased and visibility increased enough for Captain Cartwright to set his charts and continue to steer his course. From that point on, the journey was very different. The weather improved rapidly, with days of glorious sunshine and balmy breezes. The temperaments of the passengers also improved, with much good humour in evidence. The Captain had allowed the crew to dispense with their heavy serge uniforms and wear white trousers and shirts, making their days in such glorious weather easier too. Robert appreciated the change, as Daniel appeared even more dashing. His contoured chest looked well in just a shirt.

At just under halfway on their voyage, a day was declared as a special gala. It was to celebrate the ship's crossing of the Tropic of Cancer, and all manner of festivities were planned to make the day a memorable one for its company. Many of the crew had dressed in exotic garb, and fancy dress, and the Captain, resplendent in a patterned waistcoat, acted as Master of Ceremonies from his 'throne' upon the bridge. Many of the passengers entered into the spirit of things, and appeared happy to participate in the ceremony of ritual humiliation, all except Trench and his party, who sat alongside the Captain and watched the proceedings with forced expressions of goodwill on their faces.

A shrill cacophany of notes blew from a sailor's pipe, the main door to the deck was flung open, and a parade of crew members dressed in sheets and sea-shells stepped out. At its head, arms flung wide, a beaming grin from ear to ear, was Daniel, a sheet wound tightly around his waist like a Roman skirt, a necklace of oyster shells hanging down upon his chest. On his head was a cardboard crown draped with seaweed, and in one hand he carried a trident. He looked magnificent, and in this persona of the King of The Seas, he carried himself superbly. Charisma radiated from him, and many of the female passengers blushed as he passed, this exquisite example of manhood causing their pulses to beat a little faster. Among the watching men, Robert's heart also stirred, as he gazed adoringly at this Adonis.

Safe in the knowledge that he had the attention of all, Daniel stood on the centre of the deck and raised his arms, trident glinting in the sunlight. 'Silence, all. Who dares to cross the line of Cancer without my permission? Who travels here without my knowing?' Dramatically, he gripped the trident and swung it round, pointing it at various passengers in turn. He knew that he would have to be careful in his choice of initiate at this ceremony, it was considered almost a crime to treat a person of good breeding with disrespect. To humiliate some such person was unthinkable. He pointed his trident at Mrs Tupton, who giggled girlishly and hid her face in her hands. Then his fierce stare landed on Hamish Dee, standing on the bridge, with his arms crossed, looking bored. Everybody had been told that if they were chosen by "The King" then they would have to capitulate and partake in the ceremony, to be a good sport, whatever happened to them. 'YOU!' Daniel screamed enthusiastically at the Scotsman, who shook his head in disbelief. 'Your King orders you.' Daniel waved at a couple of his accolytes, fellow officers who had taken a dislike to Dee from the outset, who bounded up to the bridge and feverishly grabbed him by the arms. He looked pleadingly at Trench, who just waved him away, a smile on his lips for the first time in days.

Having pushed Dee to his knees in front of him, Daniel continued his search. Martenson and Fitch, the cousins, huddled together for safety, determined not to be picked. Then Daniel's eyes lit upon the merchant Barnes, who was travelling from his home in Liverpool to oversee his newly acquired plantation. Barnes guffawed heartily and joined Dee on his knees, waving his fingers at his blushing wife. One more initiate was needed. Daniel knew who it had to be. His trident pointed unwaveringly at Robert, who grinned and said, 'Who, me? What could your Majesty want with me?'

'Down on your knees, unworthy one. Prepare for the King's revenge.' Daniel was enjoying every minute. As the centre of attention he shone brilliantly and held everyone in thrall with his performance. Kneeling next to Barnes, Robert whispered, 'What is going to happen?' Barnes just raised a finger to his lips and gestured with his head toward Daniel, who was bearing down upon his three victims. At a signal from him, several of the sailors held the arms of the three and began to undo their shirts. Soon they knelt before the assembled throng, shirtless and apprehensive. One of the sailors rang a large bell, and a wooden pail was brought forth. Nodding sagely, Daniel waved a hand and let the ceremony commence.

The passengers watched delightedly as the three initiates were daubed with some kind of watery red dye, which was then rubbed into their chests. Robert was unsure, but wondered if the sailor who attended to his punishment lingered a little longer than was necessary on that particular task, letting his hands massage his chest slightly more than expected. They were also forced to wear two joined half-coconuts about their chests, in mocking guise of a woman, and had to drink a disgusting concoction of milk, beer, raw egg and chilli. Robert gave in to the fun of the day and enjoyed his humiliation, as did Barnes, but Dee did what was required with ill grace, scowling at everyone concerned, his contempt for his captors evident. Daniel seemed unaware that Dee was the wrong man to have picked, and continually tried to show him up, revelling in the cheers of admiration from the crowd. At length, the ceremony was concluded, and the newly initiated "Brothers of the Sea" were set free. Barnes collapsed into the arms of his wife, weeping with laughter, while Dee slowly climbed back to the bridge, where he whispered in Trench's ear and was excused. Robert watched him cross to the hatch and make his way down to his cabin.

The Captain came down from the bridge and began mingling, conversing pleasantly with the assembled passengers. Many of them slapped Robert on the back, congratulating him on his fortitude, glad that they hadn't been picked. That peculiar English trait was much in evidence, namely that of being happy to watch others being made fools of, but then running a mile should the humiliation be coming their way.

Barnes cornered Robert and seemed to want to re-enact the afternoon with a blow-by-blow account, for his wife's benefit, when Daniel sidled up and excused Robert from them.

'Thank you. I was in danger of a ritual boring to death.'

'Never mind that now, come to my cabin as soon as you can.' Daniel had a mysterious air about him, and without disclosing any further information, he turned and went below. This was puzzling, and as Robert hated puzzles, he waited for a minute and then followed.

He gave a firm knock on the cabin door, which was immediately pulled open, and Robert found himself yanked inside. Before he could react, a blindfold was hurriedly tied about his eyes. He tried to speak, but a number of hands pinioned him and began to hurriedly undress him. A voice he immediately recognised spoke softly near his ear. 'Mister Marchant... Some would say that you got off very lightly with that ceremony today. There are some of us who think that a little more should happen. Don't struggle, you'll only make things worse for yourself!' Daniel's enjoyment of the situation was evident in his voice, and Robert could picture the grin upon his face. In seconds he stood unhindered, naked, unsure as to what exactly was about to happen.

Unknown hands started to feel and rub his chest and thighs. He felt there to be three pairs of eager hands making themselves acquainted with every nook of his body. This was an unexpected experience, but, with a shrug of his shoulders, Robert decided to enjoy it. He reached out and tried to feel who else was in the cabin. His fingers met with bare flesh, muscled and hard, and he silently thanked God that they seemed to be men, not women. He was unable to tell who was in the room apart from himself and Daniel, and longed to take off the all-enveloping blindfold, and see. His fingers intertwined with someone's hair, thick and long. The skin of the unknown body was quite rough around the hands and arms. Was it one of the sailors? Surely an officer didn't have such rough skin? He put his arms wide, reaching for Daniel, but he didn't seem to be close. Without warning,his arms were held down by his side and he was unable to move. The shock of a pair of lips brushing his chest was intense. Another mouth joined the first as they licked around the chest, neck and back, then a third. All three mouths seemed practised, licking and sucking, but not going anywhere near any of the tenderer areas, avoiding the nipples. As the mouths gave his torso attention, the hands didn't stop the massaging of his legs and thighs, going just so high and stopping before they got to the groin.

Then, suddenly acting as one, two of the mouths lit upon his nipples, each one encompassed by a wet tongue and soft lips, while the third mouth started to kiss him, forcing its tongue into Robert's throat, probing and pushing. Whoever it was, he was an expert kisser. Reciprocating, Robert kissed back, their tongues meeting and sliding against each other, mouth pressed hard to mouth. The other participants lingered over the chest, sucking the nipples deep into their mouths, biting the tips with their teeth, then letting the tongues flick around the darkened outer circle.

Again without any hint of what was coming, another mouth joined the fray. Robert wanted to exclaim with surprise, but the un-named kisser's mouth kept him from doing so, as his now rigid cock was engulfed by a warm, wet mouth. It clamped about him, and began to suck greedily. With his arms held tight, Robert couldn't move. In his mind he could see Daniel on his knees, his mouth sliding back and forth along his cock, his eyes looking up, meeting his gaze. But he couldn't be certain that it was Daniel down there.

In all his experience, Robert had never encountered such sensations. Having several mouths working at the same time sent shivers through him. Each mouth was giving a wonderful feeling, and he found it hard to concentrate his reactions on just one of those pleasured areas. The slurping, biting and sucking seemed to take over his entire being, even more so when the mouth that was kissing him stopped and instantly reappeared further down his body, sucking his balls into that malleable wetness. Now that his chest, cock and balls were being attended to, Robert felt such waves of ecstatic energy course through him that he thought he would die of pleasure instantaneously. The sucking increased its tempo, the vacuum of the mouth around his prick getting higher, the mouth around both his balls seeming to want to pull them down. A climax was not far away. As if one creature with one mind, the others stopped suddenly, as though sensing his nearness to coming.

The arms that held him moved him back until his legs hit the side of what he assumed was a table. Pushed back, he sat down clumsily, the arms laying him down, and swinging him round so that his legs were hanging over one edge of the table and his head down over the other. It was an uncomfortable position, but he could do nothing about it, the others were in control. Robert had always been a man who liked to know what was going on around him. He liked to be able to sort out problems and be aware of his surroundings, but here all he could do was lay there and wait. Obviously his captors knew what they wanted, all he could do was go with the flow.

As he squirmed about, to try and lie in a more congenial position, his head was pulled down. His mouth was free but his eyes were still covered. Robert opened his mouth wide, exposing his throat. As a mouth slid itself down his own cock again, someone's solid shaft was forced down his throat, past the lolling tongue, to prod the tonsils at the back. With his head held back like this he could take the whole length easily, and so he did. It was long, and tapered down to a smallish head. He knew by its dimensions that it wasn't Daniel. The cock started to push itself in and out, a low moan coming from its owner, as Robert squeezed his own mouth tightly about it. Whoever was sucking Robert's cock was doing an expert job, as the tongue and lips manipulated it deliciously, holding firm as it engulfed the rock-hard pole. Other mouths now fell back upon Robert's nipples, the tongues working across the whole chest area, sometimes working in unison, moving to the armpits and slavering them with saliva.

The cock in his mouth started to twitch, Robert wondered what he should do. Did this person want to come so soon? Should he intensify his actions? Or should he slow, as there might be other sexual items on the menu? The choice was made for him. The cock pulled away and was immediately replaced by another one.

The head of this penis was huge, it filled his mouth, and the shaft was collossal. With great difficulty, Robert tried to take the whole of it down, but he couldn't. The width of the thing was so enormous that it only got half-way. Its owner knew that Robert was having difficulty so he backed off and left the giant head just sitting inside his mouth. Robert sucked and licked at it heartily. Somehow he managed to stretch his jaw wider than he thought he could, and before he knew it, the complete monster was inside his throat, the balls hanging heavily against his nose. Robert had heard of snakes dislocating their jaws to swallow their prey, but never a man to swallow another's gigantic cock! All the while he was still being blown expertly, that stranger's mouth knowing when to hold back and when to proceed, keeping Robert on the edge of climax.

He did all he could to satisfy this huge weapon, letting the owner do all the work, pulling and pushing, fucking Robert's mouth. All of a sudden, the gargantuan cock started to jerk. Unable to stop itself, a stream shot forth, filling his throat, so Robert drank it down, to the sound of heavy grunts from its owner. Again it disappeared and a third cock pushed its way inside his now-aching mouth. Thankfully it wasn't as big as the previous one, it was solid and straight, and filled his mouth perfectly. Wanting to do it justice, Robert slid his tongue around it, holding the cock tight, sliding the skin on the shaft back to let the sensitive head be released from its containing foreskin. Whoever he had in his mouth shuddered, and pushed frantically, jamming the prick down to the back of the throat, with quick, jabbing motions. Every time Robert sucked in, the cock twitched. The fact that its owner hadn't had much oral experience was quite evident. Robert could feel the pulsing of the veins. The stranger stood squirming and wriggling in delight, his hands clasped about Robert's throat, as if wanting to feel the length of his weapon inside. The man thrashed and whined as Robert's mouth skillfully coaxed him to orgasm, his cock stabbing wildly in the throat.

With a whimper of delight, the man's thighs trembled and Robert felt the bitter, salty taste of semen splash against his throat. He pushed his face down its length, while it shot several large bolts more. Robert's mouth was full to overflowing with the thick hot liquid and he slowly let it slide down his throat, still sucking hard on the cock itself. The stranger groaned as his cock immediately began to soften, and it slid free with a muffled plop.

Instantly, whoever was between Robert's thighs began to suck with all his might, going mad, trying to induce the very soul from it. Robert knew that he could hold back no longer, and he shot, into the mouth, which suckled on its load, like a baby on its mother's breast. Drawing down every last drop. Robert lay, listening to the sounds of the room. Whoever else was in there was now obviously beating themselves to climax. He could hear the shuffling, rubbing sounds of masturbation, and in but a minute he heard a small cry from his left side and felt hot blobs of semen land across his chest, followed by another yelp of satisfaction from between his thighs and more warm fluid splatter across him.

Not wanting to be the one left out, he grasped his own still-solid knob and started to jerk, his fingers pressed firmly around the swollen cockshaft, working it to explosion. He began to shake, an eruption building up, as the head of his cock grew larger. With a moan, his fingers opening and closing, he came in a great arc of spunk, landing in smalls pools amongst the other's streaks of come. He collapsed back on the table, still moaning, still grasping at his half-hard cock, breathing heavily.

The suspense was now too much. Robert sat up on the table and pulled the blindfold from his head. Blinking slightly, as his eyes adjusted to the light in the cabin, he looked about him, amazed. Still standing between his thighs was Daniel, grinning sheepishly, while around the room stood three other naked men. Robert recognised one of them as the sailor who had rubbed ink on his chest during the ceremony, a wiry, muscular man called Soames, whose short cropped hair gave him an adoring look. The remaining two he saw to be other members of the crew. One was the Third Mate, a quiet man named Quilter, who was the one with the enormous cock, which hung, half-hard, between his legs, still a sizeable thing, and the other was one of the cooks, a swarthy young man called Zenos.

Robert rubbed his eyes and gave a look of surprise at Daniel. 'Well. That was certainly an experience. How did you know that these other men would want to participate?'

With his throaty chuckle, Daniel put his arms around Robert's neck. 'It is not difficult to recognise a kindred spirit, you know. It was obvious that they preferred the company of men, like I do, and in conversation with them, they expressed their interest in you. We cooked up this little party a couple of days ago, knowing that we would be having only a few official duties to perform today, and would have some time off. Say you enjoyed yourself!'

'Oh, I did. It was one of the most exciting things I've ever encountered. The sensation of being taken by more than one was indescribable.' He turned to Quilter, who stood by, watching keenly. 'I must say I was surprised by the size of your prick, Mr Quilter...'

'Please call me Luke.'

'...Luke, I have seldom encountered one with such astounding dimensions.'

Quilter's hand stroked his semi-erect penis. 'I can quite believe you, Sir. When I was at boarding school, you can imagine that I endured much ribbing. By the age of twelve, I was almost as big as I am now, but I soon gained the other boy's admiration for my stamina. Many of them would try and sneak into the wood with me to experience it at its fullest. Not many of them went back disappointed.'

'I'm sure, Luke. Have you ever met a man who could accomodate it up his arse?

'No. I have often wondered what that would be like. But when the thing is erect, no-one seems to be able to take it.' His eyes narrowed. 'Perhaps you would like to try sometime...?'

Unable to resist such a challenge, the memory of Crook's enormous apendage fresh in his mind, Robert nodded, leapt to his feet, and grabbed the swinging member, giving it a gentle squeeze. 'I think that might be an interesting experiment, what say you, Daniel?'

The First Officer patted Robert's bottom, his sparkling grin covering his face, and said, 'As long as I can watch!' Robert turned to the cook, Zenos, who had been hovering at his elbow, his cock shrunk back to its normal size, his arms folded. He was an intense man, apparently in his mid-twenties, of mediterranean appearance, with dark hair and eyes, a mop of curly body hair, and a stocky, well-proportioned frame. 'And you, my friend. Where did Daniel, I mean Mister Good, find you?'

Zenos moved closer to Robert and stroked his fingers across the drying semen on his chest and stomach. 'I work in the kitchens. I not get much fun there.' His accent was pronounced, most likely Greek, mused Robert.

The cook continued. 'I see Mister Good, he look like he want boy sex. I do too. We have fun.' He looked to Daniel for confirmation, who just nodded slightly. 'Then I see you. You are beautiful man. I say to Mister Good can I have boy sex with you?' He gulped and carried on. 'He say he arrange. And we have others to do it as well. I like it very much.' A lopsided grin spread across his face. Robert had heard of the unusual sexual appetites of the Greek male. Having a highly developed libido, Greek men will have sex with anyone they desire, male or female. Even if they are married they will enjoy sex with their men friends, as a way to find relief, with no deeper overtones. It is only the stuffy English who think sex a bad thing, an activity to be performed behind doors, and in secret, never to be talked about. Robert often wondered how the English came to be so inhibited. He had never found an answer.

'Well, Mr Zenos, I hope that you enjoyed the afternoon? Perhaps we shall do it again sometime.' A look of joy filled Zenos's face and he flung his arms about Robert. 'Thank you, thank you.' He kissed him on the lips and then sat back upon the bed, seemingly content. A clock chimed from somewhere in the back of the cabin, and Daniel ran his fingers through his hair. 'I think it is time that we were elsewhere. Zenos, you should probably be in the galley preparing tea. And Quilter, put that monster away and dress yourself. The Captain will no doubt be in need of you. Come Robert, I think a cup of tea would be an admirable thing now!'

The hot weather continued unabated, keeping the journey ever pleasant for its voyagers. Canvas awnings had been erected on the fore deck, allowing some of the more delicate passengers to sit outside and be shaded from the blazing sun. Robert noticed that Trench kept to his cabin for much of the day, only appearing at meal times, and then only to briefly wolf down what was offered and then return to his rooms, wife in tow. Card games abounded out on deck, interrupted only by the excitement of watching the occasional school of dolphins which would swim alongside the ship and then veer off with a splash of water from their blowholes.

Throughout the voyage, Robert had been attempting to keep Trench at arm's length, the prospect of an argument with that swine a less than desirable one. One afternoon, about a week before their planned arrival in Dominique, Robert was sat on the bridge, a pair of binoculars at hand, skimming the horizon for flying fish. It was another clear, hot day, and at this time, just after lunch, most of the passengers had retired to their cabins for a siesta. Third Officer Quilter was at the wheel, and the ship was plowing its way through the ocean unhindered. The scarcity of flying fish had disappointed Robert and so he decided on a glass of orange water, to slake his thirst.

The galley was empty and so, making his way to the serving table at the rear of the room, Robert helped himself to a glass. Scarcely had he lifted the covered jug, when he heard voices outside and the handle of the door turn. One of the voices was Governor Trench. Deftly putting the glass and jug back on the table, Robert slipped into the kitchen area, through the rear door by the serving table. Holding his breath, he strained to hear what Trench was saying. The conversation was obviously half-way through.

'...I can do no more,' Trench said quietly. 'When we arrive we shall put the plan into action immediately. As I assume command of the island, so shall I start to rule with a rod of iron. Slackers, deceivers and degenerates will be the first to feel my will. What do you say to that, eh?' A grunt was his only answer, no doubt from Hamish Dee, his secretary and partner in deceit. 'I shall have that island in the palm of my hand. I believe that is the reason for His Majesty appointing me to the Governorship. He knows that I am no weak pushover, and will make Dominique a shining example of the British Empire at its greatest. We will subjugate the natives, keep all women in their place, and anyone who does not agree with me will find themselves at home in prison. And as for perverts like that Marchant...' Robert's ears pricked up, little had he expected to hear his own name mentioned. Trench continued without pause, 'He will rue the day he ever decide to trifle with me. I hope you have been keeping close watch on his activities, Dee. I shall be relying on that dossier you are compiling about him. It will be his undoing.' A cracked laugh issued from his throat, the first time Robert had ever heard him make such an unpleasant sound, sending shivers down his spine. Trench continued speaking over the sound of pouring liquid. 'No-one must know what has hit them until I am in residence at the Governor's mansion. I shall make all manner of perverted sex illegal. Anyone known to indulge in, or to have previously indulged in, sodomy will be incarcerated. I wonder if I could impose the death penalty. That is something we must look into…' Their voices drifted from the room.

Robert slipped quietly back into the room, worried thoughts buzzing through his mind. This was a very tricky situation. Trench was a bitter man, intent on being some kind of dictator when in power on Dominique. He had obviously become warped, his mind full of bigotry and hatred. This could be extremely dangerous, and certainly harmful for the hard-working, peaceful natives of the island. There must be a way to stop him. Another thought struck Robert as he poured a glass of orange water, an even more worrying thought. That dossier.

Had Trench and Dee been spying on him, keeping watch on his activities aboard *The Merry Megan*? And what exactly did he have in that dossier? Somehow Robert had to find out. There had to be a way to steal it. Otherwise his stay on Dominique, even if for a brief few days, would be untenable. Trench would make his life a misery, even arrest him if he decided to do so, and Robert would be able to do nothing about it. Things looked black. He knew that if he had details of his own dalliances in that dossier, then he would also have details of Daniel's. He couldn't let that bigoted bastard have an excuse to throw Daniel in jail. He had to think fast. Perhaps he could find a way to sneak into Trench's rooms that evening when everyone was at dinner. He could make up a plausible excuse and just slip out for a few moments. It had to be done. Deep in thought, he made his way back to his cabin, and, throwing off his jacket, lay back on the bed to think his plan out.

That evening was one that Robert would never forget. In later years he would swear that he lost five years of his lif, during the happenings of that night. Its appalling scenario would frequently play itself out in Robert's mind.

Everyone had assembled for dinner dressed in the finest attire, as they usually were. Robert had come to the table with a heavy heart, the knowledge of his intended subterfuge at the front of his thoughts. The Captain said grace as usual and everyone tucked into the delicious meal in front of them.

The conversation around the table was varied, and Robert drifted in and out of it, joining in with false interest wherever necessary. The only piece of talk that held his attention was when the Captain started to describe the rest of their journey. 'I expect that we shall be at sea for another six days. We shall head straight for the port of Ruba and dock immediately. I must warn you, though, that in the next six days we shall be sailing the waters of the Caribbean, and they are not the safest part of our voyage. As you would have been told before we left Portsmouth, this small area has been rife with privateers.'

Mrs Tupton piped up. 'Privateers? And what would they be, Captain?'

Cartwright looked at her, his tone of voice expressing disbelief. 'Privateers, Mrs Tupton, are more commonly known as pirates. Scavengers who pay allegiance to no particular country, and who scour the seas attacking harmless vessels. It is true that their numbers have greatly decreased over recent years, but there is still the chance that we may encounter such people. Now I do not want you to worry. We are a small ship, with great manouvering skills. We should be able to outrun any other vessel. I beg you to try and put this from your minds. There have been no reports of attacks in these waters for quite some time. All should be well.'

Robert chewed slowly upon a bread roll and turned his thoughts over carefully. Pirates. That would be the last thing he wanted to encounter. Especially after all he had been through so far. Still, there was nothing he could do about it if it did happen.

Putting down his roll, and taking a sip of water, Robert turned to Mrs Barnes, on his left, and coughed for her attention. 'If you will excuse me, I don't feel too well, I am afraid. I think I may have caught a little too much sun today. I shall retire to my cabin for a doze.' Nodding to the Captain, he pushed back his chair and got to his feet. Pulling out a handkerchief, he mopped at his brow, feigning sun exhaustion, and made his way out of the galley. Outside, he waited for a few moments to see if anyone followed, and then, certain that he was unwatched, he made his way to Trench's cabin.

His heart was beating wildly in his mouth as he knocked on the cabin door, half expecting it to swing open. No sounds came from within. Using a dinner knife that he had slipped into his jacket pocket earlier, he managed to pop open the latch, and stepped stealthily inside. The room was in semi-darkness. Robert pulled back the curtain over the window, letting more light pour into the room.

Where would Trench have hidden the dossier? Robert scanned the desk, and quickly opened the drawers, which revealed nothing but sheaves of official documents and maps. He made his way through to the bedroom and quickly lifted the mattress, bare boards underneath disapointing him. His eye lit upon several travelling cases stacked by the door. The top one contained jewellery and other feminine nick-nacks, the second, clothes, but the larger one on the bottom of the pile contained a variety of oddments. Robert found a gun, a bullwhip, many bags of coins, and, tucked away at the bottom, a collection of papers, rolled up and tied with a black ribbon. Swiftly shutting the case lid, and pulling open the ribbon, he saw many scribbled notes, such as

'Thursday 12th – seen in close conversation with Third Officer. They may be involved. I wonder if the Captain knows.

Saturday 14th – Disappeared with First Officer Good to own cabin. Stayed inside for 1 hour. Noises of sexual congress heard within.

Tuesday 17th – Late for dinner, as was Good. Probably had been involved with each other again. His sexual appetite seems bottomless.

With a shaking hand, Robert re-tied the ribbon and slipped the notes into an inner pocket. So it was true. That blackguard Trench had been spying on his every movement. Anger boiled and seethed through him, at the thought of that disgusting little man, keeping notes on everything he did aboard ship. He must have a more warped mind than Robert first imagined. But what was Trench planning to do with those notes? Surely no-one of any breeding would listen to such 'filth' as he would be deemed to be spouting? The majority of the passengers had taken a liking to Robert almost immediately, enjoying his charm and wit. The ladies especially would gather round him, enthralled by his many humorous stories, and taken by his handsome features. Surely they would take his word over Trench's? The Governor had proved himself to be an anti-social person, with a dislike of shipboard activities and a miserable temper. He would be laughed at, wouldn't he? Robert couldn't take the risk. It would be safer to destroy the papers, and then it would just be one man's word against another's for certain. With his flair for words and enjoyment of language, Robert would win hands down in any confrontation.

With a deep exhalation of contempt at Trench, Robert got to his feet, patted the roll of notes in his pocket and straightened his necktie. Perhaps he should rejoin the diners? The iced sorbet did look appetizing. Turning for the door, he jumped in shock, as he stared into the watching eyes of Governor Trench.

NINE

'A common thief as well as a sodomite.' Trench looked at Robert with loathing and hatred, a sneer contorting his features. 'I imagined you might not be as unwell as you seemed at dinner, and so I followed you. A wise action on my part it would appear. Breaking into another's cabin is a punishable offence. As is sodomy, of which you have been observed indulging on numerous occasions, and with numerous other degenerate members of the crew. Perhaps we should inform the Captain of your disgusting activities?'

Robert's mouth was dry, and no words came out. Trench laughed, his usual revoltingly wheezy chuckle, revelling in the discomfort of his prey. Robert was put in mind of a judge, sizing up his next defendant, assuming his guilt before hearing the case, and going straight for the black cap, delighted to be passing another death penalty.

The room was full of heavy silence; the distant creaking of the ship, and the rasping breath of Trench, the only sounds Robert was conscious of. He had to realise the enormity of the situation. 'Pull yourself together', he said to himself. 'This man cannot beat you. He is an insignificant worm, and you are the son of Lord Cedric Marchant.'

Trench folded his arms defiantly. 'I am sure Captain Cartwright will be fascinated to know what you have been doing on board his ship. He will be interested to see the notes I have been keeping on your activities, as, I am sure, will you.'

Grimly holding back his temper, Robert patted his jacket. 'Notes that you no longer possess. I have them here, and it will therefore be a matter of which of the two of us he believes. And as no-one cares a fig for you, I think I will come out on top.' He would beat this swine, and he would enjoy doing so.

A smile started to twitch at the corner of Trench's hard streak of a mouth. 'Do you honestly think I would be so stupid as to have only one copy? Your downfall, when it comes, is very important to me, and I look forward to it with great pleasure.'

Sensing that Trench may have the upper hand, Robert decided on a different tack. Sitting back on the pile of cases, he looked his enemy in the face. 'Cannot we be gentlemen about this matter? What happened between us in the past should be forgotten, surely? It was unfortunate that anything which occurred in that Admiralty office should have affected you so, but I cannot be held responsible for that.'

No response came from the Governor. He watched and listened intently, head cocked, bird-like, to one side. 'I honestly believe', continued Robert, 'that all men have the desire in them to be intimate with another man. I think it is behaviour more natural than being with a woman. A man can tell how a man feels and so can undertake certain actions... can do certain physical acts... and know the sensations they provide. Admit it... you enjoyed doing those things back then, when you went with street boys and the like, didn't you?'

Trench looked down at the floor, a moment's hesitation before he spoke. 'I did enjoy it, and I still do. The feel of a young man's firm body pressed to mine is indescribable.'

'Exactly, and so there is nothing to be ashamed of. Just because our society doesn't recognise such relationships, it doesn't mean that they are wrong. I think that as I was the first man you ever had physical contact with, you assumed that I had turned you effeminate in some way. But that is not true. You have always felt like that, deep down, and when we met, those feelings burst out. You cannot blame me for what happened in your life afterwards.'

Again Trench fell silent. Robert prayed that he had gotten through to the man. He couldn't be all bad. There had to be some spark of decency hidden in his soul. He seemed deep in thought, and he appeared to be weighing up his words before speaking them. 'Oh, but I *can* blame you, Marchant. I can blame you for everything. If, as you say, those feelings were dormant in me, they should have stayed there. I had no desire to be different from other men. The norm in our world is for man to be with woman, to procreate and further the race. It cannot be right, or correct for men to be with men, even if the sensations are desirable.'

'Just think about it for a moment...'

'I have thought about nothing else for many years. I desperately wanted to be as other decent men. I wanted a wife and a family, a career and advancement, money and a sizeable residence. All of these things cannot be had by the known homosexual in today's world.' A drop of drool splattered onto the lapel of his coat. Ignoring this, he ranted on. 'Through my hard work and tenacity I have achieved my goals, but suffered much misery and torment in the process, thinking I would be exposed as sodomite, an unnatural deviant, and fought hard to quell those desires that came upon me. Yes, I sometimes did fall from grace and partake of some young boy's inviting flesh, but I knew it was wrong. I was only doing it because you awakened that side of my nature. If you hadn't taken me to that office at the Admiralty, my life would have been happier and more complete.'

'But you cannot blame me for that. You were the one who...'

'Be silent. I know what happened and I know how miserable my existence has been ever since you dallied with me. I cannot forget and I shall damn well never forgive. I hold you totally responsible and if I can be revenged on you I shall.' Trench paused and let his tongue flick across his cracked lips. 'It seems as though the moment of revenge is at hand. I cannot envisage how you will be able to justify your exploits to the Captain.'

'Revenge is an ugly word. Is there nothing I can say that will change your mind? Nothing I can do that would soften your heart?' Robert adopted the pleading tone that always had worked with his father. A downturned head and an upward glance from a moistened eye, in tandem with a tremble in the voice, always got him what he wanted. Would it work now? He noticed that Trench shifted uneasily from foot to foot. Was this counter-attack working on him?

'What say you, Fergus?' Robert hesitated about using his Christian name but it felt like the right thing to do, in this strained circumstance.

A battle seemed to be raging within Trench. He appeared unsure. His long-standing hatred of Robert was struggling with the morality of this young man's argument. 'Perhaps there is something you could do which might sway me. Something to endear yourself to me.' His tongue flicked out across his lips again, and his hand reached down to his crotch.

Aghast, Robert watched as his mottled hand moved down. Surely he didn't mean that? Could he be swayed so easily? Would the act of Robert sucking his cock change his mind? It was an unpleasant thought. Robert kept up eye contact, purposely not looking down at where Trench's hand was fumbling for a trouser opening.

Of all the things he had done in his relatively short life, this would be one of the more unsavoury. The man in front of him had declared himself to be an enemy, and had stated his desire to crush Robert, publicly. But here he was, standing with his rapidly hardening cock in his hand, seemingly saying that a blow-job could alter his frame of mind. Should he do this? Could he do this? Robert's mind was split. Would it be that easy to change Trench's mind? Taking a deep breath, Robert knew that he had to take that risk, no matter how distasteful the experience would be.

He reached out a hand and curled it around Trench's penis. It felt cold and clammy, like a dead fish. A criss-cross pattern of knobbled veins stood out along its length. It had reached its maximum state of rigidity, and stood to attention, the foreskin just revealing a glimpse of the pinky-purple head beneath. It wasn't particularly large, but Trench seemed happy with it, gasping as Robert's hand made contact with the flesh.

Sinking to his knees, and edging forward slightly, Robert stared at this unsightly creation, held firmly in his fist. He closed his eyes and tried to imagine that it was Daniel's own beautiful prick that he was about to put in his mouth. Letting his lips move closer, Trench shivered as a waft of warm breath floated across the cock head. Steeling himself for this unsavoury action, Robert eased back the skin on the shaft, the mottled purple head emerging from the enveloping foreskin. Tiny lumps of creamy-white smegma were clumped about the lobes. Robert tried not to gag. This was the moment of truth. His mouth moved to within half an inch of this repellant apendage. His tongue flicked out and grazed the tip, making Trench's body judder with anticipation. Unable to wait any longer, the Governor grabbed the back of Robert's head and thrust himself deep in his mouth. Robert choked and resisted, pulling away, backing off from the offered cock. He couldn't bear it. It was a vile thing and he just couldn't go through with the oral attention that Trench desired.

'Well? I should get a move on, my friend. I haven't got all day. Or I may have to make my way to the Captain's cabin soon…' Trench was revelling in his superior position.

There was no way out. Robert had to do it. He closed his eyes again and opened his mouth.

Before his lips could make contact with the clammy flesh, a thunderous splintering crash sent him sprawling to the floor. A canon-ball had whizzed past Trench and imbedded itself in the wall by the door. A jagged, gaping hole lay in the outer wall. Suddenly all hell broke loose. A bell began ringing wildly, and cries and screams filled the air. Robert leapt to his feet, pushing past a stunned Trench, who fell to the floor, gibbering madly, acutely aware of how close the cannon ball had been to his head. Bounding out of the room, Robert ran up to the deck, surveying the pandemonium there. Less than a quarter of a mile away lay another ship, flying the Union Jack. As Robert watched, the flag was slowly lowered and another ensign was raised. He recognised it with a deadly certainty — a grinning skull, sitting above two crossed white bones, bearing testament to the intentions of its owners. Robert looked about him for the Captain, who was up on the deck, issuing orders to his men. Pulling himself up the ladder to the bridge, Robert gripped Cartwright by the arm. 'What is happening?'

The Captain seemed a little dazed, his coat unbuttoned and his hair unkempt. 'I thought it was another British ship, joining us for the last leg of the journey, but when it fired upon us... well, look at the flag they are flying now.' His voice trembled, and he started wringing his hands. 'Pirates! They tricked us... If they catch us, then we are all dead. We must try and outrun them.' He started shouting at his crew again, ordering more sail to be raised. Glancing about the deck, Robert knew their situation was grim. He saw men loading the heavy iron guns on either side of the ship, and could see a man standing guard at the long-gun canon at the bow, but they seemed incapable of any defence against the dozens of weapons that the other ship had trained on them.

Both ships exchanged fire. A canonade of shots ripping through the rigging of *The Merry Megan*, bringing it crashing to the deck. Thoughts of the terrified passengers filled Robert's mind. There had to be a way of getting them off the ship. If any of the women were unlucky enough to end up in the pirate's clutches, then who knew what awful fate might befall them. These lawless buccaneers were notoriously fierce, and no woman's virtue was safe in their company.

Dashing back down through the main hatchway, he began banging frantically on doors, calling out for people to come to the galley immediately. Daniel had obviously beeen thinking along similar lines. They bumped into each other at the corner of the first floor corridor. 'Are you alright?' Daniel's worried face lightened considerably as he spied Robert, who nodded and said, 'We have to get people off this ship.'

'I know.' Daniel took Robert's hand and squeezed. 'We have two small boats, which should be enough.'

Robert looked about him at the chaos, and gripped Daniel's shoulders firmly. 'That's good. We should put the ladies, and as many of the men as we can, in them and set them to rowing. We can't be far from land now. They might have a few uncomfortable days, but it will be better then being captured and violated by these pirates.'

'Agreed. You take this deck and I'll go down to the next. Tell them they cannot take anything large with them.'

The gathering didn't take long, once people knew the gravity of the situation, and as they huddled together on the main deck, they watched the pirate ship sail ever closer with undisguised fear. Many of the women were crying, holding on to small cases and boxes, carrying their jewels and other nicknacks. The men stood by, trying to appear brave in the face of the piratical barrage. At a signal, the boats were lowered with a splash, and the women began to climb hurriedly down. It was apparent that all the men would be unable to fit in the boats, and so lots were drawn. Mr Russell was able to join his weeping wife, as was Mr Tasker, who also gained a space in one of the small crafts.

As the filled rowing boats pulled away, to much wailing and anguished crying, Robert looked about the depleted deck. A bright flash from the pirate ship sent a shot plowing into the bridge. The wheel was smashed into fragments, splinters of wood and metal sent flying. Daniel suddenly re-appeared carrying a cloth bundle. Hastily unwrapping it, he revealed a haphazard collection of weapons; guns and pistols, swords and cutlasses, which he started to hand out to the remaining male passengers and crewmen.

'There is nothing else for it but to fight.' Daniel's voice had a harsh tone. 'I cannot find the Captain, and must assume he is dead. I have taken command in his absence. Their ship is faster and stronger than ours, so we have no choice. Take a weapon and do not be afraid to use it. God save the King.'

Another shot whistled overhead, causing everyone to duck. The sound of the pirates' victorious chanting floated closer, and the vessel seemed to be almost upon them. *The Merry Megan* was a wreck. Its masts hung dejectedly, ropes and rigging drooped about the battered deck. The bridge had taken a severe battering, the bridge cabin completely smashed in.

The remaining men lined the deck, staring out at the ever-closing pirate ship, guns, pistols and swords held in shaking hands. The attacking ship turned about in the wind and hove to, bringing itself about, alongside *The Merry Megan*.

With cries of delight, the pirates swarmed aboard, leaping athletically over the deck rails. A dark-skinned man leapt at Robert, hands outstretched, but Robert moved quickly, jumping to one side and giving a sharp thrust with his cutlass, driving it home between the pirate's ribs. He gave a terrible groan and fell to the deck, his eyes bulging from their sockets.

All about Robert was carnage. Guns were fired, swords clashed, men screamed in the agony, writhed in death throes. Sweat poured down his face as he dived into the fray, slashing madly with his cutlass, slicing and parrying, sparks from clashing steel flying in all directions. He ducked as a huge curved blade swung over his head. Spinning round he came face to face with a pirate, a scarf about his head, eyes gleaming, his smile of triumph revealing jagged, blackened teeth, the fearsome sword in his hand. He lunged at Robert who parried, meeting the stroke powerfully. They fought hard, and although Robert was the taller of the two, his opponent was wiry and well practised in the art of the fight. They careered about, knocking into the remains of the mast, and, as he fell back, Robert's sword became tangled in the rigging and he had to swerve his body to avoid the pirate's blade being thrust into his side. Pulling his sword free, he leapt forward, aware that his opponent was beginning to tire, his breath coming in short rasps. Standing back to regain his balance, Robert lowered his cutlass for a moment. The pirate took his chance and rushed at him, sword outstretched. Robert knelt and swiftly raised his cutlass with a mighty push, sending it upwards, feeling the contact with skin and bone as it found its target.

Glancing about him, Robert saw Daniel grappling with a viscious-looking man, a knife held securely between his teeth, trying to clamp his hands about Daniel's throat. Robert flew forward and slid his sword into the back of the pirate, who fell to the deck, clutching his stomach, a torrent of blood spewing from his mouth.

'Thank you, Robert! I thought I was done for.' Daniel smiled weakly.

'I think we will be done for. We cannot possibly win against these bastards. There are more of them than us and they seem inexhaustible.' As he spoke, the mass of pirates on board stopped fighting, sheathed their weapons and pulled back toward the deck rail. Members of the *Megan* looked on quizzically. Silence stole over the marauding pirates as a large man walked across from the other ship, striding confidently over a wooden plank, tied in place with rope from the rigging.

He stepped onto the deck and looked about him. The pirates gave a hearty cheer and raised their hats and weapons high. This was obviously their leader. He was tall and imposing, towering over every other man aboard. His hair was black, swept back from a high forehead, and tied in a ponytail with a silver ribbon. Beneath the swathe of hair was an impressive face, high cheekbones, and large, dark eyes which glittered with an air of suppressed danger, complemented by long, curling lashes. The mouth was firm, and had full, almost feminine lips. A very attractive man indeed, Robert thought to himself. The body was muscular and well-proportioned, wide shoulders tapering to a narrow waist. He was exquisitely dressed in a spotless white blouse with puffed sleeves, slashed open to the waist — the slash revealing the dark curls of hair that sprouted on his exquisitely formed chest, and his stomach, a ripple of muscles glistening with sweat. A golden heart-shaped medallion hung from a chain around his neck and nestled among the curls of hair. The multipatterned cotton breeches he wore were cut so that they emphasised his legs, the thick muscles of them, leading to a huge, almost indecent, bulge at his crotch. His voice when it came was surprisingly soft, but had a hard edge, with just a hint of a mediterranean accent. 'Where is the Captain?'

Daniel stepped forward, saluted, and answered. 'We are assuming that Captain Cartwright is dead. I have take command. First Officer Daniel Good. And may I ask who you are?'

The pirate chief took a deep breath, which emphasised his broad chest, before speaking to the assembled company, radiating an aura of charisma and power. His arms spread wide, he addressed the waiting people before him. 'As the divine genius Shakespeare once said... *"Ships are but boards, sailors but men: there be land-rats and water-rats, water thieves and land-thieves."* Allow me to introduce myself, I am the captain of this band of brigands and water-thieves that you see before you. My name is Jose Luis Felice Castillo de la Hoya.' Murmurs of disbelief came from the crew of the *Megan*. 'Some of you have no doubt heard of me.'

Daniel gulped. Jose de la Hoya was a name that filled all hearts with terror. He was the leader of the most feared band of pirates in the Caribbean, a band of marauders who had frequently escaped capture, who were rumoured to be almost mythical. They had terrorised this patch of sea for several years, stealing, looting and killing for their own murderous ends. De la Hoya surveyed the depleted crew and sniffed the air, like a wine connoiseur. 'You are a very small crew, Mr Good. And I see no female travellers on your ship.' He gestured to a gnarled, grizzled-hair pirate by his side. 'Check below, Medina. I want everyone brought up here. Phoenix, Moon-boy, you go with him. If anyone you find tries to resist, just rip their guts out.'

Medina and his two young-looking henchmen darted off to search the rest of the ship. De la Hoya turned back to Daniel. 'If some of my merry men find that your women have jumped ship they will be most displeased. Pray that they find some, or you will see what they are like when they get really angry.'

Daniel seemed lost for words. The power of this man had sapped his will. Girding his loins, and puffing himself up to his fullest, Robert stepped from behind two of the sailors and addressed the pirate leader. 'All our female passengers have gone. Your thugs will have no sport there. I am sorry they will not be able to indulge in any rape, but there it is. I don't know where you come from, but in my country we have morals and scruples... something you obviously know nothing about.'

De la Hoya's face creased with a wide smile. His bronzed features looked even more handsome. Robert watched as this astounding man moved closer to him. He moved stealthily, like a panther, and as he stepped closer, his cock could be seen swinging freely in the cotton breeches. That slumbering weapon seemed to possess monstrous dimensions. 'In your country? Do not try to tell me of your country. I was educated in your glorious England, at Eton to be exact, and so I know all about your precious social etiquette, and your manners, and your adoration of the female, placing them high upon a pedestal, not touching them until marriage. I know all about your stilted society, with its repressed minions. But look around you, my friend… we are in my kingdom now. Here I reign supreme. I am the law and I have your lives in my hand. Cross me at your peril.' He bent his head and let his mouth brush Robert's ear. 'But there are ways to keep me happy. Ways to fulfill me, and many of my crew. I am sure you understand. *"He that will enter Paradise must have a good key."*' His lips were inches from Robert's face. 'I hope that your key is of a sizeable proportion.' He moved around Robert as though sizing him up, the back of his hand grazing his buttocks, making him shiver. 'What is the matter, my young stud?' De la Hoya brought his face in closer again, Robert could smell sweet rum on his breath. 'Nothing, someone walked over my grave, that is all.'

The pirate laughed, a full, rounded guffaw, filling the air. 'Ha! *"The paths of glory lead but to the grave."* You must make sure those words are not a presentiment of what is to come.' With a sweeping wave of his arm, de la Hoya spoke to his crew of privateers. 'Bring them all aboard, and put them in irons. All except this one.' Nodding at Robert, he started to cross to the pirate ship. 'This one amuses me. Take him below.'

The next few hours passed in a blur of images. The remaining crew and passengers of *The Merry Megan*, including Daniel, Martenson and Fitch, Barnes and Tupton, and a limping Hamish Dee, were rounded up and herded aboard the pirates' ship. It was a sturdy vessel sporting the name *The War Queen*, with an ornate carved figure of a naked woman, topped with a jewelled crown, at its mighty prow. As the men were led aboard *The War Queen*, Robert noticed the absence of Trench, no doubt killed in the fracas. He was glad. That despicable beast deserved to die.

The captured men were taken below and placed in the hold, solid metal manacles clamped about their legs. The decimated hulk of *The Merry Megan* was roped off and towed along in the wake of the pirate's superior vessel.

Unable to protest, or to ease the plight of the others, Robert was lead by a rather fey Carib Indian pirate into the depths of the pirate ship. This strange individual wore a coloured scarf about his head, from which protruded ringlets of crimson hair, and a sarong about his waist, which swished as he walked. His hands were bedecked with rings, the fabulous jewels catching the light and shining beautifully. He wore feminine garments, and moved with a slight swing of his narrow hips. When he spoke, it was with a light, reedy voice. 'You should count yourself lucky, my dear... if Captain de la Hoya has taken a liking to you, it means your life will be saved. If you are wise you'll do what he asks, however strange.'

This was unnerving. Robert gulped. 'What do you mean by "however strange"?'

The pirate tweaked Robert's cheek with a bejewelled hand, the fingernails long and painted. 'Ooh, lady. You'll find out soon enough.' They had stopped by a door at the end of the passage. 'Now this is your cabin. He'll be with you shortly.' He looked at Robert with dark, doe-like eyes and pushed the door open, gesturing for the young man to enter.

Gingerly stepping into the room, Robert heard the door click shut behind him, and a bolt on the other side slide home. The interior was in semi-darkness, and was unlike any cabin Robert had seen before. It was certainly large, and was hung with drapes and silks in the manner of a harem. Dozens of candles glowed contentedly in various shaded nooks, and incense burned somewhere, giving a faint sickly smell of lavender and roses. There was a table with two chairs, an ornate writing desk against one wall, and at the far end lay the bed — surprisingly, a canopied four-poster with the same lush draperies at its sides. Around each of the four wooden posts were tied black silk scarves.

There was nothing for Robert to do but wait, so, pulling off his boots, he sank back on the bed, hands clasped behind his head and tried to visualise his current situation. He had to be a little grateful that at least he was still alive. Few travellers who find themselves attacked by pirates live to tell the tale. This strange but powerful captain had kept the crew and passengers of the *Megan* alive. But for what purpose, Robert was unsure. He tried to picture Daniel, below in the hold, no doubt in chains, and hoped that he was alright. It seemed that de la Hoya had chosen Robert for some reason, and if he did what this pirate wanted and gained his trust, then he might be able to keep the prisoners living. There appeared to be no choice.

As Robert's eyes began to close, and he felt himself drifting off into a light doze, the sound of voices came from outside the door. As it was unbolted and swung open, he heard de la Hoya speaking. '...Make sure that my orders are followed to the letter. And now... I do not wish to be disturbed.' Robert sat up and watched as de la Hoya closed the door and softly entered the room. 'There you are, my young friend. I hope you have made yourself at home.'

His tone of voice was soothing, his manner genial and kindly. 'Because this is where you now are... home.' He sat on the bed and ran a hand through Robert's hair. 'I do hope you realise why you are here?'

'I think so. You want me as a... companion, shall we say?'

De la Hoya chuckled, a soft murmuring laugh. 'You are a very perceptive young man. What is your name?'

'Robert Marchant. I already know yours.'

'Good, Robert. But I need to know if you are willing to become my *amour*, my love-slave. I have a prodigious appetite for sex, and need to indulge myself frequently. You seem to be an energetic and inventive young man, and I hope I have found someone who can accommodate my whim. What say you?'

There appeared to be little else to do but nod his head in acceptance. Robert enjoyed sex, and de la Hoya was a very attractive man. If all he had to do to keep his life was become the plaything of this man, then why not? Pleased with this reaction, de la Hoya stood and slowly began to pull off his black leather boots, before carefully placing them by the side of the bed. He then pulled his shirt over his head, revealing his broad chest, undoubtedly a magnificent specimen of manhood. The muscled shoulders and arms were smooth and brown, with curls of hair sprouting around the firm, manly breasts, which stood hard and proud, the nipples large and perfectly round, jutting out fiercely.

Without a word he slipped from his cotton trousers, his legs thick and hairy, the cock swinging free, perfect and pendulous. Robert gasped in admiration at this appendage, not yet hard, but still a frightening sight. Its chunky, mushroom-shaped head was circumcised, and it hung at the end of a thick shaft, something like the circumference of the arm of a baby. Robert knew that this was the biggest cock he had ever seen, but hanging as it did from the loins of this astonishing man it seemed totally right and in place.

De la Hoya stood with his hands on his hips, staring down intensely at Robert, as if waiting for him to make the first move. Swinging his legs round to sit on the side of the bed, Robert looked back at the pirate, not wanting to appear too eager to get to grips with that phenomenally singular column. The pirate sensed the unease in his new plaything, and extended a hand. 'Come.' Gently leading Robert across the room, he pulled back a velvet curtain which covered a large wing-chair, raised upon a dais, and fitted with stirrup-like supports for the feet and leather straps around the chair's arms. De La Hoya setled himself in the chair and looked down at Robert, raising one eyebrow. 'Let me see what I have here. Get out of those clothes, now.' That last word was said with a slight hardness in his voice, a dangerous edge quite obvious in him. Robert knew better than to annoy someone such as this, and so quickly began to unbutton his shirt.

'Slowly, Robert, slowly.' De la Hoya folded his arms, and sat back as if he were a wealthy patron selecting a fine work of art. 'A young man's body is a thing of joy. Do not rush the unwrapping of it. Take your time. Tantalise me. Show me your creative side.'

This was unexpected. Deciding to do whatever he had to, Robert's hand moved up to the remaining buttons and popped them undone, one after the other, turning his back on the pirate, as he slipped the shirt from his shoulders. He could hear a murmur of appreciation at the fine contours of his back. Flexing his arms, he showed the muscles and sinews in that back, letting de la Hoya admire it at its fullest extent. He hoped that the scarring from his beating on *The Valiant* was not too obvious. De la Hoya didn't seem to think so. 'That's very good. Just what I meant. Carry on.'

Robert pulled at his stockinged feet, sliding off the cotton sheaths, then unbuttoned his breeches and let them slide to the floor. Kicking them to the corner of the room, he stood in just his lower undergarments, which he gripped by their waistband and pulled down to the floor, bending forward, showing his firm buttocks off to his delighted captor. Using one hand to cover his rapidly growing genitals, he turned to face the pirate. A swathe of hair fell over one eye, giving him a boyish appearance which he knew to be irresistible. Lifting both hands, he spread his arms wide. 'Do you like what you see?'

Licking his full lips, de la Hoya leaned forward in his chair, his gaze unbending and direct. Saying nothing, he opened his arms, as if wanting to embrace Robert in them. Moving to him, Robert was caught up in a giant bear-hug, the warm, solid arms encircling him in a tight hold. He could feel the strength of the man all about him, and knew that if it ever came to a battle between them, there would be no contest – he could never beat him.

Robert could smell that sweet aroma of rum, mingling with the heavy pungent odour of tobacco. In this moment of embrace, Robert sensed that although de la Hoya was a dangerous man, a thief and a murderer, he also had a tender side, a breadth of passion and emotion that was a sigificant part of his character. It would be worth remembering this if he had to do any future bargaining with the pirate.

After a while, the pressure of the embrace eased, and Robert was released. Still silent, de la Hoya pushed him to his knees in front of the chair, then rested his feet upon the stirrups, his thighs held wide apart, his massive cock and balls hanging readily between them. This was a position of power and Robert knew it. The pirate seemed to want to appear superior to his prisoner. Glancing up, he saw an expression of disdain and desire on de la Hoya's face. 'I think you know what to do, don't you... boy?'

Without a moment's hesitation, Robert nestled between the thighs, inhaling deeply the musky odour from the pirate's groin, its evocative scent making his head spin. 'Yes, Captain.'

De la Hoya leaned forward and grabbed Robert roughly by the hair, his fingers intertwining painfully. 'You will call me master, is that clear, boy?'

'Yes, master. Whatever you wish.' The pirate's fingers eased their grip on his hair, and Robert knelt back between his captor's thighs.

He took a while to examine the monster cock that sat in front of his wide eyes. Its head was downy soft, and a gentle pinky-brown in hue. An opaque pearl of pre-come shone at the end, before gently sliding down the V-shaped valley and down the length of the shaft, disappearing into the mass of curled pubic hair. The shaft itself had a mighty circumference, even though still soft. The moment of truth had arrived. Robert wet his lips and kissed the tip, a gentle peck, making de la Hoya shudder. He opened his mouth wide and encircled the cock head, sucking it into his mouth. The pirate gasped, and gripped the arms of his chair. Robert heard the gentle clink of the buckles attached to the chair's restraining straps.

The cock was filling with blood, its size increasing swiftly. Unhesitating, Robert slid his mouth down the length of the cock's shaft, more easily than he had expected, because of its half-hardness. Memories of Third Officer Quilter and his gigantic organ flashed across his mind. Had it been bigger than de la

Hoya's? Robert guessed that the pirate's would be slightly larger, when erect and ready for action. It was now growing rapidly harder in his mouth. With a sigh of admiration, Robert began to work his lips along the solidifying shaft, pushing down with his mouth as he knelt further forward, inch after inch easing down into his throat. The skin was silky smooth, with no hint of veins or arteries, just soft flesh all the way down. The head of the cock touched the back of his throat, and relaxing his tongue helped it to slip past his tonsils. Robert flicked his tongue back and forth across the underside of the shaft, provoking a groan of utter satisfaction from de la Hoya. Filling his mouth with saliva aided the lubrication of the organ, and, surprised that he was able to engulf the whole thing without choking, Robert really set to. His hands gripped de la Hoya's immense thighs as he laved the now-hardened cock with his wet mouth, sometimes sucking it down to the bushy base, sometimes just pulling back and licking around the swollen head, each change of sensation provoking a groan of enjoyment from the pirate. As Robert downed the enormous piece of meat, his chin grazed the soft hairs at the base, brushing the heavy bollocks in their hairy sac. They hung low, cradled between his sweating thighs, occasionally tightening with the thrill of arousal.

De la Hoya reached forward and grabbed the back of Robert's head, holding him forcefully in place as he started to buck his hips, fucking the hot, wet mouth, using regular, pounding strokes, filling him up then sliding back until just the tip remained in place. This hammering became faster and more powerful. Robert forced himself not to choke on the hardened bulk. The pendulous balls tightened again, a sure sign that a climax was about to arrive.

Without a word, de la Hoya released Robert and pushed him back on his haunches. He looked up at the pirate with anxious eyes. 'Is something wrong?'

De la Hoya gave his comforting, warm laugh. 'No, boy. In fact everything to the contrary. That was delicious, but I haven't finished with you just yet. I have no wish to be brought off too soon.'

Taking his feet from the stirrups and standing up, de la Hoya knelt by a large chest by the side of the chair. He lifted the lid and pointed at its contents. Robert looked in, amazed at what he saw. A collection of silver manacles and chains, ropes and leather thongs, whips and paddles, as well as a number of simulated cocks of various sizes. Leaning over, Robert picked up one of the fake penises and examined it. It was about ten inches in length, obviously carved from some kind of bone. De la Hoya stroked Robert's back as he spoke. 'These are my constant companions on each voyage I undertake. If I cannot find some willing young stud to service me, then at least I have these for company. Are they not magificent? A souvenir from a trip to the Far East some years back. Those orientals are sublime in their devotion to sex, and all its intriguing options. They are carved ivory, and feel absolutely incredible, as I am sure you'll find out soon.'

Taking the ivory dildo from Robert's hand, he helped him to his feet and led him gently to the bed. 'Lay down.' De la Hoya's voice now had a threatening quality, a sharp edge that betrayed his dangerous side. Obeying, Robert lay back on the bed. Silently, the pirate grabbed a wrist and began expertly fastening it to one of the bed posts with the silk scarf that was tied about it. In a moment, Robert was held fast, unable to move, his hands and legs bound to the mahogany posts, his body spreadeagled and vulnerable.

De la Hoya stood at the foot of the bed and gazed down at his prisoner. His tone was creepy, a look of evil on his face. 'What a delicious sight. A young, virile man, powerless and in my grip. I can now do anything I like to you, love you or torture you, inflict ecstasy or agony… and there is nothing you can do to stop me.'

TEN

De la Hoya moved stealthily around the bed and knelt up on it. Straddling Robert's chest, he positioned his cock at Robert's mouth, and pushed, plunging it down the throat, at its fullest penetration, blocking his windpipe. Unable to breath properly, Robert eyes bulged, tears springing to them, as he choked and coughed, but the cock stayed firmly in place. The pirate laughed menacingly. 'You can take it, my fine young stud... as you've already shown me. Now suck me hard... do you hear me, boy?'

Concentrating, Robert tried to beat down the wave of panic that was rising within him, and took deep breaths through his nose. The collossal prick began to fuck his mouth again, harder and fiercer this time, as if he were being punished. Usually Robert loved the feel of another's cock in his mouth, but this was no pleasure at all. He closed his mind to the sensation and attempted to give what thrill he could to his dominator. The pummelling, forceful fucking was unending. His mouth was being stretched beyond endurance, but he did his best. Unable to provide any sensual variations, all Robert could do was let his mouth be penetrated and used in this most basic way. The saliva that filled Robert's throat mingled with the lubrication that the knob provided, making the face-fuck a little easier. De la Hoya's hands clamped themselves about Robert's neck, the grip gradually tightening round the muscles of the throat. He seemed to want to feel his cock plundering his boy from the outside.

Suddenly, the invasion stopped — as quickly as it had started. Withdrawing, de la Hoya stood up, his rigid cock dripping with Robert's saliva. From his position on the bed, Robert stared at the huge penis,standing stiffly upwards, curving up past the navel where it slapped against the hard stomach ridges.

De la Hoya went back to his chest of acoutrements, and pulled out what looked like a silver chain with some kind of clamp on each end. 'Now be a good boy for me. This may hurt, but be brave.' The pirate gave a sinister smile and clamped each end of the chain onto Robert's nipples. He yelped as the teeth fastened about the flesh. The biting pain shot through him, radiating out from his chest. It felt like his nipples were on fire. 'Please, master. It hurts...'

De la Hoya leaned over the bed, his hand gripping Robert's throat again, his face contorted with rage. 'Be silent. The more you complain, the longer they shall remain in place. Be strong now, take the pain, and I shall be very pleased with you, boy.'

Squeezing his lips together tightly, and gritting his teeth, Robert tried to imagine that the clamps had been taken off, tried to convince his mind that he was in no pain, that any sensation about his nipples was an enjoyable one. It took a gargantuan effort. De la Hoya wasted no more time. He squatted on the foot of the bed and immediately began sucking his prisoner's cock. Robert gave a gasp, the intense pressure from down below in stark contrast to the searing agony inflicted upon his chest. He tightly closed his eyes and concentrated his thoughts and feelings on his rock-hard prick, and was surprised to find that the pain he was experiencing in no way detracted from the blowing that de la Hoya was giving. If anything, it was more erotic, the squeezing and biting of the clamps seeming to emphasise the suction of the pirate's mouth. Robert squirmed about, unable to move too far, but able to push his cock further down into de la Hoya's throat. The pirate sensed he was totally in control now, and deigned to give his boy the best sensations he could.

He drove his mouth down over the cock, imprisoning it in his experienced mouth, listening with satisfaction to the moans issuing from Robert. His tongue slurped and licked at the shaft, working around the head, his hand squeezing the base, ensuring maximum solidity. His lips enclosed the balls, sucking and pulling on them, then his mouth moved back up to the cock, the vacuum of each suck evoking a cry of joy from his captive. As if having a sixth sense, de la Hoya stopped sucking, knowing that if he carried on, his young prisoner would all too soon come.

Fumbling around under the bed, de la Hoya pulled out a china bowl half-full of water, and a bar of soap. Dipping the soap in the water, he lathered up his hands and then began smoothing the creamy white froth all over Robert's cock and balls. His hands moved expertly, slipping and sliding all round the head and body of his still-hard prick. Then, again silently, with a look of fierce determination on his face, he climbed up on the bed and straddled Robert's midriff, facing him. Squatting, he positioned his arsehole above Robert's quivering cock, stretching his cheeks apart as wide as he could. He sat back slowly, letting the cock head push at his hole and found it tight, resisting the invader. He sat up and tried again. This time the soapy head was swiftly enclosed in the ring of muscle. De la Hoya moaned quietly, then gently eased himself down the length of cock, stopping every inch or so, feeling its hardness inside him.

Robert was awash with ecstatic sensations. Unable to move or do any of the usual thrusts of penetration, all he could do was lie back and let the pirate be in charge. His cock thrilled at the squeezing from de la Hoya's sphincter. It seemed to massage the stalk of his prick, wave after wave of pressure, then relief, until it was completely embedded inside him. De la Hoya looked down at Robert, his eyes full and intense, then reached for the chain hanging about Robert's chest, the clamps still biting on his nipples. He took hold of the chain and pulled it high over the young man's chest, stretching the nipples, yanking the skin around them into peaks.

Yelling, Robert's head thrashed about on the pillow. The twin sensations, of his cock held in a vice-like grip, and his nipples tortured to the limit of his pain tolerance, were excruciating, and more intense than before. He wanted it both to stop and to carry on, loving and hating every second that passed. This charismatic pirate certainly knew how to inflict the ultimate in pleasure and pain upon his captives, and revelled in the practise. He was holding Robert on the very edge of a precipice, not letting him fall, keeping him on the edge of climax.

Keeping tight hold of the chain, de la Hoya started to haul himself up and down Robert's cock, his experienced muscle-ring gripping the shaft, letting it ram into him harder and faster, relaxing and squeezing alternately. Robert lifted his head and looked down at his dick pumping de la Hoya's arse, watching it slide back and forth, gritting his teeth at the pain emanating from his chest. The pirate was getting urgent now, his rising and falling swifter, his arse cheeks slapping against Robert's thighs, his own cock rock-solid and smacking against his stomach with each cock thrust, the bollocks jumping in their swinging sac.

Robert had to speak. His voice came in a shuddering, weak tone. 'I cannot take it any more! I am going to come!' De la Hoya grunted and pulled himself off the cock, letting it slide from his hole, slowly squeezing each inch as it popped out.

'Not yet, boy. You will come when I say you are ready, and not before.'

Standing, he moved round to the side of the bed and released the clamps. Sighing with relief, Robert watched the pirate rummage around in the chest and, with a crow of delight, pull out a long strip of leather. Attached to the middle of the strip was what looked like a small golf ball. He then produced one of the ivory phalluses, its thick, foot-long body gnarled and extremely fearsome. These were tossed onto the bed, as de la Hoya began to unfasten the silken scarves, holding Robert in place. He had hardly a moment to stretch his aching limbs before the pirate shouted at him, 'Turn over.' The dangerous edge was back in his voice again, so Robert swiftly obeyed, throwing himself face down upon the mattress. He felt hands grasping his legs, and re-tying the scarves about them, then his wrists.

All of a sudden, Robert realised that he was in a dangerous situation. This pirate seemed to have two distinct personalities. At present he was in the thrall of the less pleasant one. He was powerless, spreadeagled on the bed, unable to move an inch, his arse wide open for his desires. 'What are you going to do?' Robert's voice trembled slightly, wondering if he dare speak to the man dominating him. The answer, when it came, surprised him. De la Hoya seemed calm again, in control, but no longer filled with anger. 'You have been very good so far, boy, and so it is time for your reward. You'll enjoy this, I promise.'

Kneeling at Robert's side, he picked up the leather strap and tied it around Robert's mouth, the small ball filling his mouth, forcing it open. Robert's head fell back on the pillow. He was unable to comprehend the total subjugation that he was being forced to endure. Never had he experienced such things. In his life so far, sex had been a joyous thing between men, to be delighted in by each participant. Now he saw that there were endless variations, some having more sinister connotations, some involving pain and humiliation. He wasn't sure if he liked it, but it was certainly an education.

He could hear de la Hoya swishing the water in the china bowl again, and in a moment he felt him kneeling between his legs, spread wide and at the pirate's mercy. A muffled gasp was expelled from Robert's shaking body as the first few inches of the cold ivory dildo was driven into him. De la Hoya paused, letting him get used to the feel, allowing his shaken ring-piece to relax. When he was sure that Robert was ready, he slid it deeper inside. Robert wanted to scream, but the gag in his mouth made it impossible. Even if he could, he knew that it would be a hopeless action. No-one would come to his aid, and it might make his captor more determined to take his time.

Biting back his pain, he raised his head, and through his nose, breathed in great lungfuls of air. With a huge effort, he tried to concentrate all his efforts on relaxing his arse hole, knowing that it would be considerably less uncomfortable if he did.

Unexpectedly, the dildo was tenderly withdrawn from his body, Robert sighing with relief. It seemed like this particular tortuous session was over. His head fell forward into the soft plump pillow.

With a frightful laugh, de la Hoya jammed the phallus back inside in one swift shove. Robert pushed his head into the pillow, to deaden the sound of his muffled groans, as the fake dick was thrust inside him, rammed between the spread buttocks again and again, to the accompaniment of low, sinister chuckles from his master. Gradually, as Robert became accustomed to the piercing onslaught, his mind no longer in a state of utter turmoil, he realised that the furious attack on his arse wasn't too painful. It felt good, and with a moan, he tried to squirm his arse about, wanting to now enjoy the dildo's plundering. He shocked himself with his reaction, it was a form of rape, but it actually felt wonderful. His cock, pressed between his crotch and the mattress, was fully aroused, and seeping juice, a sign of extreme enjoyment. He felt full, the dildo reaching up inside him, pushing and probing, while his arse ached and squeezed with pleasure, the hard, even strokes coming in increasingly rapid succession.

There was now no other feeling but the fucking of his arse. No other sensation, and no other time and place but here and now. Robert had melted away and become one with the fiery passion provided by his new master. He wanted to cry out, gasping, praying for release, his arse raised high, hoping for that final euphoric explosion of climax. De la Hoya sensed this and fucked him harder still, the dildo working frenetically, deeper and deeper, his other hand moving round under Robert's stomach to grasp his throbbing cock. It took but a few swift strokes to bring him off, his whole being suffused with burning lust. The pirate felt the cock grow in his hand as it exploded, blasting forth a cascade of its juice. It pumped out an incredible stream, splashing across the bed. A rainbow of colours danced before Robert's eyes and a spasm of physical exhilaration coursed through his body, shuddering and shaking him to his very foundation. Each bolt of semen sent another wave of energy through him, but they gradually subsided, and he collapsed on the bed amid the sticky mass of his come, his breath growing slower and more regular. Robert desperately wanted to relax and curl up into a foetal ball and sleep, but he was still held fast by the scarves at each bedpost, the solid ivory phallus still deep inside his rectum.

De la Hoya sat back, leaving the dildo embedded in Robert's arsehole. 'Now I told you that you'd enjoy yourself, did I not?' His voice was low and tender. The strained anger had vanished and his nicer self was much in evidence. Robert tried to push the ball from his mouth but it was firmly strapped around his head. He started to feel slightly panicked, even claustrophobic. The walls of the cabin seemed a little closer than they should be.

The pirate stood and came round to the side of the bed. He gripped Robert by the hair and pulled his head sharply up. 'Do you really want to be released boy, hmmm?' His fingers twisted in the hair, causing Robert to wince. 'I think you have been a very bad boy and should be left here, don't you?' All he could do was shake his head. The gag in his mouth was really uncomfortable. Not a spark of energy was left in him. He tried to squeeze the carved prick from his anus, but it refused to budge. Tears sprang to his eyes, and he looked up pleadingly at his captor, who stood by his side, cock in hand, slowly stroking himself to a state of erection. 'Let me look at you, my wonderful boy.' His face had assumed a look of intensity, his eyes scanning the bound and gagged slave before him. The sight of Robert's body, trussed and unable to move, was a turn-on for him. His cock grew rapidly, and with a few sharp jerks, he was coming, shooting across Robert's back and buttocks. His balls emptied themselves, erupting a volcanic flow of milky-white spunk. His breath grew shallow, his body tensed.

After a short while, he stood and began putting his clothes back on. Ignoring Robert, he pulled on his boots and took a final satisfied glance at himself in the looking-glass by the bed. He puffed his chest out with pride and, running a hand across his smoothed-back hair, strode to the door. As if Robert didn't even exist, he unbolted it and stepped out, banging it shut behind him.

Robert stared after him in disbelief. He couldn't believe that de la Hoya had abandoned him like this, still tied to the bedpost, his legs spread, covered in spunk and with a dildo still deep within him. Try as he might, his bonds held him firm and, push as he might, the dildo was held fast inside. The light in the cabin had faded, the candles having all fizzled out, and so he assumed it was night-time. Darkened shapes loomed at him out of the gloom, and he closed his eyes. However hard he tried to doze, he found it impossible. His tied limbs were aching, his arsehole was stretched beyond endurance, and a dull throbbing continued in his arse muscles. There were moments when he wanted to die. He found it difficult to breath, and his arms and legs screamed for release. If this was what being de la Hoya's slave meant, then perhaps death was preferable. His mind wandered. Images of Daniel and William floated about his brain, interspersed with pictures of Joseph Crook, Jack the potman and Fergus Trench. In his mind, Trench was a giant, with rolling eyes and an elephantine cock hanging snake-like between his legs, the skin pitted and rotting. The head of the snake was coming towards him, rearing up and trying to force its way between his lips. Robert wanted to cry out, to make it go away, but with a start he was brought back to the reality of his current situation. The gag he was wearing was beginning to cut the corners of his mouth. How long he could stay like this without going mad, he didn't know.

He must have slipped into a light doze, because he was woken by a cold hand touching his back. Quick fingers unfastened the strap around his mouth, letting the ball slip out. His jaw had been held open for so long that it ached badly, even closing it made him whimper with discomfort. 'Sssh, there now.' He didn't instantly recognise the voice, but turning his head slightly could see the face of the feminine pirate who had shown him to the cabin earlier that evening. He had lit a candle and had placed it in an ornate holder by the bed. Speaking softly he said, 'The Captain has given orders that you are to be released.' He started to untie the knotted scarves, one by one, allowing Robert's limbs to fall free. He hesitated as he moved down to the young man's bottom, enviously staring at the embedded phallus. Slowly wrapping a hand around the end, he slid it from the extremely tender hole. Robert gave a cry as the bulbous end slipped out. 'I tried to take this one once, but I just couldn't do it,' the pirate said, in a sing-song voice. 'Anyone who can is held in high regard by the Captain. You are a real find. Mind you don't go upsetting him now. Your life could be quite comfortable if you remain his favourite boy… just think of that. Food, clothes, riches, and a powerful lover.' He sighed. 'Sounds wonderful.'

The blood had begun to come back to Robert's limbs, and he gingerly sat up, pins and needles attacking his numbed legs. 'Thank you,' he murmured, rubbing his hands about his tingling thighs. 'Who are you, though?'

'The Captain calls me Mother. I suppose it's because I look after him, like an actual mother, really. I think he realises that I am the only one on this ship who truly loves him, so he keeps me here, tending his daily needs, washing and cleaning after him, making sure his boys are looked after. Turn around.' Mother reached down and pulled a cloth from the china wash bowl, and tenderly began to wipe the congealed semen from Robert's back, pausing slightly over the faint scars left by the whipping he'd been given on *The Valiant*. Saying nothing about them, he pushed Robert back onto the bed, dampened the cloth and cleansed about his stomach, then around his cock and balls. The extreme attention they had been put to earlier meant that they lay lifeless, but Mother still seemed impressed by their size. 'Very nice. Another reason why the Captain chose you.'

Having finished his cleaning, Mother dropped the cloth back into the bowl, pushed it under the bed and pulled a blanket over Robert's naked body. 'I should try to sleep now. You'll learn to get as much sleep as you can, because Captain de la Hoya has a strange habit of wanting his fill of sex at any time, day or night. Although I think you'll be undisturbed tonight. This is where you'll stay. He has a bedroom next to this cabin. Can you see over there?' He pointed at what looked like a connecting door. 'That leads to his cabin, so he can have easy access to you whenever he wants. But I think he'll sleep deeply tonight, so just relax. I have left some food and wine on the table for when you feel hungry. Sleep well, and I'll see you in the morning.' Patting Robert gently on his slumbering cock, he slipped out. Shucking the blanket, Robert padded to the door, his legs aching with every step. It was locked. Of course. If he was such a valuable asset to the Captain's love life, then he'd hardly let him escape, would he?

Sitting back upon the bed, he glanced about the room. His clothes had been taken. No surprise there. Presumably he was expected to stay here naked, ready for his master's rampant libido to pay a call. He lay back and listened to the creaking of the ship's timbers, watching the shadows dance upon the fabric-hung walls, eerie shapes moving and swaying in the candlelight. Reflecting, Robert knew that there were worse ways to be in the clutches of pirates. Being the sex-toy of an over-amorous Captain was infinitely better than being chained up in some rotting hold. Thoughts of Daniel sprang forth. There had to be some way of getting him freed from the hell-hole he was probably locked in. It would mean gaining de la Hoya's trust, and that could take some time. The main problem was that Robert had no notion of the whereabouts of *The War Queen*, or where the ship was heading. Though it would be tough for Daniel, he would have to bide his timeuntil the circumstances were right. 'I will do everything in my power to free you,' he said aloud, his words ringing powerfully around the room.

Shifting to one side, trying to block out the dull ache from his anus, Robert saw the tray of food and drink on the table. A well-timed rumble came from his stomach, and he sat up and padded across to it. A platter of cold chicken, some cooked vegetables, a chunk of bread and a carafe of wine provided him with a hearty meal. After taking his fill, Robert crossed to the small porthole by the bed and looked out. The moon hung high in the cloudless sky, throwing brilliant streams of light upon the luminous sea. It was a magical sight. He leant on the window rim and gazed at the sea, watching it rise and fall rhythmically, as it had done since the beginning of time. How long he stood there he knew not, but as a yawn escaped him he realised that the happenings of the day had left him exhausted. Slipping onto the bed and pulling the blanket about him, he fell into a deep slumber immediately.

Robert awoke with a start. He sat up rubbing his eyes, not knowing where he was. As the realisation of his situation came upon him, he sank back against the bedhead, and focused on the figure that sat across the room. 'Good morning, Robert. You slept well, I trust?' De la Hoya was at the table, gnawing rampantly on a chicken leg, a spotless white knapkin tucked in his collar. 'Would you like some breakfast?'

Kicking back the blanket, Robert eased himself up, his body awash with aches. His arms felt like they had been subjected to a thousand press-ups, and his arse still throbbed dully. 'Thank you. I am quite hungry now.' He sat across the table from his captor, who gestured at the laden table. All kinds of exotic fruits and meats jostled with bread rolls and sides of steamed fish. He dove in, ripping apart a roll and dunking it in the bowl of hot, sweet coffee that de la Hoya had poured for him.

'I like to breakfast with my boy, it gets the day off to a delightful start. Did you sleep well?' He asked again, his voice a rich velvety texture. Swallowing the steaming nectar, Robert cleared his throat before speaking. 'Yes, thank you, especially after…' He paused for a moment, unsure as to how much he could say, whether he could be honest and frank and not make de la Hoya angry. Deciding to chance it, he spoke clearly. 'I did get to sleep, after you had me released.' He looked his master in the eye. 'Why did you leave me trussed up like a goose at Christmas? I thought I had done everything you wanted last night, and yet you deserted me, tied to the bed, completely humiliated and in great discomfort.'

The pirate leant his elbows on the table and gave a charming smile, flashing his perfect white teeth. 'You needed to know that I am in control. You do not exist but to serve me. If you understand that, then there will be no need for a repetition of that situation. Do you understand?'

'I do. I will make the best I can of my being here. I see no reason to live in misery and squalor… luxury and comfort is what I am used to, and therefore if doing what you desire will bring me that, then so be it.'

Picking up a large, colourful fruit, de la Hoya spoke gently as he peeled it with his knife. 'Good. That is what I wanted to know.' Popping a slice of fruit in his mouth, he continued, the juice dribbling down his close-shaven chin. 'You say you came from a background of luxury. Tell me your story.'

Happily obliging, Robert told de la Hoya the tale of his recent adventures, leaving out the details of his various sexual escapades. The pirate listened enthralled, asking the occasional probing question. 'And so you are the heir to an English fortune, eh?' He scratched his chin with the tip of his knife. 'I can see why you would appreciate the better things.'

'But what of you?' Robert asked. 'I believe you said that you had been educated at Eton. How did that happen?'

Settling back in his chair, de la Hoya grinned ruefully. 'It is a very long story. I am the eldest son of a Portugese diplomat. The de la Hoyas are very well respected in my native country. My father was granted the honorable post of Ambassador to the King of England's court. Naturally my mother, my four younger brothers and I went with him. I was nine at the time, and was thrilled at the difference in our two countries. My father decided that I should have the best education that England could provide, and as money was no object he enrolled me at Eton. I adored the process of learning. Books became my dearest companions, and soon I fitted in amongst the other sons of noblemen and royalty like one of their own. I revelled in the joy of the language, avidly devouring any book I found, especially poetry, taking refuge in the beauty of the word. There is really nothing as beautiful as a well-written poem. The joy of words is for me unequalled, except perhaps in the beauty of an exquisite male.

'At Eton I learned to act like an English gentleman, even though I was not one by birth. I attained success in my academic career, gaining a degree in mediaeval literature studies, and decided to see more of the country that I now loved and thought of as home. I travelled around, visiting towns and cities, seeing castles and ruins, and enjoying myself immensely. I was a handsome young man, fit and wealthy, but with no apparent interest in marriage. My father had pleaded with me to find a fiance before I set off on my journeying, but I stalled him. I was driven by a desire to explore, not to settle down.

'It was on the south coast that my fortunes changed. I found myself in a charming port. I cannot remember its name, but I recall a gang of friendly men who bought me drinks and passed a pleasant evening at cards... but then all is blackness. I recall waking up on a ship, forced to become a sailor, and spent two miserable years at sea. I tried to convince the Captain that it was not right that I was there, that I was the son of an Ambassador, but every time I tried to make my case I would be punished — either by being made to scrub the deck, or by being given any number of lashes with a cane. From that moment, I hardened myself. I exercised, I trained, and built up my body. I became strong, wanting others to be jealous of my prowess, not wanting to be the inferior dogsbody that everyone would pick on.

'It was on a naval reconnaisance mission in the West Indies that our ship was attacked by a band of pirates. I was taken aboard, and watched gleefully as many of my former brutish crewmates were put to death. I begged their leader to let me join them. He agreed and so I began my new career in piracy and plunder. I learned from various old hands the way of the pirate. I discovered the joy of handling a cutlass, and the ecstasy of pillaging a harmless vessel, to steal and loot their precious cargoes. I had power. It took me many years, but I rose. Then came the marvellous day when the previous captain of this ship made me his successor. I became the pirate king. I developed a cut-throat crew who obey my every command. They know that they are with the most fearless brigand in these waters. They ignore my sexual whims — anyone who passes comment or judgement is killed. I have worked my way to the top, and will do as I desire.

'I was indoctrinated into the mystic art of homosexuality by a young Hungarian pirate on that first ship. He showed me ways of physical and emotional release that astounded and delighted me. He practised on my young body, discovering new and exciting means of achieving sexual ecstasy. I was a willing student. As before, I loved the process of learning. Every day we would find some time to secretly experiment on each other, driving one another to previously unfullfilled heights of pleasure. It was on a voyage to the East that I discovered manuscripts detailing Chinese and Asian sexual secrets, and purchased some of the toys that you saw last night. Those times spent with Tomas, for that was the pirate's name, were some of the happiest times of my life. And now that I command my own ship, I have the opportunity to indulge myself in those wonderful times again, with any like-minded crew member – and there are many aboard – and with any willing stud that wanders into my web.'

He took a swig of coffee, swilling it around his mouth, letting his tastebuds savour each atom of its rich aromatic texture. Robert sat, amazed, staring at this powerful man who had risen from wealthy beginnings to be the charismatic leader sat before him. 'I can hardly believe what you have told me,' he said after a few moments silence. 'The similarities in our lives are remarkable. To think that you, too, fell foul of a press gang, entered the clutches of a group of pirates, and that by various routes we ended up on the same ship, both uninterested in women, both willing to take chances. I am glad you told me what you did… it has made me understand you a little more, and if I am to stay with you…well, I would need to understand what makes you work, and what drives you. I think I am a touch nearer to knowing that.' He reached a hand across the table and stroked de la Hoya's cheek. The pirate ttook his hand and kissed the palm softly, then lowered his gaze and spoke quietly. 'I am a complex man, Robert, but not a bad one. I have made the most of what that fickle bitch "Life" threw at me. You must too. Be my friend and my lover, make your home here with me and we could be happy. Please forgive me if I show you my temper. I have a cruel streak which I usually keep hidden, and sometimes it rears its head... mostly during sex. You must do as I wish then, and all will be well. Do not take it personally, it is as if I have two personalities, and they jostle for position.'

Robert listened with a supressed intensity. The picture that was unfolding before him was astonishing. Certainly he knew no reason why he shouldn't make the most of his current situation. To be pampered by a man such as de la Hoya, who could make sex exciting and different would be a wonderful experience. He would go with whatever happened and wait. Wait for the moment when he may be able to release the other prisoners and make good their escape. It would not be easy, but something was bound to present itself.

'You seem to engender real loyalty in your crew.' Robert's voice cut through the enveloping silence, jolting de la Hoya's thoughts back to the present moment.

'I do indeed. Men like that appreciate a powerful leader. Any sign of weakness is pounced upon. They know me well, and work well under my guidance.'

'Do they not miss having a home, somewhere to call their own?'

'But they do. We have settled on a small island, some distance up the coast, inhabited, I believe, by a few native tribesmen. It was once the hideaway of a French merchant and missionary. The story goes that he was more interested in the bodies of young children than the good book. The natives rose up and killed him and his household. His mansion sat empty for many years until I discovered it, and we have made the south part of the island our base of operations. Every now and then, the tribesmen rattle their spears to show their displeasure, but I string one of them up, flay him alive and they go back to their mud huts, leaving us in peace. That is where we are headed now.'

Robert's mind whirred with this new and fascinating piece of information. If the ship was to dock at some island base, then it increased the chances of escaping. There was little chance of getting off a ship in the middle of the ocean, but if they were soon to be on dry land... He kept his face a blank, not wanting de la Hoya to notice any changes caused by this intriguing news.

'How soon will we be there? I long to be on land again. Life aboard a ship can be tiring. I want to smell the air, and walk barefoot on the beach. Perhaps we can?' He looked up through his fringe of hair, pouted his mouth boyishly and waited for an answer. It was a long time coming. 'Perhaps. We shall be there sometime tomorrow, and then we shall see.'

'And can I have some clothes? I feel rather uneasy being naked.'

De la Hoya licked his lips and stood, pushing back his chair with a shrill scrape. 'Not for the moment. I like to see my boys unclothed. The nude form of a young man is one of nature's greatest creations. I like to see it as nature intended, besides...' he stopped and moved round behind Robert's chair, draping his arms around his neck, his hand tweaking the still-sensitive nipples. '...Besides, if they are nude then they are less likely to conceal any hidden weapons, and less likely to want to escape.' Roughly grabbing Robert by the hair, he yanked his head back and planted a kiss on his lips. The taste of coffee and mango mingled in his mouth. Robert opened his lips wide and let his tongue respond. They kissed passionately for a moment, then suddenly de la Hoya pulled away. 'I have things to do. Amuse yourself, Robert. There are some interesting items in my trunk... feel free to experiment. Alternatively, there are a number of books in the desk drawer. Goodbye for the present.' And with a toss of his luxuriant hair, he was gone, the door locked behind him.

The rest of that day passed slowly. Robert had little to do but lay back on the bed and read. At one point his inquisitiveness gor the better of him and he knelt by the wooden chest, heaving back the lid and sorted through de la Hoya's collection of toys. The memory of his rough handling with the large ivory dildo weighed heavy on his mind as he rummaged through the strange items. He examined every piece with a sense of intrigue, wondering what each item was for, what each strap or tube did. Perhaps he would soon find out.

The only disturbances that day were the frequent entries of Mother, who came to clear away the breakfast mess and later brought lunch and dinner. When he first appeared, Robert nervously pulled the blanket over his lower half, suddenly feeling a little shy, and annoyed at being forced to stay naked. Mother just clucked and spoke in his wheedling voice, as he cleared the table, 'Ooh, what is she like? There's no need to go all coy, young lady. I have seen it all before... admittedly, though, yours is one of the nicer ones.' He put the tray back on the table and,whipping the blanket back, gazed lovingly at Robert's cock and balls. 'Very nice. You don't mind, do you?' His gem-encrusted fingers wrapped themselves about the cock, and squeezed tightly. 'Mother's perks!' he said cheerily, as he massaged and coaxed the dick into life.

Robert was stunned. This strange pirate had some very odd ways, but, under the make-up and silk clothes, was actually quite attractive. His black skin was smooth, his features slightly negroid, his hair dyed vivid crimson, and his lips painted with a faint scarlet tint. He'd never met anyone so flamboyant before. He had heard of men that dressed as women... *en travesti*, he had heard it called. But had never seen such a creation with his own eyes.

He watched as Mother began to wank his hand up and down his cock. The silver bangles about his wrist jangled with each stroke. Even if Robert had wanted this to stop, his prick gave a different impresssion, growing harder and longer with the Carib's fondling. The slim, nimble fingers started working at the head. A bubble of lubricant emerged and was rubbed into the velveteen knob, moistening it, evincing a sharp intake of breath from its owner. With his other hand, he reached down and wrapped his fingers around the balls, hanging heavy, weighing them and rolling them around like marbles, then pulling the sac, emphasizing the full erection of the cock.

Mother leant forward and, letting his lips part, flicked his tongue around the chest, leaving a wet trail of saliva about the puckered skin of his nipples. The trail led down to the stomach, where he began licking and sucking about the navel. Robert ached for this man to swallow his cock, thrusting his hips up and pushing his firmness out for attention, whilst leaning back on his elbows. With a clatter of jewellery, Mother quickly parted Robert's thighs and settled between them, his face now only an inch from his sweating glans. Robert closed his eyes and urged every muscle in his body to stiffen as, without a pause, Mother began to lick along the underside of his shaft, slathering it with saliva, slurping merrily, sucking the balls into his mouth and swinging on them, a delighted hum emanating from his throat.

Then, mercilessly, Mother pushed his mouth down, swallowing the whole stiffened length, Robert writhed on the bed, shoving his groin up, forcing the cock into the wet maw of the Carib's throat. His hands held the back of Mother's head as he pushed his mouth over the swollen cockhead and down the shaft. Mother's tongue could feel the blood pumping through every inch of the phallus and he licked at the engorged plum, his large lips working furiously as they stretched about the fat dick.

Robert looked down with wonderment at the sight of his manhood being swallowed by a black face, the contrast between his pale white skin and the dark, slavering hole was immense. He sighed with pleasure at the blowing that this strange man was giving him. He was certainly no novice when it came to servicing a cock, and he was definitely enjoying doing it. Stifled groans of enjoyment came from Mother, who was now sucking frantically, his head bobbing, his hand grasping the base of the dick, squeezing every iota of stiffness into it. He relaxed and contracted his throat muscles, as the cock plowed in and out, pushing down past the base of the tongue, and back again. The thick root of his cock was held in the tightest grip Robert had ever experienced. The continuous sucking was creating thrilling surges of lust through his entire body as he fucked the mouth with a hot, regular pounding, seeing the black lips contort and move about his massive cock.

Momentarily, Robert could feel the rolling tide of come building up in his balls. He held on tight to the Carib's head, grunted and began coming. The first shot splashed against the back of Mother's throat, and was swallowed eagerly, the salty-sweetness flooding his tongue. Holding back a choking cough, he drank lustily, savouring each drop, sucking and tonguing until Robert's shuddering body fell back upon the bed, exhausted.

Wiping the spunk from around his mouth and licking his lips, Mother sat up between Robert's legs and gave his cock a final friendly squeeze. 'That was very nice!'

Robert grinned uneasily, and sat forward, crossing his legs. 'But should you have done that? What if de la Hoya finds out?'

Throwing back his ringlet-covered head, Mother emitted a short, reedy laugh. 'You need not worry about him. He knows. He is a very generous man. He will let me have some sport with his boys, because he knows there is nothing serious between me and them. Besides, it is a sort of thank you for looking after him. I must say he has found a marvellous specimen in you, my dear.' He stood, straightening his sarong and patting his crimson hair. 'But be warned.. I am not the only favoured member of his crew that might visit you. There a number of pirates who are the "homo" way, and so they'll be allowed to pay a call. Of course, is up to you if you want to entertain them, but you will only make the Captain angry if you refuse.'

Robert frowned, deep lines creasing his forehead. 'It very much looks like I have become some kind of prostitute, doesn't it?'

Taking up the breakfast tray, and slipping through the door, Mother giggled. 'Well done! Now perhaps you'll relax and make the most of your new profession.'

Surprsingly, after Mother's revelation about other possible visitors, Robert was left alone for the rest of the day. Apart from the cheery Carib with his trays of food and drink, he saw and spoke to no-one. De la Hoya didn't even put in an appearance. Possibly he had spent himself the previous evening and had no desire for more of Robert's body.

Immersing himself in several beautifully bound books, Robert passed the time by delving into the legends of King Arthur and the tales of his knight's adventures. Occasionally glancing out of the porthole for any sign of land, Robert found the time actually rolled by quite quickly.

As he was finishing his supper tray, the door swung open and de la Hoya stood framed in the doorway, its small dimensions emphasising the enormity of his stature. Robert stood and faced him, hands on hips, waiting for him to enter.

'I shall not be disturbing you this night,' the pirate said in a tired voice. 'I have much on my mind and would make poor company. But I have here several of my crew, who have expressed an interest in getting to know you better. I know you'll agree.' He stood back and let two young men enter the room, both looking sheepishly at Robert's unclothed frame. 'Meet Phoenix and Moon Boy. Even though they don't appear so at present, they are insatiable lovers. I think you'll enjoy yourself.' Withdrawing, he pulled the door and left the three young men alone.

'Well, my name is Robert. How do you do?' Formality seemed a strange convention in these circumstances, but Robert didn't know how else to proceed. He took the chance to examine the two young men, the one called Phoenix slightly taller and chunkier than his compatriot. He was about twenty-five or so, and long, black hair fell about his face, which was still boyish, but marred by a vivid red scar which ran from below his left eye to his chin. His eyes were dark and watery, with short lashes and thick bushy brows which crossed his forehead, meeting in the middle. His chin was encased in a short, neat, goatee beard, which lengthened his face, giving him a stronger appearance. Moon Boy seemed much younger, eighteen or nineteen possibly, slim, with brown, tightly curled hair which exaggerated the shape of his rounded head. He had an angelic sadness about his countenance, with deep, dreamy brown eyes, flecked with specks of white, resembling the surface of the moon, no doubt leading to his nick-name.

Both the men were wearing similar clothes — plain blouses with ruffled cuffs, dark breeches and some kind of sandals with leather thonging about their ankles. Robert waited, arms folded, wondering what to do next. Phoenix and Moon Boy turned to each other and made that decision for him. Moon Boy dropped to his knees and began to unfasten the buttons on Phoenix's breeches. Then, reaching in a trembling hand, he unfurled the semi-rigid penis. It was of an average length, but was exceedingly thick, ending with a huge circumcised head, which narrowed to a sharp tip. He nuzzled his face into the groin, avoiding contact with the dick, inhaling the odour of his comrade, before slipping the head of it into his mouth, licking it energetically. The boy settled back on his haunches, as if ready to indulge in some good sucking.

The pirate Phoenix gasped as Moon Boy slid the entire pole down his throat, slapping his tongue against the ridges on the shaft. He seemed to become manic, sucking and tonguing, eager with desire for this meaty stalk. His head was a blur, falling and rising with flashing rapidity, taking the cock down, ignoring the gasps of surprise from above.

Phoenix's cock had fully hardened now and was standing to attention, curving perfectly up, the head purple and pulsing, the entirety covered in saliva. His legs began to judder, and he grasped the back of Moon Boy's head for support. Both the pirates had seemingly ignored Robert, carrying on with this astonishing floor show for their own benefit. Robert's own limp cock had started to fill, and was jerking up, getting harder as he watched the young, attractive Moon Boy devouring Phoenix's stiffness. The older one was now breathing heavily in short, rasping grunts, then without warning, he pulled out of Moon Boy's mouth and let fly with a stream of silvery come. It streaked upwards, in a great arc, followed by another and another as his cock pumped out, leaving a creamy trail across Moon Boy's face.

By now Robert was completely enthralled. His mouth was dry as he took the scene in, his hand wrapped about his own cock, jerking roughly, just holding himself back from the edge of coming. This was definitely erotic. He had never watched anyone else getting amorous before. Moon Boy looked up at Robert, sperm dripping from his unlined face onto his shirt, leaving darkened, damp patches, and he gestured with his head. 'You like?' His voice was soft and friendly, and heavily accented. Phoenix also turned to face Robert, his cock still hard and jutting up from the opening in his breeches, and still covered with saliva and spunk.

Moon Boy shifted a little and held out his hand to Robert, who took it and was pulled closer to him. With a smile that spread across his whole face, Moon Boy leant forward and took Robert into his mouth, his tongue working furiously, as though he hadn't had enough from Phoenix. His sucking was superb and masterly, drawing it down, filling his throat, and letting it slide back when he judged the moment to be right. This way he kept up a constant wave of pleasure, an on-and-off suction that left Robert gasping.

The sheer bliss that Robert was feeling was abruptly brought to an end, as Phoenix pulled Moon Boy to his feet and pushed him back on the bed. His hands set about his clothes, expertly plucking them off him and leaving the boy laying naked before them both, before expertly shucking his own, allowing Robert to get a good look at their bodies. Moon Boy had the amazing blush of youth, a smooth body which was completely hairless, with narrow hips and a well-developed chest. His cock was erect and waiting, not as thick as the one he'd just been blowing, but much longer, a smooth, narrower shaft culminating in a large, drooling head. Phoenix complemented him admirably, a well-built man, with muscles where they should be, and a broad, manly chest with curls of soft hair over it tapering down to wide hips and thighs.

Phoenix moved to the bed and pulled Moon Boy to the side of it, raising his legs in the air and exposing his arsehole, resting his legs over his shoulders. He nodded to Robert and gestured with his head toward the other side of the bed. Robert moved round and watched for a moment.

Letting a huge drop of spit fall onto his cock, Phoenix pushed at the tight opening. The head of his cock jammed itself inside, forcing a cry of surprise from the boy. With one more almighty thrust, he slid fully in, and began to fuck him in slow, regular strokes. Robert leapt up on the bed and positioned himself over Moon Boy's mouth, lowering his arse until he felt the tender flicker of a tongue at his hole. He shivered, as Moon Boy got to work, licking and sucking frenetically, washing the hole with his spit, pushing the tip of his tongue inside the ring of sphincter muscle. This made Robert cry out with delight, relaxing those muscles to let the tongue further in. He sat up and down, encouraging further action, all the while not taking his eyes from Phoenix, who was relentlessly fucking Moon Boy.

Desperate for another blow-job, Robert pulled himself up and plunged his cock into the youngster's mouth, feeling it touch the back of his throat, and seeing Moon Boy's eyes bulge as he gagged momentarily and then began sucking in earnest, revelling in the double attention, his mouth full as well as his arse. Phoenix was ramming harder, pummelling and stretching the inner passage, its warmth holding his cock fiercely within. Robert held his hands under Moon Boy's chin, feeling his stiff rod filling him as he fucked the mouth. The boy's body was jumping with every thrust of Phoenix's dick, whose bollocks were slamming against sweaty arse cheeks. His mouth's suction and release began growing and fading with each penetration of his backside, working in rhythm with the anal attack. He may be young, Robert thought, but he knows how to suck a cock. The sensation of his tight mouth was so incredible that Robert had to know how his arse felt.

Lifting himself off, sliding his cock out of the expert mouth, he moved round to Phoenix's side. The older boy could see what Robert wanted and so eased his prick free from the confines of his fellow pirate's hole. Positioning himself so that his cock was ready to enter, Robert knelt on the side of the bed. Moon Boy looked pleadingly up at him, desperate for his length to plunge inside him. Spreading his arse cheeks wider and thrusting himself forward, showing the trembling hole, Moon Boy let a short cry escape his lips 'Now... do it now.'

With a flash of pain, the cock was inside him. Even if he had changed his mind, it was far too late now. He felt the initial pleasurable probing as the first few inches eased inside. Then he was totally penetrated, and the depth of the cock made him squeal. His fingers twisted and turned on the blanket, gripping and releasing the soft cloth. He could feel that Robert's cock was bigger than Phoenix's, longer, and with a much thicker circumference, and he marvelled at the friction it set up, as the sides of his arse wall stretched to take the whole solid length inside him.

Robert was excited beyond description. The groans of pure pleasure and pain that Moon Boy was giving made the moment more of a turn-on. He could feel the heat of the young pirate's arse rising and falling, allowing the regular invasive strokes to go unhindered. He could also feel the youngster's body tensing and relaxing with each thrust, holding each in-breath as the rigid cock plunged deep. Moon Boy must be feeling each push of the embedded weapon right to the tips of his toes.

Never had the young pirate known such a pounding from another man, never had his young arse been subjected to such a passionate fulfillment. The throbbing of his heart sounded in his ears, the beat growing in speed with each downstroke of Robert's dick.

Reaching forward, Robert began to pinch and squeeze Moon Boy's nipples, letting his fingers seize upon the small, pointed pinnacles of flesh. Moon Boy's head began to thrash about on the bed, the two incredible points of connection between him and de la Hoya's new boy sending his brain reeling. Not wanting to be left out of the action, Phoenix squatted on the bed by Moon Boy's side, and plunged his mouth over the end of his young, twitching prick, rolling the head around like a plum, pulling the skin of the shaft down to the base, letting the newly-freed sensitive head enjoy a good tonguing. The cock was reacting as desired, jerking and pulsing, oozing lubricating juice. His mouth slid down, lips clamped to the shaft, teasing their way down to the skin at the base of it, nestling his nose in the fragrant curls of his pubis hair. The cock was deep in his throat, wet and snug, although his tongue still hung out, slavering across the balls, licking them with obvious delight.

The moans and thrashing of the helpless youngster increased dramatically, his eyes wide, his mouth gulping for air, between the cries of astonished ecstasy. In his life so far upon the high seas, he had experienced sex with men, mainly either Phoenix or de la Hoya, but never had his firm young body had so much pleasure as now, his nipples, cock and arsehole all getting feverishly worked on. Robert's cock was fucking him so fully, and Phoenix's mouth was slurping and sucking him so amazingly, that he could feel his juices boiling and surging. He wanted the triple sensation to go on forever, but he knew it couldn't. As Robert pushed further up, he felt the head of his cock touch some deep trigger, and a tumultuous wave of lust washed over him. He exploded with a shout, the first bolt hitting the back of Phoenix's throat, who rapidly pulled away. He swallowed the first wave greedily, but then sat and watched, thrilled as more of his friend's spunk erupted, flowing forth, shooting in torrential streams across the firm stomach.

Phoenix couldn't hold back any longer either, kneeling up and pounding his fist about his own aching tool, coaxing the very seed from him. In a second he grunted and shot out a wad of cream, landing on Moon Boy and blending with his already spent juice. His fist jerked and pulled as an endless amount poured forth, until he shook and sank back on his heels, empty and replete. Throughout this double climax, Robert continued to fuck Moon Boy's arse, waiting for the moment when he could pull free and come. This was it. He slipped out from the encircling hole and came, his cock jerking as it ejaculated its bubbling load, each spasm making Robert grunt. As the last hot drip trickled from the slit in his aching cockhead, Robert fell forward, lying across Moon Boy's chest and stomach, the sticky mass of come adhering to his own body. Phoenix also fell back on the bed, his arm across Robert's waist, his hand fumbling for his cock, which he held in his fist, manipulating his fingers, massaging the slowly softening pole. A warm glow of satisfaction coursed through all three, as if they were one contented creature. The heat from their bodies merged and melded, their hearts beat in time with each other. Robert's head was against Moon Boy's smooth young chest, and he rose and fell with the regular breaths the boy took. He found himself fading away, drifting ino a state of unconciousness, when a short, scuffling sound brought him back to life.

It appeared as if it came from the wall at the far side of the room, near the connecting door. Pushing Phoenix's arm gently to the side and easing himself off the bed, his hair peaked on one side with congealed spunk, he padded across to the door. He tried the handle, which didn't give, obviously locked. He put his ear to the wall and listened. Nothing. It was then he noticed a darkened painting on the wall by the door. It was of a family group, children playing merrily on a hearth rug while their adoring parents looked happily on. The head of one of the children seemed slightly darker than the others, and, on touching the canvas, he felt that it was slightly deeper indented, as if the shape of the head had been cut out and replaced.

A sinister thought crossed Robert's mind. This was a peephole. From the other room. Put there so that de la Hoya could watch him at anytime he wanted. Had the pirate chief been watching his session with Phoenix and Moon Boy? If he had, then that meant he had another strange fantasy... voyeurism. Robert stored that fact away at the back of his mind in case it would sometime prove useful. It also showed that he must enjoy watching his boy having sex with others. This might be a way to get Daniel released from below. Perhaps if he offered to perform with Daniel, de la Hoya might be interested in watching their bodies at work on each other.

The sound of the door being unlocked made Robert jump and he sped back to the bed, throwing himself down on the mattress. Phoenix and Moon Boy sat up sleepily. De la Hoya entered, and sat on the end of the bed. The sight of three naked young men should have aroused him, but Robert guessed that he had just wanked himself off in the connecting room and so was a little weary.

'I hope that you were entertained, Robert? I assumed that you would have had a rather dull day, and so thought a little variety might give you some pleasure.' Moon Boy had lain back and spread his legs, his nimble hands slowly playing with his genitals, toying, almost daring de la Hoya to react. The pirate chief smiled indulgently. 'Haven't you had enough, you bad boy?'

Moon Boy grinned and turned to face Phoenix who was still sitting at his side, eyes focused on his leader. The older boy also started to play with his cock, seemingly knowing what was on Moon Boy's mind. Robert could see what they were playing at, and spoke quickly. 'If you will take these two temptresses away, then perhaps I could finish my supper and get some sleep.'

De la Hoya smacked the two pirates on their swelling pricks, making them wince, and pulled them up with his powerful arms. 'Out... before I lose my temper.' The two young men lept sharply off the bed and began dressing, throwing their clothes on randomly, eyes fixed on de la Hoya, before scampering to the door. A quick, appreciative glance back at the naked Robert, and they were gone.

'Very enjoyable. Where did you find them?' Robert sank back down on the bed, plumping a pillow behind his shoulders for support. He could see that the pirate was eyeing him, a look of triumph on his face.

'They were aboard a ship we commandeered some months ago. They only spoke a little English, but it was obvious in their body language what kind of men they were, and that they enjoyed the pleasures of the flesh. Manly flesh in particular. I took them under my wing and let them have free reign with my boys. They enjoy the experience as much as my boys usually do. You did enjoy them, I hope?'

Robert licked his dry lips. He wanted a drink of wine very much. Standing, he crossed to the table and poured out two large goblets. Handing one to de la Hoya, he sat back, crossing his legs, arranging his cock and balls to their best advantage. He was aware that the pirate watched him closely at all times. 'I did enjoy them. They seem very, how shall I put it... enthusiastic. Moon Boy is certainly an expert cock-sucker. I detect your fair hand there... I am sure you gave him some private tuition. Am I wrong?'

A mighty laugh poured out of de la Hoya, as he sat on the bed and stroked Robert's thigh. 'Quite correct! He was willing to learn, and I relished the prospect of teaching him. I assume he then practised his discoveries lustily upon Phoenix... an energetic young man.'

Taking a mouthful of wine, Robert savoured its rich fruity bouquet. 'Can I ask you a question?' He tried to sound as unperturbed as he could.

'Of course. What do you want to know?'

'You have used the phrase "my boys" on several occasions. I assume I am not the first young man who has stayed with you in this way?'

An amused chuckle was de la Hoya's first reaction. After a swig of wine, he continued with the gentle thigh-stroking, before his tone changed slightly, his features creasing, and a darker look sweeping across his ebony eyes. 'You would be right to assume that. Over the years I have had many such companions, though I admit you are one of the highest quality. I admire your spirit, and your willingness to adapt yourself to the situation. Some of my boys have taken a time to realise their good fortune in being found by me. They have had to endure numerous such evenings as you spent yesterday. Until they learned to relax and accept me as their master, their lives were fairly uncomfortable. Some of them weren't even interested in men. Some were married or had a chosen girl back at home... Those ones proved to be a real challenge. Can you imagine the thrill of penetrating a virgin heterosexual arse? The squeal of pain and shock is delicious, even more of a potent sound than the one made by a willing partner.' He paused and slugged down more wine. 'Have you ever truly loved another?' The question came out of the blue, rather stunning Robert.

After a moment's hesitation, Robert swilled down the last few drops of wine and sat up, head down, eyes fixed upon a damp patch on the blanket. 'I actually think I have. The problem is that I didn't realise it at the time. His name was William and we came into each other's lives back home. We were separated at sea, and I don't even know if he is still alive. Deep down in the depths of my soul I believe that he is. I know that somehow he didn't perish in the North Sea, and is waiting somewhere for me to find him.' He stopped, amazed at this revelation. He hadn't fully realised this stunning fact before. He did love William. A dull ache started up in the pit of his stomach, a longing for the man that he had lost. 'Have you ever loved?' Robert raised his eyes, meeting de la Hoya with a steely gaze. The pirate answered slowly, picking his words carefully, and speaking with a great sigh. 'I did love my last boy, very much. His name was Jean-Paul. He was found aboard a French vessel, bound for the Americas. He had been sold as a slave and was scared out of his wits. The poor young innocent had been kept chained in the Captain's cabin, used as an occasional outlet for his vile temper. When I found him he was a mass of sores and bruises, shivering with fear and hunger. I killed the callous bastard of a Captain… slit him open from stem to stern, as a matter of fact, and swept his remains overboard for the sharks.' A dangerous gleam was in his eyes and his tone became colder. 'I took Jean-Paul aboard and cossetted him. Gave him food and warmth, tended his injuries, and helped him back to full strength. He was so grateful that his love for me was overwhelming. He was a beautiful lover, tender and giving, with no thought of his own satisfaction. I had never found any boy like him.'

Robert waited until de la Hoya had stopped, the pirate's eyes moist with tears. He hadn't known that there was a tender side to this man. Perhaps this could also be exploited. 'What happened to him?'

'He died. Something on our island bit him, a snake or a spider, I am not sure, but he died from poisoning. It was a slow, agonising death. I sat with him holding his hand until the last, until the last wheezing breath croaked from his limp body. It was the hardest thing I have ever had to endure. Up until that moment, I thought I was strong, but the devastation and loss was unbearable.

I was deeply affected and became very depressed for months. I did finally pull myself together. That was almost a year ago now. I vowed never again to fall in love with anyone, and so put myself through that kind of heartache again.' He stopped. His eyes seemed very far away, and his shoulders drooped, his whole body overcome with the emotion of those memories. Shaking his head as if to dislodge them he said, 'I am sure you understand, Robert.'

This was a revelation. Robert hadn't expected de la Hoya to have such depths, to have suffered so in the name of love. He just didn't seem the type. All the drive and energy seemed drained from the man, and so, with a deep breath, Robert took his chance. 'I also recently became acquainted with an officer on board the ship you attacked. His name is Daniel. I developed a real fondness for him in the weeks of our journey west, and it really pains me to think that he is suffering, held in chains in the bowels of your ship.' He looked up through his fringe, trying to work his boyish charms again, widening his eyes and pouting. 'Can you not release him? He is a very beautiful young man, with a stunning body, and perfect blonde hair, who you would, I am sure, find rather delightful. He is a highly sexual man, adept in many things. He is well-endowed, not at all shy, and would probably show his gratitude to you in many ways. Please think about it.' He paused again, licked his lips, and leant forward, taking de la Hoya's hand in his. 'We could do things for you. I am sure you'd enjoy watching us in action.'

The pirate was silent. Robert could see his mind working, the great brows furrowed in thought. 'I shall think about it. Now get some sleep. You will have a busy, tiring day tomorrow.' The bed creaked as he stood. Then, placing the goblet on the table, he moved to the door. Turning back, he gazed at Robert, looking his naked form up and down. 'Goodnight. Sleep well.'

ELEVEN

Robert slept exceedingly well that night. Not long after de la Hoya left, Mother appeared and fussed about the cabin, tidying the supper things and blowing out the candles before tucking the blanket neatly about Robert and, with an affectionate pat on his crotch, jangling nimbly from the room.

It was the excited shouts and cries from above that woke him next morning. Rubbing the sleep crusts from his eyes, he scrambled to his feet, barely noticing the breakfast tray that had obviously been brought in while he was still asleep. The view from the porthole was astounding. *The War Queen* was nearing the shore of an island, no more than a mile away. From this distance it looked a green, lush place, with tall trees holding sway over a wooded promontory. A little further on was an outcrop of rocks and boulders, creating a natural harbour, into which they were now heading.

Realisations flooded Robert's now wide-awake mind. One of the reasons this band of privateers had never been caught was no doubt the fact that they would be difficult to spot, hidden in this small but useful cove. The shouts from above increased as the sails of the ship were being brought down, allowing the vessel to ride the rolling tide into the harbour. As they rounded the promontory, Robert's eyes grew wide with wonderment. The island harbour was unlike any place he'd ever been before. It was as close to paradise as he could imagine. Majestic palm trees waved in the gentle breeze, growing up the side of a jagged mountain, until petering out, leaving the giant peak to rise uncovered into a fluffy band of cloud that obscured its tip. The bay itself was a perfect semi-circle. Robert was reminded of childhood visits to Lulworth Cove in Dorset. All along the length of the harbour, the waves lapped gently at a golden strip of sand, fringing the abundant greenery that grew beyond. As he looked up, a rainbow flock of birds flew overhead, shrieking wildly, moving and swooping in the breeze.

The cabin door swung open, making Robert jump. He looked around and saw Mother, with an armful of clothes. 'Here, my dear. You'll need to wear something, as we're all going ashore shortly.' Dumping the jumbled collection of garments on the bed, he waggled his fingers playfully and left, with a toss of his crimson hair.

At last. Robert dived at the bed, rummaging through the rough assortment. As much as he admired his body, and liked others admiring it, it would be a relief to put some clothes on. A short singlet, cut at the arms, and a pair of cotton shorts seemed appropriate, with a pair of leather sandals for his feet. Feeling much surer of himself, he sat at the table and quickly wolfed down some breakfast.

Soon he heard the rumble of the anchor being lowered, a sure sign that they had arrived. Robert sat on the bed waiting anxiously. Now that they had reached their destination, things would be different. With luck, de la Hoya wouldn't keep him locked up, would let him have a reasonably free reign to do as he wished. He had high hopes that he could get Daniel released from his bonds, to try and make life easier for him. A knock came at the door, and it banged open. Outside, Moon Boy looked cheerily content. He beckoned for Robert to accompany him. As Robert stepped through the door, the young man fondled his buttocks, grinning lasciviously. Pinching the boy's cheek, Robert allowed him to lead the way.

As they emerged onto the deck, Robert shielded his eyes against the brilliant glare of the sunlight on the lapping waves. Keeping his hand up for shade, he watched as the operation of going ashore continued unabated. A small rowing boat was being brought alongside, and cases and trunks were being loaded aboard.

De la Hoya approached Robert, brimming with good humour. 'Good Morning, my little one. Welcome to my island. Welcome to Baruga, which is my home, and I dearly hope you will be able to treat it as your home. The boat will take us ashore, climb down.' He helped Robert to clamber down the ladder, to jump aboard the small craft and nestle amongst the stacked cases. De la Hoya swiftly joined him, sitting at his side, his meaty arm about his shoulders. With a nod from him, the boat pulled away, and several shirtless pirates began to row towards the shoreline, grunting with the effort, their muscular arms aglow with exertion and sweat. The pirate, too, had a healthy glow about him, viewing the approaching shore with pride. He hugged Robert to him and shouted aloud,

' "The Common sun, the air, the skies,

To him are opening Paradise!"

'Your wonderful poet, Thomas Gray, a master of words, he could encapsulate the whole world in one short sentence. Do you not agree?'

Robert had nothing to say and, turning his head back to the ship, saw the prisoners of *The Merry Megan* being led onto the deck, blinking in the violent sunshine and shuffling along, the rusty metal leg restraints hindering their progress. Scanning their gaunt, unshaven faces, Robert couldn't see Daniel at all. With a sinking heart, he wondered if he was still alive. He heard a commotion and saw Hamish Dee being led out, shouting at the crew, but unable to escape his chains. Then, with a sigh of relief, he saw Daniel stepp out on deck, his hair unkempt, his face covered with stubble, and a dejected stoop about his gait. Robert bit back a cry of anguish at the sight of this proud man in such a shambolic state. Closing his eyes was all he could do.

Turning back to face the shore, he watched as the sandy beach grew closer, as the boat cut its way through the gently foaming waves. The sea about him was of such a deep, vivid blue, that it looked as though it were made of liquid sapphires, shot through with tiny specks of silver, as small fish turned and darted about in the luxuriant depths. A warm breeze blew across his face, hair streaming behind him, and he pondered that if his life were to be lived out in this place, it wouldn't be a bad spot to end up. It only took a moment for him to realise, though, that this tropical wonderland wasn't his home, and never would be. It might be paradise, but it was paradise with bars. Whatever situation he found himself in, he must always be on his guard for a way to escape, a way to free himself, and others if possible, from the clutches of the charismatic de la Hoya and his crew.

De la Hoya patted his arm and pointed ahead. Rounding the wooded promontory, Robert saw the first few white colonnades of a grand house appear from a clump of trees. Nearing the shore, he could see that it was an example of architecture at its finest. The imposing columns led to a greek-style portico above the front of the house, the windows were shuttered, and the great wooden doors slowly swung open to greet the master of the house. Some way behind the house, a dense woodland grew, as if shading and protecting the pirate's lair from wayward intruders.

In a few, heaving strokes, the rowing boat pulled up alongside the rickety wooden jetty. De la Hoya leapt from the boat and extended a bronzed arm to

Robert. Clambering onto the planks, Robert saw a group of men hurrying down from the house to the jetty, anxious looks on their faces. As de la Hoya saw them, he opened his arms and a broad grin swept over him. 'I am home! I hope you have been looking after the old place for me?' The group of four young men nodded vigourously as if they were obedient dogs, waiting for a treat from their owner.

Turning to Robert, de la Hoya put hia ram about his shoulders and squeezed proudly. 'This is Robert. He will be living with me, as my new boy. You will do anything he asks you, and you will do everything you can to make him comfortable. Is that clear?' The men again nodded and gave Robert welcoming smiles. One of them, a tanned young man with a taut body, wearing only a flowery sarong about his waist, stepped foward and put out his hand. 'Welcome to Baruga. I hope you'll be very happy here. My name is Felicia, and I am the head houseboy. If you desire anything at all, just call for me.' He spoke English impeccably, and Robert wondered if he imagined a twinge of a Welsh accent. Wherever he came from, he was an attractive man, with close cropped hair atop a rounded firm face and piercing eyes that seemed to bore deep, a sign of great strength of character. He clicked his fingers and another of the retinue appeared at his shoulder. 'Jonno, take Robert up to the house. Show him to his room. Everything is ready for him. I shall take care of the master.' The pale-aced young man bowed his head and gestured for Robert to follow him as he set off along the jetty, his tight cotton shorts showing his muscular arse off to great advantage. De la Hoya nodded to Robert, and with a sweep of his hand waved the way to the house.

As he walked slowly after Jonno, Robert noticed the other two servants, who had been hanging back slightly. Their nervousness at de la Hoya's presence was extremely obvious. It took only a second for Robert to realise that they were twins. The had identical brown hair and eyes, their bodies were of the same toned shape, their faces strong and manly. Each held the other's hand. They bowed their heads as Robert passed, watching him stride by.

The heat from the sun was beating down quite mercilessly now, and the shade of the house, when they reached it, came as a much-needed coolness. Jonno let Robert enter the large, studded front door first and ,as he walked inside, he gasped. The floor was of a mottled marble, and along each wall of the entrance hall were velvet and brocade chairs, whilst the walls were hung with magnificent full-length portraits of various noblemen and their wives. At regular intervals stood shoulder-high marbled plinths topped by exquisite oriental vases and bowls. Robert paused at one and recognised it as a perfect example of the Ming dynasty. Somehow he didn't expect to find such beauty in the stronghold of a group of notorious thieves and murderers.

Jonno lead the way forward to the staircase, which stood broad and imposing in front of them. It curved round and up to the first floor and a long corridor with rooms on each side. The servant stopped at the end room and opened the door, which swung open noiselessly. Again Robert was stunned by what he saw. A king-sized bed, hung with gorgeous drapes, luxurious French furniture, superlative paintings and porcelain. It was a treasure trove.

Crosing to a small ante-room at the far end, Jonno opened another door and smiled. 'Would you like a bath, Master Robert? I have one prepared for you.'

The thought of a warm soak did sound appealing and Robert nodded in delight. 'Yes, that would be marvellous. Thank you.'

A slight nod was the only reaction as Jonno held open the door for Robert to enter. In front of him was a large, ornate bathtub sitting atop tiger-claw feet, filled to the brim with soapy water. Faint whips of steam arose from the inviting surface. Jonno moved to his side and pulled the singlet over Robert's head. Then, kneeling, he helped Robert to slip out of his shorts. As he knelt, he ran his fingers up Robert's thighs, tracing lines with his fingertips. Their soft touch sent a shiver down Robert's spine. 'Ye Gods!', thought Robert, 'de la Hoya knows how to pick servants and crew. This one is bursting with desire for me.' Looking down into the eyes of Jonno, the pleading gaze staring back, desperate for some attention, desperate for some solid piece of male flesh. Knowing that he was now on de la Hoya's home territory, it suddenly struck Robert that he should try and be a little careful. Now that he was in a position of some respect among the staff, and of some trust from his pirate master, he didn't want to ruin it. If he was caught with his dick in this servant's mouth, what would the chief say? As the warm breath from Jonno's mouth played across the head of his cock, Robert threw caution to the wind and grasped the back of the man's head. He had to have that wet, willing mouth around him now.

The moment of contact made Robert gasp, and throwing back his head he let out a long hiss of breath. Jonno was also breathing heavily, and with one swift movement he plunged his mouth down the cock. He wanted to swallow it whole, to suck it right down to the swinging bollocks, further and further into the deep wetness of his rippling throat.

Robert's breath was now coming in short rasps. He forced his cock down Jonno's throat, feeling his tongue squirming about it, filling him with his stiffness. The pressure was increasing and making the cock grow harder, if possible. Jonno was now gripping the base of the shaft with his fist, trapping the blood which had sped to its swollen head. This was incredible. Robert looked down at the servant, whose bobbing head was working fast and hard. 'Look at me,' he commanded Jonno in a trembling voice, trying not to sound too unsure. The young man raised his eyes, keeping up the extraordinary sucking motions. Robert stared down in thrilled ecstasy. He loved the sight of the entire length of his cock disappearing down another man's throat, and this man knew what he was doing. Little triumphant sighs of joy were coming from Jonno as he slurped and sucked. It seemed a labour of love, as if he hadn't had the chance to suck on a dick for a very long time. Robert decided to give the man value for money and began bucking his naked hips, thrusting down, fucking the pliant throat with vigorous strokes, pumping for all he was worth, determined to shoot a full load down this man's hungry throat. He was close to coming, could sense the end approaching as the seed started travelling and, with a shout, he came, his balls tightening, a creamy jet launching into the depths of Jonno's mouth, who drank it down greedily, savouring the bitter-sweet saltiness, swallowing lustily each jerk of spunk. As the last drop trickled down past his tongue, Jonno looked up and wiped his mouth with the back of his hand. 'Thank you.' His words came from the heart, and somehow touched Robert. This seemed a genuinely friendly and kind person. He was glad to have given him some pleasure.

'I should bathe now.' Robert felt his cock slowly drooping and he could feel the pull of the water, his skin crying for a little pampering. Jonno gave a small bow and without looking back, he pattered from the room.

The bath was extremely invigorating, and having towelled and dressed himself, Robert thought he should try and explore the house and grounds. The handle of the door turned easily and,looking down the deserted corridor, he moved quietly toward the grand staircase.

Downstairs was still a hive of great activity as pirates and servants bustled about, carrying boxes and trunks in through the front door, the occasional shouted oath ringing out as Felicia tried to stop them banging into the furniture. There was no sign of de la Hoya. With a deep breath and his heart thudding in his chest, Robert started to descend, his sandals slapping on the cold, marble steps. Felicia looked up as he approached and inclined his head. 'Are you feeling refreshed?'

'Yes thank you, Felicia, is it?'

'That's right. I was christened Felix, but since I started my new life with the master, I thought a new name would be appropriate. Careful there!' He waved his hand angrily as the two twins carried in a large wooden chest, which they knocked into the door frame as they entered. 'I have never known such clumsy boys as those two.' He flapped his arms in an annoyed fashion. 'You'll have seen the twins, Castor and Pollux. I don't think they are of use to anyone, but the master has a soft spot for them. He likes to sometimes amuse himself with them... you'll probably find out why one of these days.'

Robert raised an eyebrow. 'Can I look around?'

'Of course. You may go anywhere you wish. Except near the holding cells. They are out of bounds to everyone.'

'What are they for?'

'That is where any prisoners are kept. I believe the Captain had a good haul of men this time. Should keep him going for quite a while.'

This was a puzzling statement. 'What do you mean by that?' But Felicia had moved away, straightening a chair which had been pushed aside, and hurrying through a door ahead of them. Robert followed, and walked through the door, entering the drawing room, a large, airy salon, again exquisitely decorated, with many chairs along the walls. Through the drawing room was the dining room, with a long polished table, already laid with silver and cut-glass. Emerging and heading for the entrance hall, Robert noticed a small door at one end of the hall. He turned the handle but found the door locked. A cellar, perhaps?

He stepped outside the front door and had to gasp as the heat radiating from the shimmering sand was intense. After a few moments of adjustment, he crossed the front of the house, noting with some sadness that *The Merry Megan* was lying tattered and torn in the becalmed waters of the cove. At the far end of the house, he saw some distance away a small grey-brick building where two pirates stood guard. Obviously the holding cells where the men from the ship had been taken. Casually, he began to whistle quietly to himself, and with his hands clasped behind his back, sauntered in the building's direction. As he neared, the pirates slovenly demeanour changed and they snapped to attention, pointing the barrels of their muskets at him menacingly.

Grinning as if he had made an unintentional mistake, he changed course and strolled up the path past the holding cells. At the rear of the mansion were several low-slung dormitory-type buildings, where a number of pirates were lounging about in hammocks, smoking and swigging from a large pottery jug. A couple of them nudged each other as Robert passed and said something in Spanish, which produced great guffaws of laughter from the rest of the men. Walking by, Robert smiled, and noticed that the majority of the pirates were fairly young and fit. Probably hand-picked by de la Hoya, he guessed sarcastically. All eyes were on him as he sauntered up the path and so, stretching his arms up, he pulled the singlet over his head, revealing his firm torso. Many of the men sat up and made low comments to each other. Was there anyone in the crew who did not prefer the male sex? Robert was seriously beginning to wonder.

The area behind the crew quarters swiftly became densely tropical — there were trees and plants in various states of growth, the chirping of insects and the sqawking of birds coming from somewhere in its verdant vegetation. He decided not to risk going any further.

On returning to the house, he met de la Hoya standing on the veranda at the front of the house. 'So do you like my little place?' His voice had a strange tone to it, inquisitive, but with a hard edge.

'It is very impressive. You have a superb collection of porcelain and fineries.'

The pirate seemed to swell with pride. 'I do. Most of it collected from some unfortunate ship or another. Other pieces bought on my various travels. If I cannot enjoy the fruits of my labours, then what is the point of doing what I do? Do you like your room?'

'It is marvellous, thank you, extremely comfortable.'

'Good.' De la Hoya gestured to a couple of white whicker chairs that sat on the veranda, separated by a low table, on which was a tray, two glasses and a pitcher of some bubbling, milky liquid. Sitting down, de la Hoya poured out two large glasses and offered one to Robert. 'You should enjoy this, a local concoction with coconut milk, rum and a few indigenous spices. I have christened it a "Pirate's Kiss". It should relax you.'

Robert sniffed at the frothy liquid and wrinkled his nose. 'I feel quite relaxed anyway,' he said, before putting it down on the table-top. De la Hoya looked slightly peeved and left his own glass untouched. Staring out to sea, watching a group of pirates on board *The Merry Megan*, stripping her sails, and coiling ropes into piles, he spoke with that now-familiar hard edge. 'Did you enjoy the attentions of young Jonno? He sucks cock with a interesting enthusiasm, does he not?'

Unsure of how to answer, Robert watched the pirate's face, which gave away nothing. His unflinching countenance turned to stare at Robert. 'I know everything that goes on in my house. I have eyes and ears everywhere. Do not worry, I give most of my servants free reign to do as they please. Jonno asked, and he therefore received.' He stroked the massive bulge in his thin, cotton trousers with one finger, tracing the outline of his cock, which had started to swell. 'You may be *my* boy, but I expect you to be available for sexual service when requested by any of my crew.'

Robert stared at the growing bulge, fascinated by its size, watching the flimsy material strain to hold down the enormous knob. De la Hoya continued, his eyes still on Robert. 'You should know that you are nothing but a plaything for me and my crew. Remember Phoenix and Moon Boy? They speak very highly of your talents in that department, and are desperate for another session with you. All I demand is that when I want your company, day or night, you are ready, and open-minded enough to do as I want. Play fair by me and you shall have a pampered existence and want for nothing.'

'Except my freedom.'

'Precisely. Do you agree?'

With a nod of his head, Robert acceeded. 'As to the house and grounds, you may go anywhere you wish. You may take advantage of my library, I have a fine collection of classics. If you wander off, I would advise you to stay within calling distance, as the natives can sometimes be a little difficult. I wouldn't want you to go for a stroll and end up on their supper menu. Not with a body like yours. That would be a waste. And of course it goes without saying that you will not attempt to speak to any of the prisoners. If you even think of trying to help them escape, you will suffer the consequences of your actions, and most painful that will be.' De la Hoya sat back with his hands clasped behind his head and closed his eyes. 'Now leave me. I wish a little peace and quiet. Go to your room and I will be with you in a while. Take your drink with you.'

There was nothing else to do but obey. Glass in hand, Robert climbed the staircase and walked ponderously back to his room. There was much to think about. Somehow he had to find a way to get to the prisoners in the holding cells. If he could release them then perhaps they could get away from the pirate's clutches. *The Merry Megan* would be of no use at all, now that it was being broken up. With a small, if inexperienced crew, they might be able to sail away on *The War Queen*. Alternately, if they armed themselves, they could escape through the jungle, and if necessary fight any natives that should come upon them. Guns and muskets should be a match for spears and chanting, surely? But how to get to the prisoners? There must be a time when they were left unwatched. He would keep a close eye on the movements of the guards, and see if an opportunity presented itself. Perhaps at meal times, or crossovers. It would take a few days, but he had to be vigilant.

Crossing to his bedroom window, Robert pushed his face against the pane of glass. He could just see the holding cells. It should be easy, then, to keep constant watch. In the meantime, he would continue to play the whore, to service any of de la Hoya's men as desired him, and do it well. He knew how to pleasure a man, and so he would make de la Hoya proud of him. He needed to earn the trust of the pirate. The more trusting he was, the more relaxed he would become.

The clock on the mantel read five o'clock. He was feeling a little hungry and thirsty. Remembering the drink he had brought up with him from the veranda, Robert took several deep gulps. It was deliciously creamy, but had an odd kick to it, and a flavouring that he didn't recognise.

As there was little else to do, he watched the guards from the window, standing easily by the cells, arms folded, chatting nonchalantly to each other. One of them, a heavily built man with a bushy beard and a scarf about his head, had a large bunch of keys dangling on a chain at his waist. Could he be the one to keep surveillance on? Was he in charge, or did he just pass the keys on to whoever was on duty next? Robert became so engrossed in this line of thought that he didn't hear the door open. A cough made him leap and spin around. De la Hoya stood with a pitcher of the same creamy drink, and a stony look on his face. 'I am sorry the view is not that spectacular from this part of the house, but you'll find it much cooler in the mornings, due to the shade from the trees.' Placing the tray upon a table, he crossed to the window and looked in the direction Robert had been so intent upon. Saying nothing, he then poured a generous helping of the tropical brew into a silver goblet and held it out in front of him. 'Here, you must be thirsty, drink this.'

Licking his dry lips, Robert found that he did suddenly have a raging thirst and so he took the goblet and drank greedily. A moustache of froth sat on his upper lip, and with his hand he wiped it clean. 'I am so thirsty... and hungry. When will we eat?'

Again the pirate stayed silent, his only response to pour another large goblet of the "Pirate's Kiss", and hand it to Robert, who again downed the frothy nectar.

De la Hoya smiled at last, and placed the pitcher down. 'It works best on an empty stomach. I should lie down, because you will be feeling the effect shortly.'

This sounded ominous and Robert was about to demand to know what was going on, when a strange sensation began to creep over him, a tingling in his toes which slowly flooded up his legs and across his whole body. His head started to swim, and he had great difficulty in focusing his vision on de la Hoya, who stood, hands on hips, smiling in a sinister fashion. The pirate's grinning face blurred and twisted, as did Robert's stomach. A wave of nausea churned in him, and he fell back on the bed, clutching at the bedclothes. A soothing warmth was now seeping through his being, spreading out from his groin, and unsure as he felt, Robert knew that he was desperate for sex. His cock had swiftly grown to its maximum girth and length, throbbing and aching for attention. He was unable to resist as de la Hoya bent over his limp body and pulled off his singlet, then tugged down his shorts, allowing his hardened cock to spring free. De la Hoya swept him up in his arms and headed from the room, carrying him naked and unresisting down the staircase to the hall.

Robert wasn't sure if he imagined a large group of men milling about at the foot of the stairs, and was even less sure of where he was then carried. His eyes closed, a throbbing black drowsiness overwhelmed his consciousness, and he collapsed, inert in the pirate's strong arms.

TWELVE

'Make sure he cannot move.' A strident voice cut through Robert's mind as his eyes opened and a sea of blurred images swam before him.

'He is secure, Sir.' Robert's fuzzed mind recognised the dulcet tones of Felicia, and he vaguely made out his face hovering at his side. He tried to get up, but found he couldn't move. Another wave of sickness poured over him, as he felt like he was floating in mid-air. Blinking rapidly to try and focus on his surroundings, Robert sensed that he was hanging in some kind of harness, on his back, with his hands and legs tied to the supporting chains. His legs were elevated and pulled wide, and his arse was exposed and helpless. A dull throbbing resounded in his head. Every time he turned it to look around, the picture before him disintegrated into a whirl of colours and shapes.

Taking several deep breaths seemed to help momentarily and, opening his eyes wide, Robert could see he was in a darkened, high-ceilinged room, which was hung with half a dozen or so similar harnesses in a line, all occupied except the one nearest to him. As he watched, he saw another helpless man being placed in the harness, legs and wrists strapped into place. It took a few seconds for his eyes to focus on the unconscious body of Daniel, his hair mussed and untidy, his face a mass of stubble, his chest covered in purple bruises. With a shake of his head to try and clear his blurred vision, Robert saw that the two pirates fastening Daniel into the harness were the twins, Castor and Pollux. They were naked apart from leather thongs which just covered their prodigious cocks and bollocks, and which, after rising up the cracks of their arses, were tied tightly about their waists. One of them nudged the other as he noticed that Robert had awoken. The other came round between Robert's thighs and gazed at his cock which was lying to one side, flaccid and unaroused. Obviously impressed by its size, even when limp, the pirate grasped it and gave it a squeeze, the contact with warm flesh making it rapidly respond. A raised eyebrow was the only response from the pirate. As he moved aside to let his brother have a look, Robert noticed that they were wearing earings with the initials C and P on them. That would help him to identify them, he thought vaguely, his mind distracted by the swelling between his thighs.

Pollux, for he was the second one, took a firm hold of Robert's cock and rubbed the drop of pre-come that had oozed from the tip into the head, watching closely as Robert gave a gasp of surprise.

Suddenly both broke away and moved to Daniel's head. Castor slapped his face in an effort to bring him round. Robert watched, helpless as Daniel started to wake, murmuring something inaudible, his head lolling to one side. After a couple of minutes he was conscious enough to look about him and take in the situation. When his eyes lit upon Robert, he tried to speak, but couldn't, emotion choking his words.

The twins moved along the line waking the next suspended man, who Robert saw was one of *The Merry Megan*'s crew, Soames, the sailor who had partaken in the blindfold sex after the Tropic of Cancer festivities. Still woozy, Robert managed to speak calmly to Daniel, whose eyes pleaded for an explanation. 'It is alright. We are in the pirate's headquarters. Just try and relax, and do what they ask, and we'll be unharmed. It was the drink. The "Pirate's Kiss". Don't take it again...' His voice trailed off as another fierce wave of nausea rolled over him. Daniel sank back, biting his lip, his eyes brimming with tears.

An almighty shouting started, making Robert look up. It sounded like the rantings of Hamish Dee, who he then saw suspended at the far end of the room. His huge, bear-like body was as naked as the rest of them, a covering of reddish hair sprouted at his chest and led down to his groin, his huge uncut cock lolling between his legs, impressive even when unexcited. His attempts to free himself were totally ineffectual, and after a few minutes of struggling he realised the efficacy of the chains and straps holding him secure. His head fell back and he muttered profane-sunding oaths under his breath

The throbbing in his head was easing slightly, so Robert took the chance to scan the room in more detail. He saw to his surprise that all six harnesses were now filled, all the occupants naked and unable to move, the remaining two harnesses filled by the cousins Martenson and Fitch. Facing the line of strung prisoners was a chair on a dais, with two low-slung stools each side. Around the walls were many chairs and tables, and a variety of wooden contraptions, similar to village stocks, and to vaulting horses. The walls themselves were hung with strange looking whips and bats, as well as numberless dildos and fake genitalia of all shapes and sizes. The air was heavy with some kind of incense, a flowery, exotic smell that pervaded every corner. Candles sat about in niches, giving off an aura of flickering unreality.

Robert guessed that they were in the locked room off the main hall, a room where the pirates presumably carried out sex sessions, or orgies as the Romans called them. Robert had often wondered what one of those ancient happenings would be like. He was about to find out.

The doors at the end of the room opened with a crash, and a stream of pirates entered, all naked except for the leather thongs. In amongst them he saw Felicia looking tanned and aware, and Mother still bedecked with baubles, but with her head strangely bare — the red hair was obviously a wig. Then came Phoenix and Moon Boy and the big bear-like guard from the holding cells. So he was into this as well. Robert stored the information for future further use.

They lined up beneath the chair and dais, and waited. Moments later, de la Hoya entered, wearing nothing but a red satin robe, which flowed about him, billowing as he moved. His body was impressive. His cock was half-hard, bouncing from thigh to thigh as he walked in the room, nodding to each of the gathered pirates, who in turn bowed their heads with a look of deep respect.

Castor and Pollux were seated casually on the two low stools by the chair and they stood as he approached it. Then, with an imperial wave of his hand, de la Hoya sat down, his legs spread wide, his genitalia proudly on display.

At his signal, the pirates gave a murmur of delight and moved in groups around the suspended men, who were all now awake, but in various states of unsettled consciousness. Robert was aware enough to know that a mouth clamped about his cock and began to suck. He raised his head and saw that it was Felicia, his broad mouth working hard, bobbing up and down as he sucked, teasing the swollen helmet, swallowing deeply. His lips pressed around the shaft, his eyes closed in delirious admiration, he went at the task with vigour, enjoying the rigid pole in his mouth.

Other hands moved around Robert's body, stroking and fondling, pinching and kneading his chest and stomach. A tongue started to lick around his exposed arsehole, flicking at the few downy hairs that surrounded the puckered opening, making it clench tightly shut. His whole body was just a mass of sensations which, resist as he might, he had to give in to. A hand grasped his hair and roughly pulled his head back, his mouth dropping open. A cock was being stroked against his lips, its sweet-tasting tip brushed gently against the soft skin. Robert's mind was in a state of turmoil. From inside him, his upper-class breeding told him that this was a stranger about to violate his mouth and he should resist. He didn't know who it was and should therefore refuse, but another, baser, part of him said that it was a cock and it needed to be sucked, and he would enjoy sucking it. He found that the stranger's thighs were now placed on either side of his head, holding him down in a position of total submission. A sudden push, and the decision was made for him, as the solid dick was forced down his throat.

He relaxed his tongue and with an effort tried not to gag. Whoever was in his mouth was a big boy. The cock was wide and thick, the circumference of it filling his mouth totally. Robert tried hard to produce more saliva — the need for lubrication was imperative. Settling into the joy of the blow-job, he let his tongue waver back and forth across the underside of the cock as it slid in and out, feeling the ridges on its length while squeezing his mouth tight about it, creating a warm, wet suction that brought forth a cry of excitement from the owner of the massive prick.

Mouths clamped about his chest and began licking his nipples in unison. A steady rhythm was set up — a hard suck, pulling the tender fleshy lumps into the mouth before biting them with sharp teeth, then licking the skin with flat, broad strokes. With his head held back, and the cock pummelling his throat, Robert couldn't see who was working on him. A small part of him didn't want to know. The feeling that strangers were lavishing attention on him, and enjoying his body, was exquisite. The pumping in his mouth continued ,as did the sucking of his own cock. The tongue action about his arse had ceased, and a finger had started to probe around the crack.

Without warning, the tip of the finger entered Robert's tight hole. It was covered in some sort of slippery goo, and so it slid in easily. Then another and another were inserted, until three fingers stretched and massaged the wrinkled muscle ring, pulling it wide. As they slid away, Robert tried to cry out, the cock in his mouth stopping him, because their place was taken by a swollen cock head. His anal ring had no time to contract as the hardened end pushed inside. Thankfully, it was lubricated too. Robert's arse shut tight about the invading organ, and for a few seconds stayed like that, getting used to the feeling of fullness. After the initial shock, he relaxed slightly and felt the whole ten inches slide in, bit by bit, until it filled his very being. The cock seemed to touch a spot deep in him, bringing tears to his eyes. This multiple attention was astounding. Whoever was doing things to his body was certainly enjoying themselves, and seemed to want Robert to enjoy it too. The cock inside his arse started to fuck, poking hard and fast, each thrust forcing Robert's cock up into Felicia's mouth, who sucked eagerly with each push.

Around the room Robert could hear cries and shouts of pain and delight. Some of the prisoners were accepting their fate, but some were still fighting. He could hear the angry voice of Hamish Dee, crying out all manner of foul names, swearing to kill his violators, but he broke off every now and then to gasp, as he was no doubt being subjected to the same attention as the rest of them. There were sounds of satisfied moans from the direction of the cousins. Robert desperately wanted to know if Daniel was alright, but with his head held firm between the pirate's thighs, he couldn't move.

Robert's sphincter ring was starting to ache a little from the ramming it was being subjected to, and he dearly wanted a break. As if his captors had read his mind, the fucking of his arse and mouth and the sucking of his cock stopped. The mouths on his tits continued ,though, and ,raising his head, he saw Castor and Pollux working in unison, each pulling away on their engorged pricks, both blessed with genitalia of enormous proportions.

Having slid the monster pole from his throat and stepped back, the man moved away, and Robert managed to see that it was one of the Spanish pirates he had seen lounging by the dormitory block. He watched entranced as the pirate walked around the harness and positioned himself at Robert's well-used hole. With one almighty grunt, he pushed his cock inside. Now that Robert's mouth was empty he cried out with alarm. The thickness of this rod was greater than the one before, and even though he had gotten used to that penetration, this was even more painful. The massive girth of the Spaniard's knob stretched his anus wide, wider than he wanted. Again the lubrication helped, but the ploughing of his arse was too much for him to take.

Lifting his head and giving a pleading look at his invader, he raised his voice and called out to him. 'Please stop. I cannot take any more.'

With a heavily accented, dark voice the pirate just laughed. 'Ha. No, I think you like this. My fuck is good. Take it all and shut fucking mouth.' He pounded away with a harsh ferocity that made Robert whimper. Gritting his teeth, he tried to imagine that there was no sensation from his arse, that there was nothing there but a huge empty hole. With a grim determination, Robert looked about him, taking in the carnal scenes which were unfolding everywhere, the flickering shadows giving the appearance of some hellish arena, the heat growing and making the bodies glisten with sweat.

Many of the pirates were young and fit, their bodies browned and well-formed. In spite of himself and the situation he was in, Robert found the sight of so many lithe young men exciting and erotic. The sight of the prisoners lying in the harnesses, unable to resist, unable to stop the useage of their bodies by the man-hungry pirates, was also a turn-on. The picture of the huge, meaty body of Hamish Dee, his thighs spread wide with his cock hanging impressively between them, while the big bear-like pirate repeatedly shoved a long, cock-shaped pole inside his arse, would stay with him for many nights to come. The Scotsman thrashed about, cursing and wriggling, his wrists and ankles held fast.

At Robert's side, Daniel was having an easier time of it. Phoenix and Moon Boy were at either end of the harness. Phoenix was crouched between his thighs, sucking lustily on his bollocks, slipping first one then the other into his mouth, rolling them around his tongue and letting them pop out before doing it again, each time with renewed vigour. Moon Boy was cradling Daniel's head in his arms and kissing him energetically. Robert could see that Daniel was responding to the attention, his cock standing proudly up, twitching with the occasional spasm of enjoyment. He seemed okay, and so Robert lay back his head, mightily relieved.

A sharp slapping noise filled the room, and Robert looked about him to try and see what was happening. It was de la Hoya,who stood on the dais overlooking the sexual carnage and clapped his hands for attention. The pirates stopped whatever they were doing and watched him intently. Some of the prisoners were left with phalluses embedded in them, some lay with another man's cock still in their mouths, waiting for the next move.

De la Hoya stepped down from his vantage-point and walked along the line of harnesses, like a sergeant on parade, inspecting his soldiers for any sign of scruffiness. As he came to each suspended prisoner, he would fondle theircock and balls and nod appreciatively at whichever pirate was nearest, his own knob swaying menacingly before him, half swollen. On reaching Dee, he stopped longer and spoke, his powerful voice resounding around the walls, so that everyone could hear him. 'Surely you will have realised that to struggle is pointless? All you do is wear yourself out, and frankly the sight of a man such as you resisting his fate is more exciting than if you were to lie back and accept it. How does Lucretius put it?' He stood fondling his cock and balls, encouraging them to grow, their length and girth increasing little by little until they stood erect and fearsome.

'"*Suave, mari magno turbantibus aequora ventis, E terra magnum alterius spectare laborem*"... or I should say... *"It is pleasant, when the sea is high and the winds are dashing the waves about, to watch from the land the struggles of another."*' He paused, as if savouring the moment. 'Immortal words and so true.'

Taking hold of Dee's cock, he stroked it lovingly, pulling back the foreskin, revealing the purple glans beneath. With his other hand, he gave the pole in Dee's arse a little slap, making the Scot wince. Dee eyed the pirate with a look of utter venom, gasping a little as he tried not to become aroused by his manipulation. The pirate's touch, however was superlative, and unable to stop it, Dee's cock began to fill and swell with blood, growing harder with each squeeze, until it rose, thick and pale, from the reddish bush of hair at the base, meaty and significant. Even de la Hoya seemed impressed. 'Very good, Mister Dee, you are a quick learner. In the words of the genius Chaucer... *"And gladly wold he lerne, and gladly teche."* I see you have much to show us here between your legs. But I would warrant that you have had little sexual contact with another.'

Dee growled, and spoke roughly in a cracked voice. 'What is that to you?'

'Oh, come now,' said de la Hoya, 'all I wish to know is if this charming creation in my hand has had much experience. You may as well tell me, because you will stay here until I get my answer.'

Taking several deep inhalations of breath to steady his temper, Dee met de la Hoya's gaze. 'Take this fucking thing out of my arse and I'll tell you.'

'Dante, if you would oblige Mister Dee.' The leader nodded at the bearded pirate who slid the pole from Dee's backside. A groan of relief escaped the

Scotsman's lips. 'I had a wee girlie once, she was to be my bride, but she died of pneumonia. We never consumated our passion, no.'

De la Hoya smiled. 'Well it is time we righted that wrong.' He knelt, and swiftly took Dee's cock in his mouth, swallowing the whole shaft, until his nose was buried in the reddish pubes. Dee cried out, his voice cracking with emotion. 'Fucking hell. What are you doing to me, man?'

Without a pause, de la Hoya sucked on that cock, his warm mouth engulfing the Scotsman's meat, his own manhood rising stiffly toward his stomach. Many of the pirates gathered about, watching as their leader demonstrated the art of sucking a cock. He was at times slow and tender, licking around the helmet, then at times furious and energetic, plunging his head down, taking the complete rod down to the back of his throat, pumping it for all he was worth. Sensing that Dee was on the point of ejaculation, he pulled away and wiped his mouth with the back of his hand. 'There, Mister Dee. How was that?'

Dee stared at him, unsure of how to answer. 'I… that was such a feeling like I've never had before.'

'I knew it. Suck a man's cock and his heart and mind will follow.' He looked around the room. 'Would anyone else like to sample Mister Dee's supply?' The twins, Castor and Pollux appeared at his side, like two eager puppies.

Standing aside, he let the twins at Dee's cock, their technique quite unusual — one would linger and lick thoughtfully, while the other would go at it with devilish enthusiasm, swallowing and sucking down the meat in a frenzied asault, swapping positions every few seconds. Hamish Dee didn't know what had hit him. He threw back his head and cried out surprise. Leaving the twins to service Dee, de la Hoya walked along the line until he came to Daniel. Taking the young man's cock in his hand, he examined it with interest, and turned to look at Robert. 'Is this the one you were telling me about on board my ship?'

Robert nodded. 'I see that you have very good taste. Delightful, yes delightful. I should have listened to you. I believe you would have provided an amusing floor-show for me… and my men. Still, perhaps we can save that for another day.' He knelt between Daniel's thighs and gave his cock a lick, sliding his tongue along the shaft, taking the tip into his mouth. 'Hmm, very nice.'

He turned back to Robert. 'I think you may have some competition here, boy.'

Standing, he positioned himself between Robert's thighs. 'I think it is time I had a little fun.' He spoke loudly for the benefit of the room, and a small murmur of appreciation bubbled through the attentive pirates. 'You may carry on. Enjoy!' With a burst of laughs and cheers, the crew went back into action, resuming their passionate encounters with the helpless prisoners. Dee was still lying motionless and, against his better judgement, enjoying the blowing of Castor and Pollux, who were enthusiatically giving their best.

De la Hoya scanned the activity with a condescending smile, and turned back to Robert. The pirate's cock was now solid, towering up from his crotch, the velvet head full and wide. He waved at one of the pirates across the room, who hurried to his side, holding a glass jar of an opaque gel. Smearing it over the whole of his hardened cock, he positioned the tip at Robert's aching hole. 'I know you've been waiting for this, you fucking little bitch.' He sneered demonically, his eyes dark and glowering, and with one brutal thrust, he pushed himself inside. The pain was indescribable. A cry of surprise and agony flew from Robert's throat. It felt like a red hot poker was being buried in him. The swollen stiffness of de la Hoya's cock seemed to want to split him in two. 'This is what you love, isn't it? You want a good hard fucking.' De la Hoya's voice assumed the hard edge that Robert had heard before, and knew that it could spell danger.

'Say it, boy, say what you want.' The pirate gritted his teeth as he fucked, his pounding strokes growing in intensity.

Giving in to the moment, and becoming the sex slave that he now was, Robert drew in a deep breath and cried out in a voice soaked with passion. 'YES! FUCK ME! FUCK ME LIKE A DIRTY WHORE! OH GOD, FUCK ME!'

De la Hoya's eyes grew wide, this had done the trick. He slammed harder and harder into Robert, filling him up, his heavy bollocks slapping against the sweaty arse cheeks, in total control over the boy he had under him. His domination was complete. This was the ultimate joy in life, to fuck the life out of a captive boy, a boy who couldn't resist, who was screaming for mercy. This was it. His deep thrusting became faster. He screwed up his face and began to breath noisily. Robert could see that he was about to explode. It was time to help him along. 'Yes... come on... fuck my arse. Come on, shoot your spunk in me... oh yes!'

The pirate threw back his head and gave a cry, an almost primeval scream from the depths of his being, as he pulled out and came over Robert's stomach, a shower of milky come streaked across his cock and belly, an endless stream, pumping six or seven great spurts of release, his hands grasping the harness chains, his eyes squeezed tightly shut. Eventually, as the last few drops had spattered onto Robert's balls, he hung his head and began to breathe more slowly, beads of sweat dripping down his forehead and sliding from the end of his nose, mingling with the newly shot spunk.

Robert squirmed about in his harness, rattling the chains. 'For God's sake, let me come. Please let me out of here. I want to wank myself off.' De la Hoya raised his eyes and leant forward, unbuckling the leather straps about Robert's wrists. Grasping his cock, it took only a few swift jerks for him to coax the boiling semen out. It erupted in a lava flow of orgasmic joy. Several deep groans of amazement escaped as Robert climaxed, shooting out over his own stomach, even reaching his throat, landing with a plop among de la Hoya's thick juice.

The pirate stood back, his cock still fairly engorged, and moved slowly over to his chair. With a grunt of effort he stepped up on the dais and slumped into his chair, cloak spread wide, cock slapping against his thigh.

From all around the room were coming similar cries and noises.: the sounds of multiple orgasms, of the climaxing of many men. The air was filled with the bitter, waxy smell of come, as pirates and prisoners shot their loads. A giant cry of release came tumbling from Hamish Dee, as he gave in to the sensations he was actually now enjoying and came in waves. Castor and Pollux eased the spunk from his cock with eager hands.

Robert pulled himself up and with numbed fingers managed to unfasten the straps at his ankles and lever himself down, his legs a little unsteady. Holding onto the supporting chain for a moment, he crossed to Daniel, who was lying unattended and obviously in need of release. Crouching between his spread legs, Robert nestled himself in his groin and inhaled. The smell of a man would never cease to excite him. Daniel, who had been lying back with his eyes closed, raised his head and stared down at Robert, unable to comprehend who was there. With a shake of his head, his vision cleared and he realised who it was between his trembling thighs. 'Robert, thank God. Get me out of here.'

'In a moment. Now listen to me.' Robert's harsh tone made him blink in surprise. 'Do not touch that rum drink. It was drugged somehow. Tell the others when you're back in the cells. When they come for us again, pretend to be... ' A warm hand was placed on Robert's neck and he jumped.

'And what are you doing?' De la Hoya, already recovered and seemingly in fine spirits, stood at Robert's elbow.

'Helping Daniel off. He seems to have been forgotten.' Inclining his head, he nuzzled his face into the bush of curly hair around Daniel's cock and balls. With his tongue, he played around the bollocks in their sac, hanging low and large. Opening his mouth, he slipped one, then the other inside, swirling them around in the enveloping warmth. Daniel threw back his head and gave out a low, whining moan, the suction on his bollocks an absolute delight. Robert let each ball plop out of his mouth, then let his tongue wander up the shaft of Daniel's cock. With his fist, he gripped the base, ensuring the maximum state of hard readiness.

Robert looked up along Daniel's body, over the twitching prick and the firm stomach to the rising and falling mounds of muscle at his chest. He had Daniel in his power and the feeling was strangely erotic. He could do anything he wanted, and the young man wouldn't be able to stop him. In a flash of understanding, he could see why de la Hoya had gone to so much trouble drugging the men and having them brought to this purpose-made dungeon. To have the fate of another in your hands, and to have the ability to degrade or humiliate them at will, was a powerful aphrodisiac.

He could see that Daniel was desperate to come, his eyes now holding him in a pleading, but strong gaze. Robert decided that Daniel had waited long enough. With a sharp intake of breath, he guided the mushroom-shaped head of the cock into his mouth, taking it in and encircling it with his experienced tongue. Each swirl of his tongue provoked a sigh from Daniel. Sliding more of the shaft into his mouth, Robert knelt forward on his haunches, knowing that his oral actions were as wonderful to Daniel as they were to himself. In one fast movement, he buried the cock deep in his throat, his nose resting among the pubes, pleased that it wasn't going to choke him.

The climax came unexpectedly. Daniel's cock twitched suddenly and a warm gush of salty sperm exploded against the back of Robert's throat. Gulping hard, he swallowed every last drop. Daniel gave a quiet whimper of exhaustion. De la Hoya patted Robert on the head and whispered quietly in his ear. 'Very good. I can see why your friend here is very fond of you. Come now. Time for supper.' He put a hand under Robert's arm and led him from the room. As they passed each of the harnesses, groups of pirates were unbuckling the restraints, helping the unstable prisoners to their feet and, after securing their hands behind their backs, helping them up the stairs and out to the holding cells. Robert was surprised to see Hamish Dee going quietly, without causing any sign of a commotion, his head hanging low and dejected. Something must have broken in his mind, for a man such as Dee to accept his fate without a fight.

On entering the main hall, Robert was handed his clothes by Mother, who was standing by a large wooden frame on which were hanging the clothes of the pirates who had entered the dungeon. Mother then followed them into the dining room, seating himself by Robert's side at the polished mahogany dining table. De la Hoya, still in his flowing red robe, sat at its head and waited patiently as various crew members filed in and sat around the table, its polished surface laden with cut-glass and silver.

Dinner itself was a strangely muted affair, everyone eating with gusto, but with very little conversation. De la Hoya held court, watching amused as his piratical courtiers filled themselves with delicious food and wine. Behind de la Hoya, an ornate ormulu clock struck ten, and with a wave of his hand, the pirate stood and swept majestically from the room, his cloak billowing behind his huge, muscular frame.

As the door closed on him, the crew seemed to breathe a collective sigh of relief, and small-talk started among various groups of the men. Robert turned to Mother, who was sitting, silently watching him out of the corner of his eye. 'Well, that was an interesting, not to say exhausting ,experience.'

Mother chuckled and ran his fingers over his bald head, and then fiddled with one of his colourful beaded ear-rings. 'The Captain has a vivid imagination.'

'He certainly does.' Robert cleared his throat, and twisted round in his chair to face the Carib henchman. 'How often does this kind of thing happen?' It would be useful information to possess.

'It depends on how the master feels. But usually every couple of days. Last year he held a gathering every night for a week. The men were utterly spent, but he seemed to want to go on forever. I don't know where he gets his energy from.'

That was what Robert wanted to know. If de la Hoya planned another such sex session in a day or two, then hopefully Daniel would have primed the rest of the prisoners, and told them about the danger of drinking the "Pirate's Kiss". As there would be no way to get to them and talk directly, he would have to keep his fingers crossed, and trust that Daniel had done what was needed.

As he looked about the dining room, watching the pirates in various cov-ersational groups, he felt a wave of tiredness sweep over him. Realising that he needed a good night's sleep, he made his excuses to Mother and trod wearily upstairs, pushed open the bedroom door, and fell onto the bed, sleep coming the moment his head hit the pillow.

The next day Robert saw neither sight nor sound of his pirate captor. He sat in the dining room alone at breakfast, and ate his coddled eggs in silent contemplation. Strolling out on the front veranda, he was greeted by the sight of a hive of frenzied activity aboard the wreck of *The Merry Megan*, as pirates clambered about her, unloading weapons and canons, winching them into smaller boats and rowing them ashore. All available hands seemed to be engaged on this job, busily pillaging and stripping the poor vessel of anything of any worth. He watched ominously as a small boat carrying half a dozen barrels of gunpowder were rowed out to the stricken ship and hauled aboard. It looked like the end for the *Megan*, and Robert was saddened. He had enjoyed his time aboard her, even though he had been on her by necessity rather than his own choice.

A thought struck Robert and, looking about to see if he was being watched, he slipped quietly off the veranda and crept round the far side of the house. Stopping at the end of the wall, he could see that the pirate's dormitory block was deserted. Hoping that the entire crew were busy working down at the bay, he tentatively made his way to the corner of the block. Peering in through the end window, he could see no-one. The main door was ajar, and so, holding his breath, he slid inside. The block was functionally furnished, with basic wooden tables and chairs. The rooms had bunk beds. The walls were hung with posters and illustrations torn from books, giving the place an eerie, half-finished atmosphere.

Robert rifled through bags and trunks but could find nothing of use. He had silently, perhaps foolishly, hoped that he might find a spare set of keys. Assuming that a continued search would prove fruitless, he slipped outside and, using overgrown foliage for cover, crept down to the edge of the holding cells. Just one pirate was on guard, the Spaniard who had vigourously fucked Robert the previous evening.

He had to try and speak to Daniel, or to any of the prisoners he could. Picking up a small stone, and crossing his fingers for luck, Robert threw it with all his strength into the bushes at the far side of the path. The pirate looked up and, cocking his musket, cautiously went to see what had made the noise. As he disppeared into the greenery, Robert stood on tiptoe and squinted into the Stygian darkness of the cell window. 'Can anybody hear me? Ho there!'

'Who is that?' A strained voice came floating through the bars. 'It's Robert Marchant. I do not have much time. Listen carefully. The next time they bring you that rum drink, pretend to take it, and act as if drugged. We have to get away from here, and during the sex sessions is their most vulnerable time. Wait for my signal, and be ready to attack. Tell the others.'

The voice was silent for a moment. 'I will. But I hope you are right. From what Good has told me, I am not looking forward to being violated by these brigands.'

Robert wasn't sure if he recognised the voice. 'Who is that?'

'It is Tupton. Benjamin Tupton.' Robert immediately knew him as one of the captured merchants. 'Thank God my wife escaped in that boat, before these fiends got hold of her. She would have rather died than let herself be used by them.'

A rustle of leaves from beyond the path meant that the Spaniard was probably returning. 'Just be ready.' Robert ducked away and scooted round the side of the cells. After a few moments, he pursed his lips nonchalantly and whistled a discordant tune, affected an air of disinterest and strolled around the corner, nodding at the Spaniard as he passed. The pirate grinned and licked his lips. 'You like?' he said leerily, grabbing hold of his crotch and squeezing it. Ignoring him, Robert made his way back to the house.

The discovery of de la Hoya's library made Robert's afternoon pass a little more quickly. Tucked away down a side corridor was a door that he hadn't tried before. As he entered, Robert caught his breath. The room was lined with shelves from floor to ceiling, all stacked with a multitude of impressive volumes.

Crossing to one shelf, he pulled out a fascinating selection of books, including a dusty edition of Samuel Pepys diaries, Milton's "Paradise Lost", and a copy of the "Satires" of Juvenal. Seating himself in a comfortable leather armchair, he quite lost himself in these volumes, until a fierce shouting from outside pulled him back to the present. Standing, Robert noticed that the room had grown quite dark, so he must have been immersed in his literature for most of the afternoon. Putting the work of his favourite Roman satirist down, he hurried from the room and out onto the veranda.

It seemed as though all of the pirate crew were gathered on the beach, the atmosphere among them lighthearted and jovial. One of the rowing boats was floating alongside *The Merry Megan*, and standing in the boat was Dante, the bearded, bear-like pirate, waving a fearsome flaming torch. Robert saw de la Hoya on the beach, surrounded by his loyal men, chatting to them amiably. All of a sudden the gathered crew fell silent, and de la Hoya stepped forward out of the crowd. He raised his hand and gestured toward Dante, who, with a cry of triumph, threw the flaming torch onto the deck of the *Megan*. Jumping down, he grabbed the oars of the boat and began rowing, great muscular strokes, pulling himself away from the powderkeg aboard the ship. He was nearing the shore when an almighty explosion rocked the hull, a deafening roar, and a colossal ball of fire rolled about the vessel. It would now burn for a couple of days at least.

The crew raised their weapons and hats and cheered, a victorious cry of almost satanic satisfaction. Their delight at the destruction of such a friendly ship made Robert's stomach churn. It made him even more determined to get away from their clutches as soon as possible, and by whatever means.

Seating himself on the veranda and viewing the sickening scene, Robert tried to formulate a plan. Their escape would have to be when the pirates were at their most vulnerable. He decided that the best time would be when they were half-naked and ready for one of their sex sessions in the dungeon. Suerly then their minds would be more concentrated on cock and arse than on security.

A deep mumbling erupted from the men on the beach and Robert looked up. He saw de la Hoya pointing at him and waving his hand in the direction of the holding cells. It looked like the jubilant buccaneers were in the mood for one of their gatherings tonight. This could be it. Steeling himself and closing his eyes, he whispered a short prayer to whoever was listening on high. 'Please help us. I know we haven't been on the best of terms so far... but, if you can hear me, we need your help. We have to get away from here tonight. Please... I know it is a lot to ask, but tonight we may well be fighting for our lives.'

THIRTEEN

The mumblings of the sex-obsessed pirates getting ominously closer, Robert swiftly entered the house and ran up to his room. Picking up a book on the dressing table, he settled himself into a chair and made a pretence of reading. Minutes later his door swung open. Mother came in carrying a tray with a jug of the creamy "Pirate's Kiss".

'A little something for you to drink. I know you must be thirsty.' He placed the tray carefully down by Robert's elbow and poured a frothy goblet-full. Holding it out to Robert, he stood back, hands on hips expectantly.

'Thank you. I will have some shortly.' He put down the goblet and carried on pretending to read. After a few moments he looked up over the leather-bound volume and saw that Mother had slipped away. Throwing the book on the bed, he grabbed up the goblet and tray, and carried them into the ante-room, where his hip-bath stood, still filled with his morning's bath water. With a crow of suppressed pleasure, he emptied the entire contents into the soapy froth.

Next, pulling off all his clothes, but still wearing his sandals, he lay back on the bed and closed his eyes. He didn't know how long he would have to wait before someone collected him, but he would have to be patient. Robert guessed that half an hour had elapsed before he heard his door click open, and footsteps cross the floor. Two pairs of strong hands manhandled him to his feet and then carried his limp body out and down the stairs, one holding his feet, the other with his hands under the arms. Out of the corner of his eye he saw that he was being carried by Dante and the Spaniard, who both kept up a stream of babbling chat all the time. Dante appeared to be wearing just his leather thong, Robert could feel the tickling hairs of his chest as they walked. At the foot of the staircase, they turned along the corridor and headed toward the dungeon door. Squinting carefully, Robert could see the wooden rack of clothes standing nearby. Again he prayed that this dangerous plan would work.

'Strap them in well.' Felicia's voice rang out. Through his barely opened eyes, Robert saw six other prisoners being carried down the corridor, all hanging limply, Daniel at the head of the line, as well as Third Officer Quilter, Tasker, Barnes, Hamish Dee and Zenos the cook.

With a cry of anger, Robert wrestled himself free from the grip of the two pirates. 'NOW!', he yelled. 'GET THEM!' The other six prisoners scrambled to their feet, the shock of their awakening surprising their captors. Then all hell broke loose.

Dante realised what was happening and threw his arms about Robert's neck. With a swift up-thrust, Robert parried the grip and, spinning round, aimed a punch at the man's stomach. Winded, he fell back on a chair, which smashed to pieces, sending the pirate sprawling in a heap. He lay inert, a large bloody gash on his forehead. The Spaniard gave a blood-curdling scream and threw himself at Robert, his hands outstretched. Leaping to one side, Robert pushed the pirate in the ribs. Turning his head, he saw a heavy, decorated vase on a pedestal. Grabbing it, he brought it down sharply on the Spaniard's head with a resounding thud. Splinters of china showered his body, and the impact laid him out cold.

Looking up, he saw that the rest of the prisoners were also fighting well. Daniel had one of the pirates in a neck hold and was repeatedly punching him in the face. Blood streamed from his nose, and over Daniel's fist. The element of surprise had worked to their advantage. Tasker and Barnes had also used vases and chairs as weapons and had battered their captors into unconciousness. Knowing that they currently had the upper hand, Robert turned back to the clothes rack and began hurriedly searching for Dante's keys. After a few short moments, he heard a satisfying rattling noise, and his fingers twined around the life-saving bunch.

'Let's go!' Robert span on his heels, and saw the last pirate fall to the floor, knocked out by a ferocious punch to the jaw by the swarthy Zenos. 'The cells. We must rescue the others.' Robert was in overdrive now, waves of adrenalin pumped round his system, clearing his mind, strengthening his resolve to win. 'Take those guns, we may need them.' He nodded to a pile of muskets lying alongside the front door, grabbed one tightly, and without a look back, ran outside. The light was now almost gone, which Robert was thankful for. The evening darkness would provide much-needed cover. A sudden cacophany of shouting came from inside the house. 'Quick, the game is up, they know we have escaped. Daniel, take these keys and unlock the others. The rest of you take cover behind the cell building. They shouldn't see you there. I'll try and gain us some time.' The five naked but determined men ran for cover, throwing themselves behind the cell block, into the comforting shadows it provided.

Panting heavily, Robert dived behind a water barrel and cocked his musket, aiming at the front door of the house with studied precision. A distant memory of grouse shooting at Marchant Hall flitted across his mind, the camaraderie, the thrill of the hunt. Now Robert was on a hunt of a different kind. This time his life hung in the balance. Framed in the doorway stood de la Hoya, furious, a expression of pure hatred contorting his features. Lifting his head, he bellowed up at the darkening sky. 'Where are you? I shall find you all... and when I do I shall kill you.'

With trembling hands, Robert took aim. He didn't want to kill de la Hoya, but he had to warn the pirates off, and earn a little breathing space. If they could escape into the jungle, they would be impossible to track. All they need do was keep hidden for a day or two and then, at night, make off with the pirate's ship. There would be enough experienced sailors amongst them to do it, Robert hoped.

His fingers squeezed about the trigger and with an ear-shattering retort, he fired. De la Hoya clutched at his shoulder and fell back against the door frame, gouts of blood pumping between his clenched fingers. Chaos seemed to be reigning inside the house, and with a quick glance about him, Robert dashed across to the holding cells. Daniel had succeeded in finding the correct key and was unlocking the heavy, studded door. Pushing it wide, Daniel called out to the gloomy interior. 'Come on. We have made a break for it. As quick as you can. Move!' A stream of around a dozen men burst out through the door, all naked, but too caught up with the delirium of escape to care. Robert wondered if he had ever seen such a bizarre sight — twenty or so men, all naked, all scared for their lives, running frenziedly into the jungle beyond. 'Wait for us in the first clearing you find, we will be with you as soon as we can.' Robert barked out this order, and watched the men disappear into the swathe of vegetation.

Daniel grabbed an oil-lamp from the outside of the door, and ran to

Robert's side. 'That's everyone out now. How many firearms do we have?'

'About ten in all. We will have to make each weapon count, as we don't know what we will find out there in the jungle. I wish we'd had time to grab some clothes. I know that we have all spent much time naked these last few days, but I think we'll need protection for our bodies in the forest. Oh well, at least we have gotten away....' His voice trailed off as a shot rang out across the clearing. One of the pirates was hanging out of an upper storey window, and had aimed at the two escapees.

Daniel collapsed with a scream of terror and agony. Blood spouted from his thigh, where the bullet had entered, cutting through muscle and sinew. Horrified, Robert put his arm around his shoulder and helped him to his feet. Tears of pain were streaming down the poor man's face. 'Come on... we have to get into the forest. Then I can check your wounds.' Sweating with the effort, he hauled Daniel along the path into the first overhanging area of jungle greenery. Pushing his way past bushes and shrubs, Robert was grateful for the pool of light afforded by the oil-lamp that Daniel still tenaciously held before them. For a good few hundred yards, Robert pushed his way deeper into the undergrowth, the shouts from the pirate crew growing fainter with each lumbering step. A few steps further on they emerged from the densely packed trees into a small clearing, faintly lit by a handful of twinkling stars.

Many of the men were slumped in attitudes of relief and exhaustion, many not bothering to cover up their embarrassed nakedness, and some of them looked up expectantly as the two men arrived.

As Robert helped Daniel to the ground, resting his head against a boulder, Hamish Dee crawled up to his side and tapped him on the shoulder. 'Is he alright? It looks like he has lost a lot of blood.'

Robert held the oil-lamp near Daniel's thigh and saw that, although it looked like an extremely nasty wound, the bullet had only gone straight through the fleshy part of his leg, avoiding the bone. With some effort he should still be able to walk. 'We need to stop the blood flow. Any suggestions?'

Dee stood and crossed to the edge of the clearing, crouched and ripped up a long frond of green leaf, and knelt by Daniel's side. 'This should do it. It is strong enough not to break and I should be able to tie a knot in it, too.' With deft fingers he fastened the makeshift tourniquet about the sailor's leg, above the wound, pulling it tight to keep the flow of blood to a minimum.

Robert crossed to the far side of the clearing, beckoned to Dee, Quilter, Barnes, Tasker and Tupton and gestured for them all to sit. Settling himself on his knees, adjusting his cock and balls comfortably, he started to discuss their options.

'It seems fairly certain that if we stay in the forest, the pirates won't come after us. They appear to be frightened of the natives.'

Barnes raised his head nervously. 'Natives? Don't say that we could be captured again?'

'It is a distinct possibility. But we are armed, remember. I think our weapons are a match for anything that a bunch of spear-carrying islanders can throw at us. Our most immediate problem is food and water. If we can bear it, I think we should stay in this clearing for the night. A roaring fire should keep any stray animals away from us, and in the morning we can search for fruit and berries. We may even chance across some wild game. Our main problem is how to proceed to our freedom. I think we should remain around here for a couple of days, then try and capture *The War Queen*. I am sure we could get her away from the island, if we all did our best. Any thoughts, gentlemen?'

Nathaniel Tasker raised his hand gingerly. 'Might I make a suggestion?'

'By all means. All ideas will be gladly accepted.'

He shifted about on the scrubby ground, pulling his legs round under him. 'Well, I am something of a cartographer. When I knew that I had gotten a berth aboard the *Megan*, I made the effort to collect all maps and books about where we were going in the Indies. During our voyage I studied all the various islands we might come across. I would hazard a guess that we are either on St Martin's Isle or Baruga.'

Robert sat up, intrigued. 'I think I can help... we are on Baruga. De la Hoya told me the day we arrived.'

'Excellent. Then if we can make it, I believe there is a small township on the north of the island, called Peterstown. It had a profitable harbour for a few years while tropical fruits were being exported from there. It fell into disrepair when the fruit supplies were completely decimated. Some people still happily live there. If we could find our way to that township maybe we could get a boat.'

A general nodding and murmuring of assent was the response. 'I think that could be our way off this accursed island. Well done, Nathaniel. You may well have saved our skins. How long do you think it would take to get there?'

Tasker scratched his chin pensively. 'If we can find our way through the jungle, I would say no more than three days trek. It will be risky, but I think we should try it.'

A quick glance around the circle showed everyone's agreement to this plan. Levering himself to his feet, Robert became decisive again. 'Right. We will sleep here tonight. At first light, we will set out, heading north. With the sun's help, we should be able to work out which direction we are heading in. We will take it nice and slow, so that Mister Good is not too worn out by our journey. Barnes and Tupton, can you set about lighting a fire? There must be some wood around — we will be able to light it from the oil-lamp. But I want to try and save as much of the oil as possible. It may be our only source of light in the nights to come.'

A general hubbub of activity started as Barnes and Tupton scrambled about, building a sizeable cone of wood and twigs. Dee crouched down by Daniel and tenderly wiped his sweat-covered forehead.

'How is he?' Robert knelt by Dee and took Daniel's hand. It felt cold and clammy, lifeless, like a corpse.

'Not good. I think we should leave him behind.' The Scotsman gave Robert a resigned stare. 'He'll slow us down. We do not need burdens such as this poor laddie.'

Standing, pulling himself to his full height, Robert spoke with a quiet intensity. 'He is coming with us. Even if I have to carry him myself. Is that clear?'

Dee groaned as he stood, folding his arms and staring inquisitively at the defiant young man before him. 'You have spirit, I will say that for you. I was led to believe by Governor Trench that you were nothing but a wastrel, a good-for-nothing pervert who delighted in corrupting others, including innocent children. But after all I've seen here lately, I have to change my mind. We wouldn't have gotten free from those bastards if it wasn't for you. Thank you.'

Touched by Dee's heartfelt words, Robert put out a hand. 'Let that be a lesson to you, Mister Dee. Never judge a man by what others say about him. I should try and get some sleep, tomorrow will be a long day.' Taking the proffered hand, Dee's grasp was firm and warm. Then he lay down by the fire, his arm under his head for comfort. Robert looked the man over, and realised that you could misjudge someone very easily. On first appearance, Dee seemed an unfriendly, miserable individual. Anyone would become so, thought Robert, after many hours in Trench's company. This great, red-haired bear of a man had hidden depths. Perhaps his ordeal at the hands of de la Hoya had changed him, made him look at his unremarkable existence with a different perspective. Watching the Scot lying on the harsh ground in front of him, Robert could see the advantages of becoming romantically involved with a man like Dee. He was strong and manful, he would always be there to protect you, his huge arms enfolding your smaller body, and he would probably be a good lover. He had certainly seemed to enjoy the cock-sucking that the twins had given him.

As he watched, the Scot had drifted off into a restless slumber, his head moving from side to side, mumbled, indecipherable words coming from his twitching lips. Robert wondered if he was having an erotic dream, because the big man's cock started to swell. From its slumbering position, lolling against his hairy thigh, it began to grow, blood flowing effortlessly into the pale shaft, making it stand out from his bushy crotch, until it towered up, thick and quivering, a long shadow thrown across his belly by the flickering firelight. Robert's own cock began to stiffen at this sight. He had never really found Dee to be his idea of an attractive man, but something in his newly-revealed nature appealed to him. Glancing about the clearing, Robert saw that most of the men were asleep. Zenos and Quilter were nestled in each other's arms for support, a hand curled around the other's hard cock, each giving the other gentle coaxing strokes. The supposed cousins, Martenson and Fitch, had crawled to the clearing's farthest extremity and were lying in the flickering shadow of a huge boulder, Martenson's head in Fitch's lap, his mouth gently sucking at the swollen cock that stood there.

Against his better judgement, Robert squatted on his haunches by the side of Dee. The Scot gave a few gutteral snores and rolled over onto his back, his hands falling flaccidly across his chest. This is dangerous and stupid, Robert said quietly to himself, but the sight of this tremendous prick, stiff and inviting, was too much. Cautiously, he let the tips of his fingers stroke the shaft, trailing from the massive head down to the thick base, circling the shaft with his fist and gently pulling back the foreskin. Dee shuddered in his sleep and gave a muted snore.

Bending forward, Robert moved his mouth closer to the object of his desire and let his lips close around the bulbous head, his tongue warm and active, flicking about the tiny slit. Robert trembled with supressed excitement. The thought that Dee, or any of the others, could wake and see what he was doing gave him a vicarious thrill. Closing his mind to such thoughts, he let his mouth slide down the body of Dee's cock, enjoying the fullness of his throat, letting it completely stuff him, the massive end pushing against his tonsils. Then, letting all his inhibitions and natural reticence vanish, he started to suck lustily on the cock, slurping and licking, sliding up and down its impressive length, now not caring if Dee did wake up.

He was ferocious and tender, frenzied and gentle, his lips and tongue working wonders on the sleeping man's rigid dick. It hardly seemed that he had started when he felt the shaft tighten and the Scot came, pouring out his juice in regular spurts. Robert pulled back and let the stream shoot over his face, each bolt of come landing with a gentle slap.

Standing and waiting for his own cock to subside, Robert looked down at the slumbering giant. Was that a flicker of a smile on his face?

Later, a sharp, jabbing sensation in the lower-back woke Robert. Golden-orange rays of sunlight were beginning to appear through the trees. Opening his eyes and rubbing them with the heel of his palm, he sat up and gulped.

They were surrounded.

A fierce, dark-skinned native was towering above him, a razor-sharp spear poking him awake. With a cry of anger, Robert felt around for his rifle. It was gone. Jumping to his feet, he saw with a great surge of fury and regret that about forty native Barugans were standing menacingly around the group, easily outnumbering them. They must have come upon them in the early dawn, taken their weapons, and now had the upper hand. Cursing himself for his stupidity in not having someone stay awake to keep watch, he knew that the next few moments were going to be exceedingly tricky.

Keeping his hands spread wide, and with a beaming smile, Robert bowed his head and said slowly, 'We are your friends... We mean you no harm.' Putting out his hand in the manner of a courteous handshake, he watched the native, suspicion and distrust corrugating his features. Robert had never seen anyone like this before. The native was tall, taller than Robert, with a dark, almost black skin, a headress of woven leaves hanging down about his face. He appeared to be the leader, as none of the others wore this kind of apparel. The base of his nose was pierced with a small, sharp bone resembling a shark's tooth. Bare-chested, he wore a short, sparse grassy skirt, which was coloured with dyes, and which rustled as he moved, the gaps in the grassy strips revealing his sizeable genitalia beneath.

The only response to Robert's friendly greeting was to point his spear at his stomach, and, after looking Robert's naked body over, he gestured toward the forest with his head. In a ringing tone, the native spoke to the other islanders, who, with angry gesticulations, pulled the awakening men to their feet.

'We would appear to be surrounded.' Robert addressed the naked, shaken crew. 'Make no sudden movements. We need to convice them that we are friendly and not a danger to them.' Keeping his arms by his side, Robert followed the native who had started to cross the clearing, stalking into the dense jungle ahead. The men had no choice but to follow, the glistening blades of the spears pointing the way. Barnes and Tasker helped to carry Daniel, who seemed a little brighter this morning and was able to walk slowly, with a limping gait.

The lush vegetation of the forest grew sparser the further they walked, until after about half an hour of tramping, the trees stopped and the men were amazed at the sight that greeted them. A vast clearing, filled with huts made from branches, twigs and mud, lay before them. Robert counted about twenty of these primitive dwellings and was impressed by their solidity, considering the raw materials that the natives had to work with. The huts appeared to radiate around a central space, in the centre of which was a large ornate wooden pole, carved from a tree and covered with various native images, many of them seemingly depicting sexual acts. Robert's educated guess was that the pole was some kind of totem, or fertility symbol. Tied around the pole with lengths of twine were strangely shaped pieces of a rough brownish material. As the men were led down into the village, Robert swallowed hard. The pieces of material were of a more sinister and frightening nature. His gut reaction told him that they were patches of flayed human skin.

Around the base of the totem was a gruesome collection of human bones, including a couple of skulls, one of which still had areas of dessicated skin hanging from it. Robert knew that the men now found themselves in far greater peril than they ever were at the hands of the pirates. If these natives turned out to be headhunters or cannibals, then their lives lay in the balance. Stopping by the totem, Robert cleared his throat, wanting the attention of the leader. 'Excuse me.' The chief turned and said something in his native Barugan. Again spreading his arms wide, then crossing his chest with them, Robert spoke clearly and with a broad smile. 'We are your friends. We mean you no harm.'

'I know what you say.' A gasp of surprise escaped from the men.

'You can speak English?' Robert was equally stunned by the chief's utterance.

'I speak little. I understand more.' His voice was rich and mesmeric, his eyes wide and piercing.

'But where did you learn to speak our language?' Any chance of persuading these Barugans of their good intentions had to be taken, and gaining the trust of the leader was vital.

'I work sometime before at Peterstown. I pick fruit. When settlers go away, I come back to my people.'

The knowledge that the chief had spent time among educated people meant that he might be willing to listen to their story, and to sympathise with their plight. 'That is very interesting. My name is Robert, by the way. I assume you are the leader of these people?'

The chief drew himself up to his full height, and raised his spear above his leaf-bedecked head. 'I am Ngara, leader of my people. You are slaves. We keep you here.'

'But, please...' Robert's anguished plea was cut short.

Ngara gave a cursory order to the rest of the natives, who began to herd the men toward two of the huts on the far side of the village clearing. 'You are leader? You stay.' A bony finger was pointed at Robert. The commanding tone showed who was in control.

'Just do as they want. We will be alright.' He watched as the men were split into two groups and hustled into the huts. Daniel gave Robert a look of bleak resignation before he, Tasker and Barnes were finally ushered inside. Two statuesque natives stood guard by the flimsy doors, spears in hand.

Ngara turned his back and walked toward a larger hut opposite the totem. Pausing at the door, he waited for Robert to follow. Pushing aside the woven grass door, he entered, Robert tentatively stepping after him.

Inside were a few rudimentary blankets scattered on the ground, some rough-hewn wooden bowls and a cage-like structure made out of poles, from which hung a handful of human skulls, the eye sockets filled with small candles, glowing with an eerie, inhuman light.

Ngara gestured to a highly coloured blanket, and sat cross-legged upon it, his grassy skirt spreading about his thighs. As he eased himself down opposite, Robert could see that the chief's cock and bollocks were visible, but he tried to ignore the sight of them. Right now he had to concentratre on getting his men away from their Barugan captors.

Opening his mouth to speak, Robert was halted by Ngara's raised hand, and so he sat waiting for the chief's next move. 'Where you come from?' Ngara's face was grimly set, his eyes now inquisitive slits.

'Our ship was captured by a band of pirates who live on the south coast of this island. We were held prisoner, and forced to... er... forced to keep them entertained. We managed to escape from them last night, but as you see we were unable to find our clothes. I don't suppose you could get me and the others something to wear? It is becoming rather tedious to be constantly naked.' He gave what he hoped was a winning smile and waited for an answer.

Ngara closed his eyes, and swayed his body back and forth for a few moments, deep in thought. Snapping open his eyes, he spoke with a voice now hard and determined. 'The men from south very bad. They kill many of my people, who go near. Some they torture and send back broken. I want revenge.'

This was just what Robert wanted to hear. 'I could help you. I know when they are at their weakest. With the help of my men you could plan an attack. Do you still have our weapons?'

'I do. Maybe. I will think. I do not want more of my men killed. We are smaller now. Tell me what they do to you.'

It was a tough decision. Should Robert tell Ngara exactly what de la Hoya and his crew did to the prisoners? Was this native tribesman worldy enough to understand the details of their sexual desires? He mentally crossed his fingers and spoke. 'They used us for sex. We were kept at their beck and call to be used in any way they wanted. Do you understand?'

Ngara nodded his head slowly. 'You are fuck. Yes?'

'Yes, I suppose so.' The chief nodded again. Strangely, he seemed to know what Robert was telling him.

'You like fuck?' This was an unexpected question, one that Robert was unsure how to answer. Deciding that honesty would be the best approach, he gave a wry smile and said, 'Yes, I do. And so do many of the men in my crew.'

Sitting forward, Ngara gave Robert a direct, penetrating stare, unnerving in its intensity. 'In Peterstown, I have fuck. Many man pay for me to fuck. I make much gold. They like my fuck.' He reached down and pulled aside the grass skirt at his groin, and somewhat proudly displayed his cock and balls more fully. Robert's eyes grew wide with astonishment. The chief's equipment seemed of an unreal size. The cock which was sitting limply in Ngara's hand was of a marvellous length, at least twelve inches, uncircumcised, but with a foreskin that was pulled back slightly, showing a pink head beneath. The bollocks were also immense. Round and pendulous, they hung in a wrinkled, hairless sac, the size of two small oranges. Robert had to whistle quietly in appreciation. In his recent experience he had seen and sucked some very large cocks, but this was astounding. He wondered whether it grew much in its aroused state or just filled up and stayed roughly the same dimension. Deep in his being, Robert wanted to know for sure. He wanted to find out how a black cock would feel and taste.

A soft murmuring came from Ngara's throat as he slapped his hand under the slumbering penis, bouncing it up and down on his palm, watching with pride as it began to swell and harden before Robert's astonished gaze. The foreskin shrank back a little, the pinky head poking out more, the slit at its tip clearly visible. Slowly and surely, the prick continued to grow, curving up and away from Ngara's crotch, as the chief wrapped his fist about it and started to stroke it, lovingly and with great rasping breaths. This sight was too much for Robert, who sat back on his heels, his cock rapidly growing. He was very proud and happy with his own manhood, but he felt totally dwarfed by this black-skinned monster. He noted with some trepidation that Ngara was staring down at Robert's hardening cock. 'Come.' Ngara spoke quietly but with a force that couldn't be ignored. Robert stood and crossed the floor of the hut, standing at Ngara's side. The chief turned his head and with one movement swallowed Robert's cock. His lips clamped about the base, tightening and causing it to harden more. The desire to pinch himself, and prove that this whole weird scenario wasn't actually happening was very strong.

The feelings coming from his cock were mind-blowing. Whether Ngara had sex for pleasure or just profit, Robert knew not, but he certainly did it expertly. His thick lips slid along the swollen shaft, sucking hard, letting the head slip from his mouth, and then taking it deeply down once more, accompanied by a satisfied sigh.

Robert could feel the tongue writhing against the underside of his shaft. Sometimes it protruded from his mouth and lathered his hanging balls, the sensation tickling the soft hairs that grew from them. With a deep breath, Robert knew that now it was time for all or nothing. With his cock still deep in Ngara's throat, he pushed the chieftain down, so that he was lying on his back on the coloured blankets. Squirming, Robert lay down so that they were top to tail. Ngara found a new lease of energy, going madly at Robert's saliva-covered knob, as Robert lay, with the fearsome black cock wavering inches away from his mouth.

You can do this, he said to himself, gripping the cock half-way down its solid length, his fist unable to close about its girth, slding back the skin, allowing the head to emerge. He thought back to the impressive organs of Joseph Crook and Mr Quilter, and how he had finally managed to take them in his mouth. With a little will-power he could suck Ngara's tremendous cock. He wes determined to do so. Sniffing the bushy pubes, Robert smelled a musky scent of grass and maleness. The pubes around the cock were short, with tight curls of dark hair, but the enormous bollocks were almost hairless.

Steeling himself, Robert opened his mouth and licked the pale, pink head. He could feel Ngara's body shiver with anticipation. The skin of the shaft was gnarled, with veins and arteries throbbing below the surface, but the head itself was silky smooth. Widening his mouth to its utmost, Robert took the head inside, its spongy hardness filling him completely. Letting his jaw slacken, he continued to slide down the cock, trying to accommodate it, letting his lips feed the shaft further and further down. His teeth must have grazed the skin as it slipped ever deeper, but it was obviously what Ngara wanted. His hips bucked suddenly, forcing the whole cock down. The gag reflex was activated and Robert wanted to react, but the head of the cock pushed past his tonsils, stuffing his throat to a state of totality. He stayed like that for a long moment until he realised that he had stopped breathing. Letting the cock slide out a fraction, he took several deep inhalations through his nose and continued with the sucking.

Robert loved the feeling of a double suck, knowing that while you had a man's cock in your mouth and were sucking away for dear life, your partner was doing the same to you. But this time was something special. Both men responded to the swallowing of each other and began pumping their hips, sucking and slurping the other, enjoying the double attack, gradually increasing the speed as their heads bobbed up and down. Robert felt the wonderful sensation of Ngara's tongue rolling around his helmet, before taking the cock down again. Their hands explored each other's bodies, made slippery by the rivulets of sweat that poured over their muscular torsos.

The native's body was hard, his muscles taught, his skin velvet-smooth. This man was unlike any other that Robert had been intimate with before. He seemed totally at ease with his body and the power he had, and the amazing sensations that he provided. Robert let his mouth slide off the gigantic cock and looked down the length of his body. The sight of his own solid dick being engulfed by the dark skin was ubelievable, and totally erotic. He wondered how his own mouth looked as it sunk again about Ngara's mammoth organ. Juddering shadows from the candles stretched and shrank acorss their skin. The musty air of the hut seemed to grow in intensity.

The chief stopped sucking on Robert's cock for a moment and sat up, his fist wrapping about the slippery shaft. His mouth was glistening from the coating of his saliva, and his teeth sparkled brightly as he spoke. 'I fuck you, yes?' This was the moment that Robert had been dreading. Although in the past he had taken large cocks up the arse, the size of Ngara's frightened him. He really didn't think he would be able to manage it. Sitting up on his knees, letting Ngara play with his cock and bollocks, he stared him in the eye, and with a serious tone said, 'No. I think it would be too much.' A thought struck him and he decided to chance his arm. 'Can I fuck you?'

A silent gaze was his only answer, as Ngara chewed the idea over. Had he ever been fucked before? Robert guessed not. It would be a wonderful experience to plunge his cock deep inside the black man's arse, to see and feel himself being swallowed deep in the dark, powerful muscle-ring. Ngara still remained silent, and after a few more seconds smiled, lay back and spread his legs wide, holding them up in the air with his hands.

Shuffling closer, Robert sucked on his forefinger and let it linger about the tightly clenched hole. He would have to be gentle and careful, and make this a fuck that the native would never forget. Letting the tip of his finger probe the anus, Robert pushed it inside. The black man flinched as it entered. This was indeed the first time he had allowed himself to be penetrated. Many times in Peterstown he had been pleaded with, by sailors and traders who had gladly paid for the use of his lean body. But he had always said no. He felt that to be used like that was to accept a subservient role, to become like a woman. If he ever was to let his body be used that way, he would never have the authority to return to his tribe and lead them. But now, he was the leader of his people, he had a captive white man, and he had a desire to know how it felt.

Robert was slow. He didn't want to hurt the man. This would have to be as easy and pleasurable as possible. Gradually, he slipped the finger in, bit by bit, up to the knuckle. A smile crossed his face as the knot of muscles clamped about his finger, pulsing and massaging. He now knew that he had won. Pulling the finger out and letting fall a great gob of spit onto the waiting hole, he positioned his cock-head. With a little effort, the head was soon inside, Ngara's breath coming in short, staccato bursts. 'Relax, just let it happen. Do not fight it.' Robert tried to help the chief, whose eyes were now wide and worried. Feeling the muscles ease, Robert let more of his cock slide in, pushing to just about halfway. Sensing that Ngara was about to cry out, he put his free hand over the chief's mouth, muffling his reactions. With one more firm thrust, he was inside, buried up to the hilt. Ngara's whole body tensed, but finally relaxed sufficiently for Robert to start fucking. The chief was becoming used to the probing of the rigidness in his back-passage. Watching in awe, Ngara's breathing matched the rhythm of the strokes, his eyes never leaving the sight of his first penetration, the incredible sight of the hard white pole sliding in and disappearing within him, then drawing back before another mighty thrust, and another stabbing wave of delicious pain.

The clenching and squeezing of his prick was making Robert's head spin. Ngara may be a novice at this but he seeemed to know exactly what to do. Perhaps his experiences at Peterstown taught him a lot. It was just then that Robert knew that fucking was his ultimate favourite sex act — being in a position of superiority over another man, being the controller of his pain and joy. Especially now, when the man he was fucking was used to being the one in control. He had the advantage over this tribal chieftain and it felt good. A pang of regret hit Robert, a sudden overwhelming desire to see William again and to be able to enjoy the pure delight of fucking his sweet arse-hole. Tears sprang to his eyes. Blinking them back, he fixed his concentration on Ngara. The native's previously unsullied arse was responding heartily. Ngara was now pushing his hips back, trying to swallow the entirety of Robert's cock, an expression of utter contentment on his face.

Beads of sweat broke out on Robert's forehead as he balled his hands into tight fists and fucked with a renewed intensity. If he carried on like this, a climax would not be far away. Ngara was twisting and turning on the blanket, his hands clawing at Robert's chest. The tightness of his hole was almost coaxing an explosion out of Robert, ripples of muscle contracting and expanding with each thrust. Reaching down, Robert grabbed hold of Ngara's cock and started to pull at it, fucking faster and deeper. This made the chieftain shudder, his head thrashing from side to side. He lifted his hips off the floor and began to rotate them, forcing Robert's cock to fill him in all directions, the squeezing continuing with increased pressure. A churning began to build within Robert's balls, he could feel himself getting closer to the point of climax with each successive push. Slamming his cock into Ngara's arse even harder, Robert could feel the spunk rush along his shaft. His head dropped back and a gutteral yell of relief came pouring from his throat.

Ngara was also on the point of coming. Robert's fist kept up a steady beat on the chief's cock, pounding its chunky girth, whipping his fist up and down, until he came, the orgasm wracking his body, shooting forth across his stomach and chest, as Robert came deep within him.

Leaning forward and resting himself on Ngara's milk-streaked torso, Robert closed his eyes, and let his softening cock slip from the punished hole. The chief put an arm across Robert's neck and let his fingers tangle in his hair. Neither spoke for a while, just taking in what had just happened. Robert was intrigued. Could he use the fact that they had just fucked to his own advantage? Surely now that the two of them had shared, the chief would look kindly on Robert and the crew?

Sitting up, Robert saw that Ngara was deep in thought. 'Are you alright?' he asked the chief.

'I am good. You like fuck me, yes?' One eye snapped open, quizzically.

Robert smiled at this. 'Yes. I enjoyed it very much. Was that your first time?'

'I never have fuck me before. I like. Now you are my slave.'

This was not what Robert wanted to hear. 'Your slave? But I hoped that you would be a reasonable man and let me and my crew go. We have suffered much on this island at the hands of those bastard pirates, and all we ask is to be let free, to make our way to Peterstown and to our freedom.' Ngara closed his eye again and spoke with a dark, intense tone. 'No. You stay. I like fuck with you. If you no stay, you die.' He paused. 'And others die too.'

Anger boiled within Robert's soul. To have escaped from the pirates to be held as the sex-toy of this strange native was an appalling prospect. He had to appeal to this chieftain's better nature. 'Please, Ngara. Let us go. We mean you no harm. We all have families and loved ones, back in England. It would be cruel to keep us here indefinitely.' Standing, he towered over the black chief, his hands defensively placed on his hips.

Ngara raised a foot, and let his toes stroke Robert's hanging cock, his eyes still shut. 'You stay, or you die.'

This was the final straw. There was no way that Robert was going to be the sex-slave of this man. 'No. we want to be let free.'

Ngara sighed, opened his heavy-lidded eyes and sprang to his feet. With a harsh, ringing cry, he called out in his native language. Instantly, two Barugans appeared at his door, bursting in and taking Robert fiercely by the arms. Without a pause, they pulled him outside and headed for the skin-hung totem. One of the men grabbed his wrists and pulled them sharply behind his back, standing him at the foot of the pole. The other produced some twine, and with dextrous fingers tied him securely to the totem. It must have been around mid-day by now, as the rays of the sun were beating down with merciless strength. Emerging into the sunlight after the dimness of Ngara's hut, Robert blinked and tried to focus on what was happening to him. His hands were held fast. He was again at the mercy of this tribe, naked and bound, for whatever they desired. The carvings of the totem pole rubbed against the flesh of his back, the flayed skin a contrasting smoothness. Was that to be his fate? Killed and skinned like some stray animal? And what would happen to the others? The same horrendous ordeal would be too much to contemplate.

Robert was shaken from his dismal reverie by the banging of a crude drum, made of skin tightly stretched over a hollowed-out tree stump — a sinister, regular beat, calling to the members of the tribe, calling them forth. A sharp burst from an irridescent sea-shell joined the rythms of the drum, a coarse, braying sound which made Robert shiver. A rustling from somewhere to his right, made him look through squinting eyes, and he saw the crew being herded, bedraggled, from their huts, and forced down on their knees in a large circle surrounding the totem pole. Robert could see that everyone, including Daniel, had their hands tied behind them with the same strong twine that held him fast. Wincing in sympathy, Robert could tell that Daniel was in great pain as he collapsed to the ground, trying to sit with as much dignity as he could.

Having made sure that their prisoners were seated and secured, the tribesmen lifted their spears up to the sky and, as one, gave out a fearsome cry. Their voices rose and fell, vibrating and screeching some ritualistic chant. When the crying was finished they started to dance and sway around the totem, shaking their spears, swinging their hips, making the grass skirts rustle. The drum beats and the noise of the sea-shell horn continued unabated as the tribesmen danced.

Robert caught Daniel's eye. The young sailor looked back at him with a pitiable gaze. He seemed utterly crushed, as though he knew that there was nothing they could do to stop their fate. Hamish Dee had a look of total concentration, Robert sensed that he was trying to work his way loose from his bindings. The angry set of his features showed that he wasn't succeeding. The others just sat, lifeless and dejected, hanging their heads in dismay, aware that they could soon be dead. Above them, the island's gaudy flock of parrots flew over the clearing, squawking and chattering. Circling for a few moments, they swooped close to the totem, so close that Robert could see their fantastical plumage as it caught the sunlight, a dazzling rainbow of colours. The natives increased their frenzied dancing, taking the birds' appearance as a celestial sign of approval.

A weird rattling noise started up, and, twisting his head, Robert saw one of the natives was making those odd percussive sounds with a twig and the jaw-bone of some large, long-dead animal. Every time he stroked the twig along the teeth, he stared at Robert, pointed a finger, and intoned some strange ethereal chant.

One of the natives began dancing closer to Robert's body, thrusting his face at him, a foul waft of bad breath issuing from his cracked lips. Then, stepping back, he gave out a shrill scream, held his arms aloft, and turned to face Ngara's hut.

The grassy curtain was pulled back and Ngara emerged, wearing his coloured headress, but with lines of coloured dye across his cheek and chest. In one hand he carried a sharp knife, with a carved wood handle and a curved blade. Holding the blade aloft, he called out to the skies, a deep, mesmeric call, leaving the assembled men in no doubt who was in charge. Ngara started to move toward the totem pole, shouting some strange incantation at every step, waving the knife in front of him, sometimes singing to the blade, as if coaxing it to do his evil bidding.

Gulping, Robert fixed Ngara with a steely glare, hoping to appear unafraid. A few more steps and the chief was standing before the totem, knife in hand, a crazed look upon his face, his eyes seemingly glazed over. Was he in a trance? Robert had heard of so-called voodoo witch-doctors who would take some herbal potion and enter trances, believing that their actions were being performed at the hands of some greater power. Perhaps Ngara was in such a state of mind right now. If he was, then there would be no bargaining with him.

Robert looked around the clearing. The crew were desperately afraid, trying hard to be brave, not wanting to flinch when the terrible moment came. A jumble of cries came from behind Robert. He tried to twist his head, but couldn't see. Then, with a crow of triumph, one of the natives proudly came forward, carrying a cockerel by its scrawny legs. The bird thrashed wildly about, unable to peck the native because its beak was wound closed with twine.

A hush settled over the tribe. They watched entranced as Ngara stalked around the totem, waving the knife and incanting ghastly sounds. After two circuits of the totem, Ngara stopped in front of Robert, holding the knife horizontally before him. The other native knelt on the ground, holding the cockerel out between his trembling hands. With one, swift, lightning flick of his wrist, Ngara sliced off the head of the cockerel. A vivid spout of blood gushed from its neck. A murmur of suppressed excitement rumbled through the tribesmen, as one after the other they knelt before Ngara, bowing their heads, and letting the cockerel's blood flow over them. As they stood, they presented a terrible sight, with frenzied eyes, flashing white teeth, and their faces dripping with violent red blood.

The chanting started again, this time faster, as the tribesmen began their dance once more, skipping and hopping around the circle, waving their spears, their souls given up to their leader, willing to lay down their lives for him. A clap of thunder shook through the air, the brilliant blue sky rapidly turning darker, and a chill wind began to whistle about the clearing. Ngara raised his vapid eyes and began swirling the knife around in front of him, getting ever nearer to Robert's chest.

Robert saw with horror and disgust that the chief was drooling, rivulets of saliva dripping from his mouth, beads of sweat making the grass of his headress stick to the side of his face. Tensing himself for the final blow, the agonising pain that would sear through his body as the knife was plunged into his heart, Robert gritted his teeth. He could see Ngara bringing the blade ever closer. With a mumbled prayer, he closed his eyes as the razor-sharp edge began to slice into the skin of his chest.

FOURTEEN

As Robert prepared to meet his Lord and maker, a single shot rang out. Snapping open his moist eyes, Robert gasped .Ngara stood before him, a small, bloody bullet hole in the centre of his forehead. Uttering a strangled croak, the chief slumped to the ground, dead.

A fearsome cry went up from the natives as they watched their revered leader fall at Robert's feet. Jumping up, they raised their arms to the darkening sky and a terrifying wailing started. Almost at the same time, a voice called out from somewhere behind Robert, 'Kill the bastards!' The trees and bushes surrounding the village parted and a platoon of soldiers came pouring towards them, rifles in hand.

The natives began to defend themselves, hurling their spears with some degree of accuracy, one of them catching a young soldier in the leg, sending him crashing to the ground, screaming in agony. The platoon's commanding officer was barking orders, trying to stay in control of the situation. Kneeling, he fired his rifle at an approaching native, shooting him at point-blank range through the chest. The native fell before him, clutching at the air. A volley of firing clattered out, the shots finding their targets, mowing down the attacking tribesmen. One of the soldiers rushed to Robert's aid, slicing through his bindings with a sword, letting him free. Rubbing his wrists, restoring the circulation in his numbed hands, Robert grabbed the sword and ran to the cowed crew, quickly cutting the men free. As each one was relieved, he jumped up and helped with the attack. Hamish Dee leapt upon a weaponless native and punched him repeatedly in the face until, battered and bloody, the man collapsed in an unconscious heap.

Surveying the carnage around him, Robert could see that the soldiers were rapidly gaining the upper hand. The natives had no real defence against the rifles and muskets of the platoon, and very soon every one of them was dead or lying wounded.

The commanding officer stepped forward and shook Robert's hand.

'Colonel Bursnall, at your service, Sir.' A thick-set, greying man, he had an aura of calm authority. Here was a man you could trust with your life.

Grasping the extended hand and shaking it warmly, Robert said, 'Thank you Colonel. You came in the nick of time. Another few seconds and I would have been filleted like some hapless animal.'

'Yes indeed, Sir.' Bursnall looked with anxiety at the gash on Robert's chest. 'Is that alright, Sir? Looks like a very nasty cut.'

Robert could see that the bleeding from his wound had stopped. It was only a superficial cut, just breaking the skin, he wouldn't die from it, but it might leave a scar – that he could certainly live with. Having come within an inch of losing his life, a scar would be as nothing.

'You all seem to have been through the wars, Sir.' Bursnall's manner was kind and caring. His eyes wandered over Robert's nudity, and he raised an eyebrow. 'But don't worry. We have a trusty ship, all loaded and ready to take you back to good old England. Peterstown is about half a day's walk north. If we set off shortly, we will be there by evening.'

'Again many thanks, Colonel. Er… would it be possible for my group to borrow your soldiers' jackets? We have been forced to be naked for some considerable time now, and we would rather appreciate the chance to cover up.'

Bursnall chuckled. 'In return, you will have to fill me in on the details of all your misfortunes, Sir, and how you came to be in this predicament. Certainly I can tell my men to let you have the use of their shirts. They should be enough to spare your blushes, so to speak!'

'I am very grateful. But can you tell me how you came to find us here? I thought we were beyond the reach of rescue.' The two men talked as they walked across the clearing, the vision of the soldiers tossing native bodies into a heap rather disturbing to Robert's sensibilities. 'A rowing boat containing many frightened, tired people, mostly women, came ashore on St Martin's Isle several days ago. They were suffering from heat exhaustion, but mainly still in control of their faculties. We were told the story of what happened when the pirates struck, taking over the ship, and of your quick-thinking bravery in getting the women off, saving them from a terrible ordeal at the hands of those ruthless buccaneers.' He broke off and addressed a handsome young Subaltern, who was clearing out the huts and collecting weapons, including the ones taken from Robert and his men. He snapped to attention as Bursnall approached. Robert eyed the pile of guns and swords appreciatively. 'I see you have the arms back. We may need them again before our journey is through.'

The Colonel chuckled again and rubbed the side of his sizeable nose, 'I doubt that very much.' Turning to the Subaltern, he said, 'Quinn, can you get the men to take off their shirts? I am sure they will not mind letting these poor chaps have them for modesty's sake.'

Quinn saluted and started rounding up the garments. Bursnall continued, 'As I was saying, they told us about the attack. When one of the women mentioned the name of the pirate chief, we knew that we had to come to your rescue immediately. De la Hoya is one of the most notorious brigands in these waters. We have been after capturing him for many years. Over the last few months, we have honed down their possible secret location to two islands. Because of the details the survivors gave us of the position of the attack, we decided that they must be using Baruga, as they were nowhere to be found on St Martin's Isle. Having assured ourselves that that was where they must be, we headed for Baruga. As we neared the island, we saw a plume of smoke billowing above the southern coast, and that was all the clue we needed. It transpires that they had set fire to the wreck of your ship, *The Merry Megan*, and its smouldering hulk was their downfall.

'We landed on the shore and managed to overpower them. Strangely, most of his crew were in some sort of sleepy trance, and were unable to resist. We found de la Hoya in an upstairs room in his mansion, bandaged about a wounded shoulder, sitting and watching two young male twins engaged in... well, how shall I say?... peculiar activities. We now have all those buccaneers in custody. We'll ship them back to England and thence to the country of origin of each of them to stand trial for the crime of piracy. I expect they'll all hang.'

A pang of regret crossed Robert's mind. He would be sorry to know that the pirates would be put to death, some of them more than others. Mother was a kindly soul, doing what he thought was right, and even though de la Hoya was the pirates' indisputable leader, he was, in reality, a good man turned bad. Circumstances had conspired against him, and he had acted in the only way he thought appropriate. None of this excused the fact that his men killed and pillaged, though, or that he delighted in the torment of his male prisoners.

Colonel Bursnall continued his explanation, his voice ringing out proudly. 'After a little persuasion, we were told that they had been holding you and the men captive, but that you had all escaped the previous evening, making your way into the jungle. It didn't take us long to find this clearing and we surrounded it, waiting for the right moment to attack... and here we all are.'

Robert was glad to see his men covering up their nakedness, and ,spotting Daniel across the clearing, he excused himself from the Colonel and joined him. The young sailor was still very pale, but his courage and bravery were obvious. He smiled at Robert and took his arm. 'I think we may be out of danger now, don't you?' His voice had assumed its normal, relaxed tone, a sure sign that he was feeling better.

'Yes, indeed. When we get to Peterstown, we will be able to have a good night's sleep, you can get your leg tended, and then in a few days, we will head for home. I should think that you will be giving up the life of a sailor after all this, won't you?' Robert led Daniel across the clearing, and sat him down upon a tree stump.

'Oh, I don't know. There is certainly an element of excitement about a life on the ocean waves. I have seen some marvellous places and met some wonderful people. You included.' He took Robert's hand and kissed it. 'If it hadn't been for you we would never have escaped from this damned island. Thank you.'

An embarrassed flush crept over Robert's face, and he squatted down beside Daniel, still holding his hand. 'How can you say that? It was all my fault that we went into this jungle, and got captured by these natives. Luckily we are alright now, but it is not my doing.'

'You got us away from those pirates. Some of the men were in grave danger of losing their sanity because of some of the things they were being forced to indulge in. You freed us, and that is that.' There seemed no arguing with the young man. Nodding gracefully, Robert helped him to his feet, joining the column of men who were beginning to head north, through the dense tropical thicket, toward their safe haven of Peterstown.

The welcome that greeted the rescued crew was joyous. The survivors of the *Megan* were standing in front of the small Peterstown hotel, cheering and clapping their return, although many of the women turned their heads and looked away at the indecent sight of the men's bare legs. Barnes, Tupton and Tasker flew into the waiting arms of their wives, hugging and kissing their women fervently. Martenson and Fitch hung back at the rear of the rescued group, keeping close together, but their faces were wreathed in smiles.

After much hand-shaking and back-slapping, Robert and the men were led inside the hotel and shown to some rooms. As the proprietors were not used to so many people staying there, a number of the men had to share. Daniel and Robert were quite happy to stay together in one room, as were Martenson and Fitch.

Having shared a luxurious hot bath, Robert and Daniel lay on the exceedingly comfortable bed and fell into a deep sleep, entwined in each other's arms. As if by some psychic link, they both woke the next morning at the same time, greeting the other's first waking moments with a barrage of kisses, deep and probing, tongues meeting and thrashing wildly. Resisting the temptation to ravish each other, and fighting down their rising hard-ons, they leapt out of bed at the peristent clanging of the breakfast gong. Hurriedly dressing in some ill-fitting garments that had been found for them, they made their way downstairs to the dining room.

The majority of the men and their wives had assembled for breakfast, and were standing about in chattering groups, waiting for the rest of the crew to arrive. As Daniel and Robert entered the room, a strange hush settled over it. Many of the hungry people turned and stared at the two men, some with looks of utter distaste and loathing. Robert knew that something untoward had happened, but he didn't know what. There was no hint forthcoming from the silent men and women, until a large bunch of them, standing by the window, parted to let someone step forward.

Robert had hoped never to see the repellant countenance that stood before him ever again, but his hopes were now totally dashed.

Fergus Trench stepped unctuously through the throng and stood face to face with Robert. He was dressed in elegant fineries, his hair beautifully coiffeured, and an aura of smug triumph suffused his person, a bundle of papers under one arm. 'Mister Marchant. How good to see you again.' His voice dripped with sarcasm. 'I hear that you have been through the wars. How frightful for one as well-bred as yourself.'

Biting back a stinging retort, Robert stood and faced this repulsive reptile. 'How do you come to be here, Trench? I thought you had been killed when the ship was attacked.'

Preening himself and giving a wide smile to the people listening intently around them, he continued. 'I put myself aboard the rowing boat, just before it pulled away. There was some small opposition, but as I explained to the more vociferous passengers, I was on my way to the Indies on His Majesty's business, and to intefere with that would mean a charge of treason on anyone stopping me. Quite simple really.'

'You are one of the most perverted creatures I have ever had the misfortune to meet. It does not surprise me that you fled, hiding behind the skirts of women.' Robert could hardly bring himself to look at the man.

Trench gave one of his throaty laughs, and addressed the watching crowd. 'I am very glad he used the word "perverted". That is a description that admirably fits itself about Mister Marchant's manly shoulders.' Robert could see Barnes and Tasker, as well as Hamish Dee in the crowd, watching and listening with furrowed brows. 'You see, I have a tale to tell you of perversion, a story that will disgust you all, and change your opinions of this man. Robert Marchant is one such pervert. Over the course of our journey from England, I have had cause to watch his movements, keep a note of all his vile goings-on, and with this information to rid society of one of its most unpleasant degenerates.'

A horrified burst of whispered comments rumbled about the dining room. Robert knew that the next few minutes were going to be exremely difficult. How could he defend himself against the word of Trench, a man who had the King's authority? Perhaps he could rely on the support of the men who he had helped to escape from the pirate's lair, men who knew of his bravery, and who could speak in support of his good name. The wait for Trench's next move was excruciating.

'Luckily, or perhaps I should say wisely, I brought some personal items with me in a small strong-box when I left with the rowing boat. Among the items I saved was this bundle of papers. If you care to examine them, they contain detailed descriptions of Marchant's sordid affairs, whilst aboard *The Merry Megan*, with all manner of seamen, officers and cooks alike. This proves that he is a man who delights in perverting other men, in using their bodies for his own ends, and in indulging in all manner of disgusting sexual behaviour. I happen to know that he also takes pleasure in deflowering children, satiating his ungodly lusts upon their innocent young bodies. He is a man with no morals, who will lie and cheat and do the work of the very devil himself.' Unease rippled among the stunned crowd, unable to believe what they were hearing.

Trench rubbed his chin and carried on, with the air of a desperate lawyer, testifying at some hushed courtroom. 'As His Majesty's appointed Governor of the island of Dominique, I say that I have the authority to demand this man's arrest and subsequent punishment as I see fit. I say that he should be taken outside and hung from the nearest gibbet, a fitting end to a life of debauchery such as he has participated in.'

A gasp of shock came from behind Trench, and Robert saw the rotund figure of Mrs Tupton emerge. She pushed her way to the front and spoke with a refreshing determination. 'Where is this proof you have? I find it hard to believe that a fine, upstanding young man such as this could be guilty of what you say. My husband has informed me of the harrowing time spent among the pirates in their lair, and how this young man engineered their escape from that hell-hole. Then, to be on the point of death at the hands of those horrid natives, well... I think we should all praise him, not castigate him.' She glanced around, looking for support, but many of the women hung their heads and glanced down at the ground, while the men stood, unmoved by her plea.

'May I be allowed to speak?' Robert stepped forward pleadingly.

A supercilious wave of his hand was Trench's only reply.

'Thank you.' As he surveyed the crowd, no-one met his eye. Many of the men and women stood back a little as he moved toward them. 'Ladies and Gentlemen, I am dismayed, not to say surprised by the Governor's unpalatable accusations. I do not know why he should seem so keen to have me strung up like a common thief. Before we met aboard *The Merry Megan*, we had previously known each other. I was reminded by Trench that we had made each other's acquaintance some years previously, when he used to hold the position of clerk at the Admiralty, and whilst visiting there with my father, Lord Marchant, he attempted to seduce me.'

'Lies, all lies,' Trench snorted. Undeterred Robert continued. 'Not so. He took me to an ante-room at the Admiralty and tried to be intimate with me. I was a young, blameless man, with a spotless reputation, who knew nothing of such things. All these years he has held a viscious grudge against me, blaming me for his desires. He is a thoroughly bad man, who has risen to a position of superiority by lying and cheating, and no doubt by seducing people who could further his despicable career. I ask you all to pay no heed to what he says. He is a jealous man who wants me to pay for something he was responsible for, years ago. If you listen to him, an innocent man will be punished. What say you?'

No-one moved. No-one spoke. A tangible sense of disquiet filled the air, so thick you could almost touch it. Mrs Tupton broke the silence. 'I think we should all stick behind this courageous young man, and give him our unquestioning support. Are you with me?' Indecisive mutterings and the shuffling of shoes met her question. Someone coughed and stepped forward through the crowd.

Recognising who had presented himself, Trench crowed with renewed delight. 'Ah, Hamish Dee, my old friend.' Spinning on his delicate heels, he again raised his voice for the benefit of the listening horde. 'Here is a man who can back up what I have been saying. Dee has been in my employ, in the important position of Private Secretary, for the last six months. Whilst on board our ship, he carried out much of the already mentioned surveillance on Marchant. He can verify my story, and can swear to the authenticity of the notes. Speak out man, tell them the truth.'

Dee took a moment to survey the crowd, finally resting his stern gaze on Trench.Pulling himself up to his full height, he towered above the rest of the assembled company. 'The truth, you say? I shall indeed tell the truth.' Moving to Robert's side, he pointed a finger at Trench. 'The truth is that you are a weasel of a man, a liar, a cheat and a fraud.'

'What are you saying? How dare you insult me so? I am your employer and one word from me can have you put away for slander.' Trench shook with rage, his fists balled up tightly.

'I am speaking the truth, as you demanded. Since starting work for you, I have seen with my own eyes how you twist people, how you use underhand methods to get what you want, blackmailing poor folk who cannot fight back. From the black day that you ran from the pirates' attack, like some yellow-bellied creature, I have come to realise that Marchant here is an honest and decent man. I did your bidding on the ship, spying on him as you ordered, because I believed the tales you told. Having survived many strange ordeals since my capture, I know that men will do whatever necessary to survive. I am not ashamed to admit that I partook in some unwholesome activities, and it is because I did that I am alive to tell the tale.'

Dee reached out and grabbed the sheaf of papers that Trench clasped to his chest. 'These papers are the rantings of a lunatic — a man who has held an unnatural grudge against Marchant for a perverted act that was not the young man's fault. In fact, they deserve to be destroyed.' With one swift stroke, he tore the sheaf in two, scattering the pages in the air, and with a satisfied smirk watched the pieces flutter to the ground. He addressed the company, 'There is your proof, some insane scribblings from a man with a black heart. If you believe his words, then I will have lost my faith in human nature. Robert Marchant is a good man, and deserves our gratitude, not condemnation. Any dissenters?' He took a firm stance, hands on hips, jaw jutting out defiantly. A sudden chatter of voices erupted as the company crowded around Robert, patting him on the back, thanking him and praising his bravery. All Trench could do was glower hatefully. 'You are all fools,' he screeched, heading for the door, but as he reached it he bumped into Colonel Bursnall, entering with a soldierly stride.

'Good morning everyone, I hope you are all well today. My word, what is going on here?' Dee took him to one side and explained what had just occurred. 'If I were you, Colonel, I would grasp that devil Trench by the collar and incarcerate him. I strongly believe him to be a crook, who has somehow gained the trust of people in high places. If the King were to hear of his misdeeds, I am sure he would be punished severly.'

Trench stood open-mouthed, unable to comprehend what he was hearing. 'How dare you, Dee? I am a loyal subject of His Majesty, and could have you strung up like a lamb.'

'Pipe down, little man.' Dee's face creased with a beaming grin. 'I would hurry, Colonel, before he evades you.' Bursnall immediately took control, grasping Trench by the arm. 'You had better come along with me, then. I think I can find a nice brig for you to rest in during the journey back home. The Militia would certainly be interested in interviewing you about your dealings.' Protesting loudly, Trench was man-handled out, to the jeers and cat-calls of the assembled crowd.

As the cheering and congratulations died down, Robert raised his hands for silence. 'My friends, I am touched by your faith in my good name. I will always think back to the good people I met aboard the *Megan*, and my memories of you will be joyous ones. We have all come through great adversity in the past few weeks, and even though we have all experienced much that was bad, we have survived, hopefully becoming stronger in the process. Never forget that life can be tough, that some higher power can change your life's direction on the toss of a coin. Always treasure the present moment, because you never know what is around the corner. Now I have one last thing to say… I am famished, I think it is time for breakfast!' Looking around the room, full of friendly faces, then taking Daniel by the arm, he helped him limp, slowly but surely, to the laden breakfast table.

Three days later, with full sails and replete with provisions, the *Julia Ramsey* set sail for England. As well as Robert, Daniel, Hamish Dee and the surviving crew-men from the *Megan*, she carried Colonel Bursnall's platoon of soldiers, eager to return home after their spell of duty in the Indian Ocean. Bidding farewell to the new friends they had made was difficult for them all. Deciding to wait for a ship to take them on to Dominique, the merchants and traders stood alongside the dock and waved cheerily as the *Julia Ramsey* hoisted anchor and headed east.

The sea was a deep aquamarine, the sky clear, and the sun happily blazed down upon their progress. The ship's progress was swift, picking up the South West Trade winds, and she docked five weeks later at Plymouth.

The disembarcation was orderly and precise, and as the passengers soon found themselves back on home soil, Robert had to stop himself from the urge to kneel and kiss the ground.

'Well, this looks like goodbye.' Daniel, who was much recovered, though still walking with the aid of a stick, took Robert's hand and held it warmly. They were standing by a cargo dock, waiting for a new passport and papers to be hand-delivered to them. 'I imagine that you will be wanting to head for home. Your father must have been worried sick about you, and I am sure you will be wanting to see him again. After all you told me about why you and your friend William left, I am certain he will have calmed down and forgiven you by now.'

'I hope so. Daniel… I don't know what to say. You have made the last few months bearable. I couldn't have coped with all the terrible things without you. If only we had met under different circumstances, perhaps we could have lived together... but then life is full of "what ifs", and it is pointless to dwell on what might have been. I insist that you come an visit me at Marchant Hall whenever you wish. I should say whenever you are back on land.'

Daniel gave a resigned chuckle. 'I don't think I shall be going back to sea again. With this injury I shall only be fit for a desk job. Still, I hear London would be an interesting place to work. Perhaps I'll find a fascinating position at the Admiralty.'

Roaring with laughter, Robert clasped Daniel to his breast and hugged him tightly. 'If you do, then avoid seducing any young noblemen that you may come across... remember what happened to Trench!' The urge to kiss Daniel was so strong that Robert couldn't hold back. With a quick glance left and right, seeing that they were momentarily unobserved, he did just that, letting his tongue enter Daniel's mouth for the last time. The young sailor's response was so passionate that Robert immediately felt himself growing hard, and had to pull away before the intensity of the moment became too much to bear.

Seeing the delivery boy approaching, Daniel stood back. Taking the presented documents, he smiled and turned on his heels, walking away with a determined air. Before he disappeared from sight, he raised his arm and waved goodbye, not turning back to see Robert's saddened face.

'Here are your papers, Sir. Will there be anything else?' The delivery boy stood keenly awaiting further instructions. Robert looked at him. His eagerness giving him the appearance of a puppy wanting to play. There was something about his large, brown eyes that reminded him of William. A bolt of regret and guilt shot through Robert as he thought again of the young man he had lost, and wondered if he would ever see again. During the journey home, he had often found his mind wandering to thoughts of young Master Benham, and whether he would ever find out what had happened to him after the attack on *The Valiant*. With a surge of willpower, he tried to put thoughts of the young man's body from his mind, along with images and memories of the special times they had shared.

Shaking his head to clear those intimate pictures , Robert put his hand on the delivery boy's shoulder. 'Thank you, my lad. If I had any money on me, I would give you something for your trouble.'

'That's alright, Sir. I can see you are a man of breeding. I know that toffs like you don't carry much money!'

Cheerily cuffing the boy about the ear, Robert said, 'Perhaps you can direct me to the nearest bank. I shall need to withdraw some money on my account and then I may have a little something for you.'

Following the boy's bounding steps through the bustling lanes, Robert was led to a banking establishment where he withdrew sufficient funds to buy his passage home to Marchant Hall. The boy happily took the shilling that Robert pressed into his palm and, after giving a mock salute, dashed away into the thronging streets.

After several enquiries, Robert booked himself a seat on a fast post-chaise coach to Southampton, where he could hire a horse for the final leg of his journey home.

As he boarded the coach, Robert was aware of the strange looks he was getting from the other passengers, and he realised that he must be presenting a peculiar sight in his ill-fitting clothes, and with no luggage. He settled back into his seat and the coach rattled off, leaving the bustle and hubbub of Plymouth's busy streets behind.

The journey itself passed quite amicabl, once he had made the acquaintance of his fellow journeymen, and told them, at length, the stories of his recent misadventures, leaving out the more intimate details, naturally. The passengers sat enthralled, the ladies holding back gasps of horror at the unfolding tale, hiding their faces with their fans, cooling themselves when they found their interest getting too intense. In this way the next hours passed pleasantly, and soon Robert found himself in the thriving port of Southampton, where he was able to hire a powerful black stallion to take him home.

The countryside that he rode through made his heart glad, the rolling hills and fields of crops nestling with herds of cattle eating contendly in other small-holdings. He knew that he was glad to be back, but the strength of his joy surprised even him. Nearing the Marchant estate, he spurred his steed on and as he broached the crest of the hill, and saw the gleaming white mansion again, tears sprang to his eyes. There had been moments during the recent past that he had doubted whether he would ever see his beloved home again. Whirling pictures and distant memories crossed his mind, a jumble of images… playing catch with his Nanny on the lawn, picking strawberries with his mother, playing piggy-back with his father... it was at that moment that he knew that this was his home, and he would never leave it again.

As he trotted down the slope, Robert could see that all the shutters on the windows were closed. Something was wrong. Digging his heels into his horse, he galloped across the lawn, pulling up at the front door, and leaping down from his sweating stallion. With one push, he opened the door, and entered. The house was silent. 'Hullo there. Is there anybody here?' Robert crossed the hall and entered the library, hoping that his father would greet him with a fond embrace. Again the room was empty. Tugging twice on the bell-pull, Robert waited for one of the servants to appear. Shortly Presland, the butler, stepped into the library, and gave a gasp of shocked surprise. 'Master Robert! Is it really you?' He hurried across and took the hand Robert had extended to him. 'Yes, Presland. It is me. You will not believe the story I have to tell. But what is going on here? Where is my father?'

Presland's shoulders drooped and he looked down at the fine Persian rug beneath his feet. 'I am sorry to have to inform you that your father is dead.'

Grasping for support, Robert sank down into a chair. 'Dead. It can't be true. What happened?' He looked about the room for evidence of his father. His favourite armchair, his globe of the world and his pipe rack were all still in place, so he had to be coming back to use them. He couldn't be gone.

'I am afraid it is true, My Lord.'

'Don't you dare call me that. My father is Lord Marchant, not I.'

'As you wish My Lor... Master Robert. It happened on the day that you left Marchant Hall. Unaware that you had gone, he set off that morning to ride to London, ostensibly to get an audience with His Majesty the King. He didn't say what he wanted to see King George about, but said he would be back in two or three days.'

'But didn't he see my note?'

'I assume not.' Robert rested his head on the chair back. He knew what his father was planning to do that morning — to get him a naval commission. 'Did he manage to see the King?'

The butler shuffled uneasily. 'No, Master Robert. Just outside the village, he was set upon by footpads, who attacked and robbed him. He was badly injured in the fracas when he tried to stop them climbing aboard his coach.

One of the villains fired a pistol. The shot went straight through his chest, and entered his heart. He died instantly.' Pausing to allow his words to sink in, Presland continued, 'He was buried two days later alongside your mother. Everyone thought you must be dead also, as we had no contact from you. The lawyers acting for your father have closed up the Hall, and would have sold the estate off after a suitable length of time had passed. I thank God that you are safe and sound. The Hall and estate will now pass to you, and whether you believe me or not, you now bear the title of Lord Marchant. Will there be anything else, My Lord?'

Robert stared blankly at the butler and shook his head. 'I don't think so. I would like to be left alone for a while. Can you make sure my room is prepared?'

Bowing slightly, Presland turned and quietly exited, closing the door with a faintly audible click. Robert's head was whirring with incredible thoughts. To discover that his dear father was no longer alive was a shock, but to realise that he had become the new Lord of the manor was even more of a shock. All of this was his. His beloved Marchant Hall now belonged to him, and he would never have to leave it again. He would have untold wealth, and could live in luxury for the rest of his life, doing as he pleased, without having to enter into the unwanted bonds of matrimony. The relief that flooded his being when he realised that with his new-found position he could remain a bachelor was enormous. If only he had someone to share it with. Standing, he wandered to the window, pushed open the shutter and looked out across the luscious green lawns, toward the lake. He had to think further.

Leaving the house, he walked slowly over the beautifully trimmed grass to the side of the lake, where he sat on one of the ornamental benches dotted around it. Small insects flitted across the surface of the water, while fish swam about, creating tiny ripples. Robert watched ,mesmerised, losing himself in thought, mentally swimming in the lake's cool darkness.

'Robert.'

A voice cut through his reverie, bringing him back to the present. He turned his head and tears pricked his wide-open eyes. A face that he had thought to never see again swam before his hazy vision. 'William! My God. It's you!'

Knocking his knee as he leapt from the bench, but feeling no pain, Robert took his love in his arms and held him tight. William's body was racked with sobs of exquisite relief. 'I knew you would come back to me. I just knew it.' He squeezed Robert to him. 'Now you are here, I never want to let you go.'

Prising himself free from the young man's grasp, Robert stood back and looked at him. 'But what happened to you? After the attack on *The Valiant,* I was taken aboard a ship heading for the West Indies. I have just returned this afternoon.'

William sat on the bench, pulling Robert down beside him, and took his hand, entwining their fingers. 'I floated about in the water for ages, until I was picked up by a fishing boat, who carried me back to Portsmouth. I didn't know what to do, and so stayed in the town for a few days in case you came back. I had no money and had to do a few sex jobs to pay my way. I felt so degraded and knew that you would be ashamed of me for doing it, but I had no choice. After a week, I came back to Marchant Hall, and hoped you would be here. I learnt that your father had died, and when I found out that Mr Willoughby had left, I asked Mr Presland if I might stay on as Gamekeeper. He didn't know that I had been fired, and so I have been working here ever since.'

He stopped and took Robert's face in his hands. 'I never gave up the hope that you would come back for me. Ever since the day we were parted, I thought of nothing else... I think I love you.'

The words touched Robert's heart and he put his arms around William's shoulders, pulling him close. He felt his body shaking. The sound of his sobbing was muted against the cloth of Robert's jacket. An arrow of realisation pierced Robert's heart and he knew that he also loved William. He knew that this was the man that he wanted to spend the rest of his life with. They could live happily together at the Hall, safe in the knowledge that no-one would bother them.

Lifting William's face, Robert wiped the tears from his flushed cheeks, and bent forward to kiss him. William pulled back in horror.

'What's the matter? I thought you loved me.' Robert was perplexed.

'I do love you, but somebody might see us.'

A laugh, relief mingled with the ridiculousness of the situation, bubbled from Robert. 'What if they should. All this is now mine and I shall damned well do as I please. Come here.' Their lips met, aglow with passion. The months apart had kept their desire burning for each other. Aware of the stirrings in his loins, Robert knelt before the bench and reached up his trembling fingers, unbuttoning William's pristine white shirt before slipping his hands inside, feeling for the nipples, tweaking each one to its maximum hardness. William put his hands on Robert's shoulders and looked down at him. Robert knew that he could drown in those sensual brown eyes. Reaching lower down, Robert started to unfasten William's breeches, grasping the waistband, and slowly easing them off his silky hips. The young man's cock, which had been aching for release, sprang up from his crotch, wavering before Robert's appreciative glance, the foreskin easing itself back slightly.

As Robert stared with love at the prick, it gave a jerk. Robert laughed softly and bowed his head to kiss it. His fist wrapped around the shaft, pulling back the skin, letting the head emerge gently. William shivered as a cool breeze played across his tender knob. Unable to wait any longer, Robert fell upon the cock, first kissing the tip vigorously, then sliding his mouth down it, not stopping until the entire solid mass was in his throat. It felt wonderful, the cock filling his mouth, knowing that it was just the right size. With a sigh of satisfaction Robert started to eat at William's dick, licking at the head, nipping the lobes with his teeth, popping it in and out of his slavering lips before plunging his mouth down it again. William had put both hands behind Robert's head and began pulling him down faster. The feelings that both men were giving each other were astonishing. William knew that if Robert were to continue his expert sucking, then he would soon come. As if magically sensing that fact, Robert stopped and pulled William to his feet.

Without waiting for any word from William, Robert spun him around and bent him forward over the bench, spreading his thighs, exposing his hairless arsehole to the air. His lover's hard cock sprung up, hitting the underside of the bench, his bollocks hanging down behind. Squatting down, Robert let the tip of his tongue flick across the puckered rose-bud, watching it clench and release. A moan came from deep within William and he spread his thighs wider, reaching his hands round, pulling the cheeks of his arse further apart. Robert's wet tongue slipped up and down the crack, licking greedily at the balls, sliding each one into his mouth, until both were being sucked and slurped on. Letting his mouth wander back up, Robert let the tip of his tongue penetrate the tight muscle-ring, feeling William relax himself to allow it in. He knew that the lad was ready.

Standing, Robert positioned the head of his throbbing cock at the opening and pushed. William's scream made him want to push harder, and he did, thrusting the cock deep within him. Holding William's shoulders for support, Robert fucked him ferociously, feeling the lad squirming his arse, wanting the whole of Robert inside.

Robert's skin was growing increasingly sweaty and his hips slid wetly against the cheeks of William's buttocks. His pace grew faster. Beads of sweat were falling from Robert's brow. His legs were going to sleep, getting numb, but Robert didn't care. The only thing in the world that mattered was this wonderful moment, fucking the man he loved, his swollen cock deep inside his lover's body, both men feeling as if they were one sensuous being. If the world were to end now, then neither of them would have cared a jot. They were together, and would remain together forever.

Wrapping his arms around William's waist, Robert increased his fucking even more, faster and faster, filling the tight passage-way with his hardness, feeling the friction as the skin of his cock rubbed against the warm wetness.

William's cock was bursting with the desire for climax. Reaching down below the bench, he began to jerk his fist ont his own hardened tool. A few tight strokes were all he needed to explode in a cry of delight, his ejaculation gushing between his fingers, splattering on the grass beneath. Robert couldn't hold back any longer either, and his juice poured into the very depths of William's body, each bolt coaxed by a manipulative squeeze from the lad's arse muscles. For a moment, they writhed in ecstasy, each aware of the other's enjoyment.

Soon, as his cock began to slowly soften, Robert let it slip from William's beautiful hole. Helping William up and sitting him back on the bench, Robert smiled then sank down onto the grass at his feet. He placed a comforting arm across the lad's lap and held his half-hard cock in his hand. 'I love you, William. It took a little while to realise it, but I finally know it now. No-one makes me feel the way you do. I don't know if anyone else will. Stay with me here. The Hall is now mine, and I can have whoever I like to live with me. We could be happy here, hunting, shooting, fishing, and of course, fucking! Please say yes.'

William looked out over the lake to the undulating hills beyond, and knew that he had truly found his home. There was no other place in the world he would rather be, and no-one else he would rather share it with. His answer came in a torrent of emotion. 'Yes, Robert, yes. Of course I will. I have loved you since the moment I first saw you. How could you doubt it? Just hold me tight and never let me go!'

With a grin, Robert got up, sat on the bench beside William and held him, doing exactly as his lover wished.

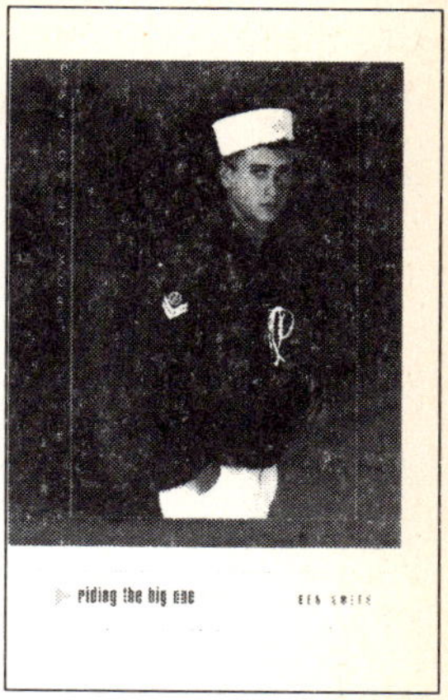

readingdirtynovels

Feeling Frisky £5.99 FIC16

A dozen hot and horny tales about the spunky adventures of young gay guys who are all feeling frisky. Includes Spanish Summer: 'I pushed him away enough to catch my breath and to let me take control of the situation. I wanted his cock and I rolled him on his back and began licking his nipples. He pushed my head down towards his crotch and I worked my tongue down along the trial of hairs leading to his cock teasing him. I went down on him right away, taking the head between my lips and lowering myself onto him. I pumped up and down a bit, then pulled off to lick the shaft and his nuts.'

Shipmates £5.99 FIC15

Rick Jackson is the beefy, polished American jarhead who, at 6'2" tall and with 9 thick inches, is always kept busy onboard ship. His career has meant that he's travelled the world and entertained far more than his share of sex-starved young guys. Marines, sailors and squaddies all come to a sticky end at the hands of this legendary lover, who always tries to be of service when his shipmates need him most.

Riding The Big One £7.95 FIC17

It's all hands on 'dick' for 18 year old Sandy in this naughty, nautical novel. School is over for our young hero and a life in the Navy beckons... 'Watch out for those hairy-arsed seamen when you're down there, Skin. It's been two weeks since most of them have had a shag or decent blow job,' warned Jack. 'Two weeks since I've had a shag,' said Willy, still gripping his delicious cock inside his boiler suit. 'So they'd better watch out themselves. I'm so bloody horny I could drive rivets in with my dick."

malexpress ltd 3 Broadbent Close London N6 5GG
24hr credit card orderline: 0181 340 8644 (live operator service sun-thur 5pm-9pm)
freefax: 0800 917 2551 orders@malexpress.co.uk
int tel: +44 181 340 8644 int fax: + 44 181 340 8885

U.S
PORN STARS
18
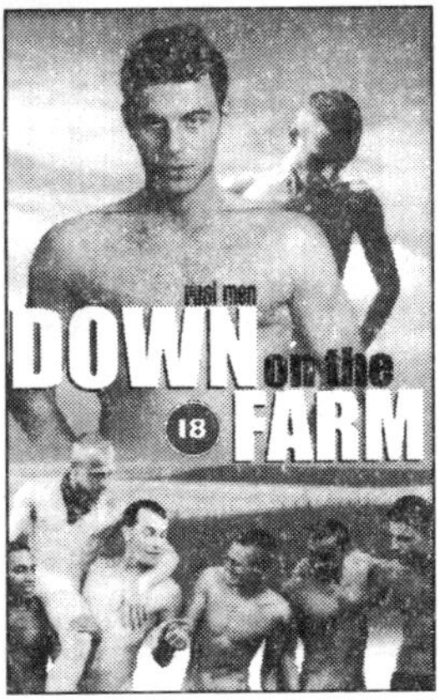
DOWN on the FARM
18

Vulcan
football shorts
18

smoothyoungguys

Sunkissed £15.99 JE13

Shot on location in Spain with natural sound and seven "enormously talented" guys. Meet blue eyed lad Alan on holiday in Ibiza where he gets it on with well-hung Rory who "likes it rough" and tattooed Pete who likes 'em big. Staying in the same villa is sexy Andrew from Blackpool and bright-eyed cuteboy Ian who can't resist Andrew's pert bum. 60 mins. BBFC cert 18

Hothouse £15.99 HOT1

Smooth, slim sexy 18 year old Richard discovers his budding sexuality in a series of adventures in London's hottest sauna. Steamy sessions in the shower followed by heated passion in the steam room leave this young guy feeling very satisfied.
BBFC cert 18.

Bel Ami Frisky Memories Video £19.99 FRM1

Join Lukas and his sexy friends as they spend a long hot summer together. Enjoying the sun, sea, sand AND each other's smooth, well-toned and tanned bodies. Getting hot and sweaty, these horny Hungarians satisfy their desires whenever and wherever they can. A must for anyone who loves beautiful boys with adonis-like bodies and angelic faces. Also includes extra behind the scenes footage and an interview with Lukas himself. 80 mins BBFC cert 18.

malexpress ltd 3 Broadbent Close London N6 5GG
24hr credit card orderline: 0181 340 8644 (live operator service sun-thur 5pm-9pm)
freefax: 0800 917 2551 orders@malexpress.co.uk
int tel: +44 181 340 8644 int fax: + 44 181 340 8885

SHOTS!

Spunky gay
18-21 year olds
get hard, suck
cock, fuck each
other and then
cum!

Straight Boys
Who Suck
Cock